Aubrin shook her head and gripped the bars. "Jaxter, you have to leave right now."

"Hey, calm down, Jinxface," I said. "I've got Maloch and Callie with me and we've got a plan."

"You have to go!" She was full-on sobbing. "Don't you understand? By coming here, it means you're going to die!"

THE GRIMJINX REBELLION

BRIAN FARREY

illustrated by

BRETT HELQUIST

HARPER

An Imprint of HarperCollins*Publishers*

The Grimjinx Rebellion

 For information address HarperCollins Children's Books, a division of HarperCollins Publishers, 195 Broadway, New York, NY 10007.

www.harpercollinschildrens.com

Library of Congress Cataloging-in-Publication Data

Farrey, Brian.

The Grimjinx rebellion / Brian Farrey. — First edition.

pages cm

Sequel to: The Shadowhand Covenant.

Summary: When the Palatinate Mages unveil their plot to take over the Five Provinces, thirteen-year-old Jaxter Grimjinx and his family of thieves must lead the rebellion to overthrow them.

ISBN 978-0-06-204935-3 (pbk.)

[1. Swindlers and swindling—Fiction. 2. Magic—Fiction. 3. Fantasy.] I. Title.

PZ7.F24614Gr 2014 2013043194

[Fic]—dc23 CIP

AC

Typography by Megan Stitt

15 16 17 18 19 CG/OPM 10 9 8 7 6 5 4 3 2 1

❖

First paperback edition, 2015

To Jim, Mark, and Pam,
who've always known the truth about the Vanguard

· CONTENTS ·

PART ONE:
★ THE CRECHE ★

· CONTENTS ·

PART TWO:
THE REBELS

· CONTENTS ·

· CONTENTS ·

PART ONE

★

THE CRECHE

1

Portents

"Portents bleed the foolish and feed the wily."

—Mendar Grimjinx, sole survivor of the Rexian Ziggurat plunder

Of all the wisdom passed down through the generations of the Grimjinx clan, the bit I think about most came from Jerrina Grimjinx, wife of Corenus, our clan father. She said, "Tomorrow's eyes penetrate yesterday's haze."

It means that when things get hectic—like when you're fighting off balanx skeletons or stopping a madman from blowing up every mage in the Five Provinces—it's hard to get perspective. It's only with time that you can reflect and see clearly what would have been obvious.

If, you know, you hadn't been distracted by all the running and screaming.

Looking back, it's all very clear to me now. The Creche, the war, the Scourge . . . each one shines brightly in my past, like a beacon leading me to my fate. At the time, you could have told me what was coming but I wouldn't have believed it. Yet the signs were all there.

I was going to die.

No expense had been spared for the Dowager's party.

The Banquet Room in Vengekeep's town-state hall was the largest, most lavish room in the whole city. Silky red draperies hung from the ceiling, framing walls that had been decorated with woodcuts depicting key moments in Vengekeep's history. Long tables buckled under the weight of roast hemmon, freshly steamed vegetables, and a collection of the best vintages of ashwine ever assembled. It would have been a party worthy of the High Laird himself.

It was a shame no one showed up.

I stood in a small antechamber tucked into the Banquet Room's north wall, hidden behind a golden curtain. I peeked out and did a quick head count.

"Twelve people," I announced in a whisper. "But they look happy to be here. You'll have a captive audience."

Dowager Annestra Soranna sat on a stool. Her hands picked at the formal gown that clung tightly to her frail frame. She hated dressing up. "*Sallah kesh*," she said, only loud enough for me to hear.

The Dowager, in her never-ending quest for knowledge, had asked me to teach her ancient par-Goblin, the language of thieves. She didn't *quite* have the hang of it yet. She thought *sallah kesh* was a form of swearing. Actually, it meant "prudent soup." I figured I'd get around to correcting her. Someday.

To the Dowager's right stood Neron, her most trusted guard. On the other side, decked out in his official uniform as Protectorate of Vengekeep, stood Da. He gritted his teeth at the news.

"Twelve!" Da said. "Well . . . that's a *good* sign. Twelve's a lucky number for thieves. There are twelve clans in the kleptocracy, twelve charters in the Lymmaris Creed. . . ." His voice trailed off as he failed to identify other ways to make twelve people sound promising.

The Dowager's nose wrinkled as Ma brushed powder onto her crooked cheekbones. "I heard Ullin Lek, the butcher, is here," Ma said cheerily. "He's the wealthiest man in Vengekeep."

Ma, Da, and I were taking turns trying to keep the Dowager from worrying that a banquet thrown in her honor had attracted so few people. Earlier, Da, who was in charge of security, had told Ma and me that over three hundred invitations had been sent to dignitaries and the nobility throughout Korrin Province. Nearly all had been returned with polite regrets. A few, Da had added, were less than polite.

"I appreciate your optimism," the Dowager said, a gentle lilt to her voice, "but we all know *very well* why there are so few people here."

Ma looked surprised. It was easy to mistake the Dowager as being doddering and unaware. In truth, a razor-sharp mind lurked beneath that befuddled exterior, ready to cut anyone who believed the facade for a second.

It was hardly a secret that her brother, the High Laird, was facing . . . popularity problems these days. His erratic behavior had been raising questions for a year now. But in the two months since the exile of the Sarosan pacifists, he'd gone positively naff-nut. Unjust taxes. Centuries-old freedoms revoked. Even his most loyal subjects were unhappy.

I had hoped to see my friend Callie Strom here tonight. But both she and her cousin, Talian, Vengekeep's mage, were absent. This suggested truth behind another whispered rumor that had slinked its way across the Provinces: the Palatinate, the mages who governed magical law for the High Laird, was also trying to distance itself from the government.

I was worried about Callie. From the letters I'd received while studying with the Dowager in Redvalor Castle, it sounded like she had come a long way in her magical training. Talian said she had a real talent. What worried me was how close she was getting to the Palatinate. If the recent past had taught me anything, it was that the mages couldn't be trusted.

I turned to Aubrin, my eleven-year-old sister, who sat in the corner, scribbling in her journal as usual. To break the tension, I tried snatching the book. But she saw me coming and did a tuck and roll to get away.

"Come on, Jinxface," I said. "When are you going to let me see what you're always writing?"

She raised an eyebrow. "It's not time," she said. It was what she *always* said when I wanted to read her journal.

The gold curtains parted and in came Castellan Jorn, chief magistrate of Vengekeep. His thick fist clutched an oversize key made of brass and encrusted with fake jewels: the symbolic key to the gates of Vengekeep. Jorn presented it to anyone of importance who visited the town-state.

He bowed low before the Dowager. "My lady," he said, "I believe we are ready to begin."

"You look marvelous, Annestra," Ma told the Dowager.

The Dowager kissed Ma, then Ma and Aubrin slipped through the gold curtain to join the others in the Banquet Room. Jorn straightened his robes and followed Ma and Aubrin.

"May I have your attention!" we heard Jorn call out, his bass voice thundering off the room's walls. "As you know, every one hundred years, the reigning High Laird throws a Jubilee to commemorate another century of benevolent rule under the Soranna family. In one month, we will mark *five hundred* years of unification for the Five Provinces!"

The Dowager cringed on hearing the smattering of polite applause. Given the mood throughout the Provinces, many people doubted the Jubilee would happen at all.

"This Jubilee," Jorn went on, "is especially exciting for Vengekeep. As per custom, members of the royal family offer their patronage to a town-state they feel most exemplifies patriotism for the Five Provinces. Tonight, we gather to celebrate that the Dowager Soranna has graciously chosen Vengekeep!"

Jorn paused, expecting applause. Silence.

"As such," he continued quickly, "the Dowager will oversee Vengekeep's celebration, offering her insight until the Jubilee begins in one month. It is now my extreme pleasure . . ."

I took the Dowager's hand as she nervously licked her lips.

". . . to introduce Her Majesty, the Dowager Annestra Soranna!"

Neron pulled back the curtain. A smile lit the Dowager's face. We walked into the Banquet Room to meek applause from the stateguard and Jorn's overzealous cheers. But most of the guests stood immobile and frowning. The Dowager waved as she took her place at the head table next to the Castellan.

"Good people," the Dowager said, "it is I who feel honored to be among you tonight. For centuries, the High Laird's Jubilee has served as a symbol of your sovereign's devotion to these lands we all forge day to day. . . ."

As the Dowager continued, I spotted Aubrin trying to get my attention. She wiggled her eyebrows and jerked her head. I looked where she was motioning. All I saw were the people of Vengekeep. Ullin Lek, the widow Bellatin, Abrinar Benrick, the cobbler. Nothing out of the ordinary.

Then, just as the Dowager started describing her plans for Vengekeep's Jubilee celebration, the widow Bellatin—a frail old woman who'd devoted her life to teaching girls to be proper ladies—stepped forward and flung her arm toward the Dowager.

Splat! A large, juicy blackdrupe struck the Dowager's chest, exploding in a mess that left the front of the Dowager's gown stained purple. The Dowager's jaw dropped.

Immediately, a retinue of Provincial Guards—the Dowager's protectors—was upon the widow, holding her stick-thin arms at her sides. But the widow strained against them, her face flushed with rage.

"The High Laird is bleeding the Provinces dry!" Bellatin

said with a roar. "The money I inherited from my husband should have kept me for life. Now I am nearly destitute, thanks to the High Laird's new taxes."

I swallowed hard. The widow had been one of the wealthiest women in town. The idea that she was poor seemed inconceivable.

Da, two stateguards at his side, approached the widow. "Arrest her," he said with a sigh.

"No."

The Dowager raised her hand as she spoke. The Provincial Guards released the widow. The Dowager smiled at Bellatin, even as the widow stared back defiantly.

"Tomorrow," the Dowager said, "you will come to the Grimjinx house and we will discuss your grievances. I have the High Laird's confidence. Perhaps I can—"

But the widow would hear no more. She gathered her skirt and stormed from the Banquet Room. Everyone fell silent.

Mortified, Jorn jumped to his feet. He fumbled to hand the Dowager his napkin, which she used to mop up the mess down her front.

"So," Jorn squeaked, "you were saying about the Jubilee?"

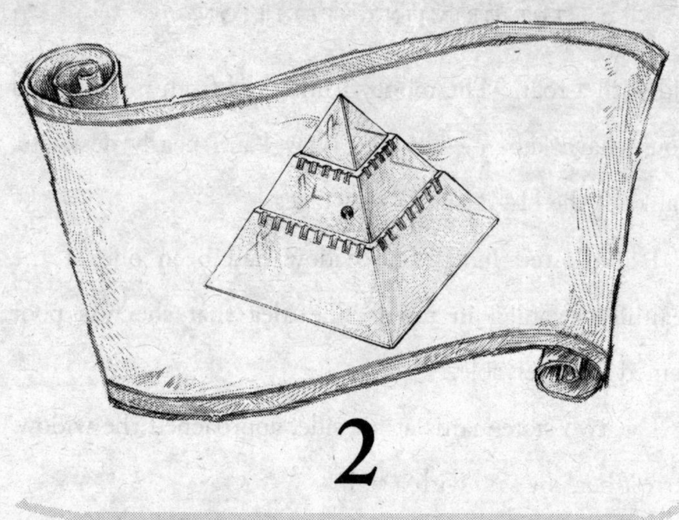

2

Jaxter's New Shadow

"Plan twice, steal once."

—Yevill Grimjinx, creator of the Grimjinx family code

The rest of the banquet was a quiet, miserable affair. Not exactly the celebration Jorn had intended, I'm sure. He'd hoped to show the Dowager off like a prize. Instead, when we finished eating, the Dowager excused herself and we all walked back to my parents' house in silence.

The second we were home, she snapped her fingers at her soldiers. A tall, broad-shouldered Satyran woman with a neatly trimmed brown beard stepped forward.

"Luda," the Dowager said, "from here on, you are Jaxter's

bodyguard. Your duty is to protect him at all times."

A *bodyguard?* I knew Luda by reputation. She could be . . . intense. The horns that stuck up out of her helmet looked sharp enough to gore an entire herd of cargabeasts with a single swipe.

"Your Majesty," Luda said in a deep and determined voice, "the boy will always be safe while I am around. This I pledge!"

I looked up at her in mock skepticism. "I'm not sure she's qualified."

If I hadn't just been placed in her care, I suspect Luda would have ended me right then. The Satyrans of Rexin were proud warriors. She stomped her cloven hooves and thumped her breastplate with her armored fist.

"I have defended the Tor of Belos against the marauding hordes from the Rexian bileswamps!" she bellowed. "I have slain a herd of rampaging sanguibeasts on a stampede through the farmlands of my home! I have—"

"It was a joke!" I threw up my hands. "You have jokes on Rexin, right?"

From her stony look, I guessed they didn't.

"Dowager, this isn't necessary—" I started.

But the Dowager's face was very serious. "I'm sorry, Jaxter, but if I'm in danger, you're in danger. I should have assigned you a permanent guard months ago, following the affair with the Sarosans. After tonight, it's clear I can wait no longer."

"But—"

"Jaxter!" An edge in the Dowager's voice sliced the air. She looked exhausted, angry, and defeated. She closed her eyes and her face relaxed. "There is no discussion. Good night."

Luda snapped to attention, her armor clanging, and she bowed to her sovereign. The Dowager nodded in return, then made for the stairs. Aubrin fell in next to the royal, taking her arm.

As the other Provincial Guards took their posts, Ma eyed Luda with curiosity. The Satyran had already attached herself to me like a second shadow.

"If you ever give up your job as a guard," Ma said, looking Luda up and down, "you should consider a life of thievery. You'd be very good at stealing objects on the top shelf." She paused, hoping Luda would crack a smile.

She didn't.

Da said, "And where will you be sleeping tonight, Luda?"

Luda folded her hefty arms. "I do not require sleep. I will hold vigil outside the young master's bedroom and protect him, as is my charge."

"Yes, well, nothing like a good vigil," Ma said. "Get some rest, everyone. Big day tomorrow."

"Indeed," Da said, grinning at me. "*Someone's* got a birthday."

With all the attention being paid to the upcoming Jubilee, I was worried people had forgotten my birthday. Of course, if they had forgotten, I had a plan. I was glad I didn't have to use it. After such a tense evening, waking everyone up at dawn with noisemakers would have been frowned upon most likely.

Hand in hand, Ma and Da went upstairs. I followed, with Luda at my heels. Walking past Aubrin's room, I found my sister sitting on the windowsill next to her bed. She leaned her head on the glass, gazing up at the two moons passing side by side against the night sky.

"Not tired, Jinxface?" I asked, standing in her doorway.

It was several moments before she looked at me. Her eyes, normally bright and mischievous, seemed sad. Even her smile lacked its usual energy.

"I'll be in bed soon," she said quietly.

"You were trying to warn me," I said, "about the widow. How did you know she was going to throw fruit at the Dowager?"

Aubrin shrugged. She slid from the sill and crawled under the covers of her bed. As she blew out the candle on her night-stand, she whispered, "It's good to have you home, Jaxter. Get some sleep. Don't forget what Kolo said: *Volo ser voli.*"

My chest tightened. Those words—a par-Goblin proverb meaning "Yesterday is today"—had been haunting me for months. It was the last thing Kolo, the former Sarosan leader, had said to me.

Just before he was imprisoned in a shimmerhex, Kolo had tried to warn me about . . . I still didn't know quite what. It had something to do with the Palatinate and the Great Uprisings. But all information about the Uprisings had been outlawed hundreds of years ago by Mannis Soranna, the first High Laird. How could Kolo know anything about the Uprisings? And how was I supposed to learn?

For the last two months, I'd used my position as the Dowager's apprentice to gain access to the biggest libraries in all the Five Provinces. If any record of the Uprisings existed, it would surely be available to royal eyes only. But not even the darkest, most unused shelves with the oldest, dustiest books held any answers.

My obsession worried the Dowager. I'd never told her exactly what I was looking for. I had only the words of a possible madman to go on, after all. But she could tell something was upsetting me. This trip to Vengekeep was supposed to be relaxing. Now, between my frustration with Kolo's warning and the disastrous banquet, relaxing was proving harder than I imagined.

I kissed Aubrin on the forehead and went to my room. There, I found Maloch Oxter, stripped down to his breeches and sitting cross-legged in the hammock Da had slung above my old bed. Like Kolo, Maloch's da had been trapped in a shimmerhex for the role the Shadowhands had played in stealing from the High Laird's vaults. Maloch, who worked for the Vengekeep stateguard to hide the fact that he was a thief, had moved into my room so Ma and Da could continue to teach him thievery.

As a result, my room now had a distinctly . . . *sweaty* smell.

Maloch was hunched over, whispering to a small, glowing crystal cupped in his hand. The second I entered the room, he muttered something and tapped the crystal. It went dark.

I smirked. "How's Reena?"

Our friends Reena and her brother, Holm, had left the Provinces with their parents and the rest of the Sarosans. But Reena and Maloch stayed in touch with a pair of magical crystals Maloch had stolen from the Dowager. It was all kept very quiet—Reena's people didn't exactly like magic—but I got the impression Reena and Maloch talked a lot.

A lot.

Maloch stretched out and stared at the ceiling so he wouldn't have to look at me. "Fine. The Sarosans have started over again on an island. They're very happy."

"And Holm? His poetry any better?"

Maloch could only smile. "Worse than ever."

I changed into my nightshirt. "How are things coming along with the new Shadowhands?"

Ma had restarted the elite group of thieves, and Maloch had signed on as the first recruit. As a stateguard apprentice, he could get information on criminals from around the

Provinces who might make good Shadowhands.

"Slowly," he said, clearly unhappy. "Your ma's very picky about who we let join."

Maloch was anxious to have the Shadowhands back in operation. He hoped their first heist would be to steal the other Shadowhands—including his father—from the Palatinate Palace, where they stood as glass statues.

"Trust Ma," I said. "She knows what she's doing."

I put out the candles and crawled into bed. I was seconds from sleep when a thought popped into my head that would keep me awake for hours.

How had Aubrin known what Kolo had said to me? I'd never told her.

In fact, I hadn't shared Kolo's last words with anyone.

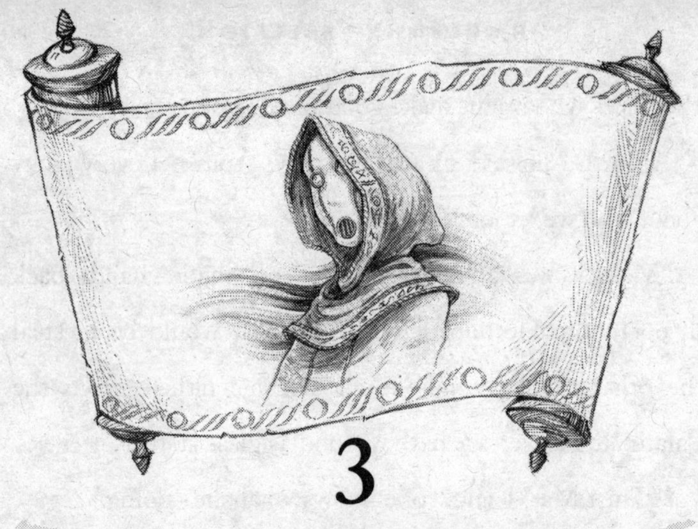

3

The Sentinels

"An accomplice is only two silvernibs
away from being a snitch."

—*The Lymmaris Creed*

Every birthday, for as long as I could remember, started with me waking to the scent of freshly grilled singe-meat sausages wafting up from the kitchen downstairs. The morning of my thirteenth birthday, I awoke to the smell of sweat and rotten eggs.

I opened my eyes to find Maloch's bare foot a hairbreadth from my face. He lay unmoving on the hammock above, his leg dangling over the edge. Grimacing, I slid onto the floor and crawled quietly out the door. Just outside, I ran headlong into Luda, standing at her post.

Maybe she really didn't sleep.

"It's my birthday," I announced, stepping around her. "In thieving circles, it's traditional to hug the birthday boy."

"I am not a thief," she said stiffly. "And I do not hug."

Given that her arms were as big as mokka tree trunks, it was probably for the best.

I resolved to forget about Kolo and the Uprisings and the Jubilee and just enjoy being thirteen. Luda shadowed me downstairs, where we found my family already gathered around the table near the tallest pile of singespice flapjacks I'd ever seen.

"Happy birthday, Jaxter!" Ma and Da cried. Aubrin pulled out the chair at the head of the table for me.

Once Maloch and the Dowager came downstairs, we all dug into breakfast. As was tradition, I led us in a spirited rendition of the Grimjinx birthday song. Standing on my chair, I threw back my shoulders and belted:

"Birthday! Birthday! Steal another year!
Eat up all the scorchcake till it disappears!
Getting what I want is fun!
Hide your purses, here I coooooome!"

Ma and Da linked arms and joined in. Every verse got louder and louder. We were in rare form when we got to verse twenty-three, which glorifies past birthday conquests. By then, though, Maloch and the Dowager were looking a bit glassy-eyed, so we cut the song short. I sang the other fifty-five verses in my head.

Next came the presents. I unwrapped Ma's gift first and found a set of new green velvet pouches to replace the ones I'd lost. They even came stocked with a healthy supply of the twelve essential plants I used to counteract magic.

From Da, I got a new leather wristband with a secret compartment to hide the vintage lockpicks he'd received when he turned thirteen. They'd been passed down through the Grimjinx family for almost three centuries.

Aubrin gave me a pair of vallix skin gloves, capable of handling cursed items without contracting the curse. Ma passed me a package from Nanni, my grandmother, delivered just yesterday. Inside, I found my very own official copy of the key that opened the Grimjinx family album. Now I could do what every thirteen-year-old Grimjinx had done for years: throw away the duplicate key I'd secretly forged when I was seven.

I wasn't expecting anything from Maloch but he surprised me. "Since you're here for a month until the Jubilee starts," he said, "I'm giving you kioro lessons. You need to learn to defend yourself."

Of course Maloch's gift involved hitting. And sweating.

Finally, the Dowager handed me a scroll sealed with a purple wax disc bearing the Soranna crest. "It's a royal pardon," she said. "Good for one nonviolent, relatively harmless, but most certainly illegal shenanigan at a future date. Use it wisely."

I thought Da was going to faint dead away. He gripped Ma's hand excitedly, his mind no doubt making plans for our next family vacation/heist. I didn't have the heart to tell him it was a joke. The Dowager had given me my gift before we left Redvalor Castle: an antique spyglass.

Usually, a thief's thirteenth birthday celebration would have lasted all day and into the night, with fistfuls of scorchcake and endless rounds of Shave the Grundilus. Just my luck that on *my* thirteenth birthday, everyone had responsibilities.

As we cleared the breakfast plates, Da prepared for a meeting about Jubilee security, the Dowager braced herself for a day discussing celebration plans with the Castellan, and

Ma talked about her phydollotry shop appointments.

"But," Ma said, "the festivities will continue tonight with a birthday dinner fit for a High Laird."

All the while, I kept my eyes on Aubrin, who'd barely touched her food. She was quiet and withdrawn, just like last night. I hoped I could get her alone to find out why she was upset.

Luckily, Ma gave me the perfect opportunity. Before heading out, she handed me a coin purse. "Why don't you three"—she indicated Maloch, Aubrin, and me—"head to the market and get a hemmon we can roast tonight?"

Then she and Da left for their jobs while the Dowager went upstairs to don her head-of-state robes. I placed the coin purse into Tree Bag, the satchel that Kolo had given me.

Maloch went to the corner of the living room where he stored his apprentice armor. "Count me out," he said. "I'm going to get some broadsword training in."

"Maloch," Aubrin said, frowning, "we never see Jaxter anymore. Can't you skip *one* day of training?"

Tears pooled in her eyes. Her lower lip trembled. Maloch instantly looked remorseful. In the two months Maloch had been living with my family, he and Aubrin had grown close.

Which meant he was now completely under her thumb. "Fine. But not because I want to spend time with Jaxter. I, um . . . I need to buy some oil so my armor doesn't rust. Lemme get some money." Maloch disappeared upstairs.

Aubrin turned to me. The tears were gone and her frown was now a devious smile. She pointed to her head. "Do you see this face? It is a *weapon*!"

"Well played, Jinxface," I said, and we bumped elbows.

Even Luda had to concede, "I fear your cuteness arsenal."

Brassbell Promenade was uncommonly quiet when we arrived. A rumble of distant thunder just beyond the valley had scared most market-goers into returning home before the storm hit. Several merchants were hoisting heavy cloth awnings to protect their wares.

Along the way there, I kept Luda distracted while Maloch and Aubrin competed to see who could pick the most pockets before we got to the butcher. Aubrin brought out Maloch's fun side. I think having a sister made him less of a garfluk.

When we reached Lek's shop, Aubrin was the clear

winner, having nicked nearly three times more loot than Maloch. She celebrated with an odd little dance that involved shaking her hips, raising her arms in the air, and grunting like a sanguibeast. Luda stared blankly. She had *no idea* what was going on.

Without warning, the wind picked up. A woman selling monx cried out as her awning collapsed. A baby started keening in her mother's arms. A street musician plucked his oxina and played an Aviard lullaby. As these things happened, Aubrin's head spun around to watch each of them. First, the awning collapse. Then the baby. Then the musician. She had a strange look in her eyes. Like she recognized all of this. Like it had all happened before.

Thunder rumbled, closer this time. Aubrin slowly looked up. Tears slid down her cheeks. "It's time," she said.

"What are you talking about, Jinxface? Time for what?"

The air above us crackled. A ring of blue energy formed just over our heads. Together, Maloch and I pulled Aubrin away from the vortex in the sky. We knew quickjump rings when we saw them. Luda crouched, ready for anything.

Two hooded figures fell from the glowing circle. As they landed on the cobblestone street, there was a snap and the blue circle vanished. The new arrivals wore dark green robes with magical sigils embroidered in gold around the hem of their cowls. They pulled back their hoods, revealing leather masks with metal grids where the mouths should be and round, silver lenses in place of eyes.

Palatinate Sentinels.

The Sentinels were elite mages, highly skilled in spells beyond the grasp of ordinary mages. Whereas the Palatinate governed magical law, the Sentinels enforced it. Most often, that meant they hunted down rogue mages.

Both Sentinels had their spellspheres resting in their palms. The taller mage stepped forward. "Aubrin Grimjinx!" she called out, turning her head from side to side.

Maloch and I shared a look. What could my little sister possibly have done to warrant a visit? Had she picked a mage's pocket?

Aubrin gently pulled herself from my protective grip. With perfect posture, she walked right up to the tall Sentinel. "I'm Aubrin Grimjinx."

"Come with us," the smaller Sentinel said, beckoning with his free hand.

Aubrin nodded. The tall Sentinel held her spellsphere

aloft and chanted in the magical language.

"Hang on a minute!" I shouted. Maloch and I rushed forward. "What's going on?"

"Jaxter, please," Aubrin whispered. "You don't know what you're doing." It was like she wasn't my little sister anymore. She was suddenly very calm, very mature.

"We're keeping these naff-nuts from taking you anywhere," Maloch said, clenching his fists.

Naturally, Maloch considered violence first. I opted for diplomacy. "Our father is Protectorate of Vengekeep. Let's go talk to him. You know, without weapons and magic and . . . meanness."

"The Palatinate does not recognize the authority of Vengekeep's Protectorate," the shorter Sentinel squawked. "Stand aside."

"It's okay," Aubrin said. "I'll go with them."

"The zoc you will!" Maloch said. He and I each grabbed one of Aubrin's arms and pulled her away.

The mages advanced, spellspheres sizzling with power.

"Uh, Luda," I called out, "remember that pledge you made . . . ?"

But the Satyran was already on the move, charging forward with a determined war cry. Her furry hands flew up to her shoulders where she kept two broadswords crisscrossed over her back. With a tinny *ssshhhk!*, she drew the swords from their scabbards and leaped in front of me.

The tall Sentinel spoke a single word. A cone of smoky gray light shot from her spellsphere and struck Luda. The Satyran's back arched as her face clenched in a silent scream. A second later, she collapsed like a limp doll.

Before I could check on Luda, the tall Sentinel spoke again. More gray light spiraled from the spellsphere and came right at me. I clutched Tree Bag and braced for the inevitable pain.

But nothing happened. As the gray light touched me, it exploded into a shower of harmless white sparks that disappeared as they hit the street. I looked at the Sentinels. They looked at me. Clearly, that shouldn't have happened.

Maloch charged. Bent over, he drove his head into the stomach of the smaller Sentinel. As the pair fell, they tumbled and brought the tall Sentinel down with them.

A crowd of people had formed a circle, murmuring and

pointing at the melee. Using his hand-to-hand kioro training, Maloch fought to keep the Sentinels from using their spellspheres.

"Go!" he shouted to me.

Grabbing Aubrin's wrist, I pulled her through the assembled throng and ran.

"Jaxter!" Aubrin protested. But I was hardly paying attention. My mind raced with options, trying to figure out the closest, safest place to hide.

Then it hit me: the Dowager! The royal family could overrule the Sentinels. I led Aubrin back toward our parents' house. If we were lucky, the Dowager hadn't left for her meeting with the Castellan.

Lightning flashed and rain started to fall as I hurried Aubrin through the backstreets and alleys of Vengekeep. Splashing through puddles, we turned the corner and saw our house ahead. I pulled Aubrin tight to me and yelled to the two Provincial Guards at our front door, "Get the Dowager!"

One guard ducked into the house while the other moved, as if coming to help. But before he could get far, the air above us lit up and hummed. The two Sentinels dropped from a new glowing ring and stood between us and the house. The tall Sentinel chanted. Red light encased the guard, freezing him to the spot.

I stepped in front of Aubrin and shook my fist at the shorter Sentinel. “Don’t make me get brave!” I warned him, my voice cracking. “Bad things happen when I try to be brave.”

I fumbled with my pouches, searching for something to help us escape. But Aubrin laid her hand on my wrist. I looked down. She was smiling, soft and innocent. “Jaxter,” she whispered, “it’s okay. You need to trust me. I’m going with them.”

I stood there, slack-jawed. Aubrin threw her arms around me and squeezed. Then quietly she stepped over to the Sentinels, took a deep breath, and winked. The sizzling ring of energy in the sky changed from blue to green. It lowered around the Sentinels and Aubrin. A flash and they all vanished.

The Provincial Guard, freed from the red light, shook his head and looked around, almost as if he’d forgotten why he was there. A moment later, the other guard emerged from our house with the Dowager in tow.

"Jaxter?" the Dowager called out from under a thin parasol. "What's happening?"

By now, the rain was falling so hard that the entire world blurred. My clothes grew heavier as I soaked up every drop. I stood there, staring numbly at the spot where my sister had disappeared. I couldn't even form the words to explain it.

"Jaxter!"

The shrill voice came from behind. I spun around to find my friend Callie Strom racing down the street. Her fists pulled at her gray apprentice robes, hoisting them up over her shoes as she ran. She doubled over as she reached me, trying to catch her breath.

"Am I too late?" she asked, her eyes searching the neighborhood frantically.

The Dowager met us in the middle of the street. "Someone tell me what's going on."

My head had started to spin. I could feel my left hand twitch. My lungs hurt. And I couldn't stop staring at that spot on the ground.

Aubrin.

"Jaxter!" Callie grabbed my arms. Her puffy cheeks and

red eyes told me she'd been crying. "Did they already take her?"

"Take who?" the Dowager demanded.

I nodded, stupefied. "Yes," I said. "Yes, she's gone. She was here and then she— Wait. How did—? Callie, did you know the Palatinate was coming to take Aubrin?"

Callie shook as she sobbed. "O-only s-since th-this m-m-morning."

"How could you know?" I asked.

She buried her face in her hands. "Because it's *all my fault!*"

4

An Ancient Decree

"The only difference between a lie
and a truth is the telling."

—Manjax Grimjinx, former commander of the Provincial Guard

"There's a very good reason."

Ma had been repeating this for the last hour. It was less convincing each time.

My family had gathered in the parlor of Talian's home. As a member of the Palatinate, Talian could explain what had just happened to Aubrin. "You wait and see," Ma continued. "It's a mistake or a miscommunication or . . . or something. We'll get it straightened out. Aubrin will be home by sundown. All very simple."

Da put his arm around her. Their weak smiles told me that neither believed what Ma was saying. The Palatinate had dispatched *Sentinels* to take Aubrin. There was nothing simple about this.

"Some mistake," Maloch said with a grunt. His tussle with the Sentinels hadn't ended well. He sat in a high-backed chair, his bandaged leg on a tuffet. A large gash on his cheek had just started to scab over. A dark red ring around his right eye promised to turn black and blue in the days to come.

Am I to blame? I wondered. I'd been discreet while researching the Great Uprisings. Maybe word had gotten to the Palatinate. It was very possible Aubrin's abduction was a warning: stop poking your nose into the Great Uprisings.

Da winked at me. "Some birthday party, eh?"

I groaned. So much for relaxing.

A sob from across the room broke through the sound of the rain outside. She'd been so quiet, I'd almost forgotten that Callie had banished herself to the corner. She hadn't stopped crying since she'd met us in the street.

The Dowager, who had been admiring a glass cabinet filled with phials of sparkling magical elixirs, moved to comfort her. "Callie," she said in her singsong voice, "please explain what you meant when you said this was your fault."

Callie eyed my family cautiously. Ma and Da gave the sofa a pat, inviting her to sit next to them.

Callie joined my parents and blew her nose on a handkerchief. "It started this morning. Every day, as part of my magical studies, I have to read several history books and report back to Talian on what I learned."

She pointed to a very old leather book on the table. The cover said *A History of Seers* in green-tarnished copper letters. "I was reading about the history of prognostication in the Five Provinces. The book says that seers are very rare, only a handful are born every generation. Even still, they all share some unique traits. For example, all seers have green eyes. And all seers are left-handed. And . . . and . . . all seers are silent for the first ten years of their lives."

The room fell quiet but for the ticking of the nearby clock. Ma and Da joined hands and I knew we were all thinking the same thing. Aubrin had green eyes. Aubrin was left-handed. And Aubrin . . .

"No," Ma said quietly. Her lips pulled back into a pained smile. "No."

By now, Callie was sobbing again. "And . . . and I just

casually mentioned to Talian that Aubrin had only started speaking about eight months ago. And that none of you knew why she had been silent for ten years . . ."

Da was on his feet, pacing behind the sofa and breathing heavily. Ma wrung her hands. All this nervous activity got to Callie and she started wailing.

"I'm so sorry!" she said. "I didn't realize this would happen. As soon as I told Talian, he contacted the Palatinate Lordcourt. I ran as fast as I could to tell you. I didn't know they'd come so quickly."

"Way to go, Strom," Maloch barked. "You'd turn in your own uncle, wouldn't you?"

Callie shot him a hate-filled look but didn't say a word.

I stared straight ahead, letting it all sink in. This had nothing to do with my investigation into the Uprisings and the Palatinate. This was about . . . my sister? A seer? She was a lot of things. A con artist. A pickpocket. But a seer? How could I not have known that?

It seemed obvious now. The night before, when she'd tried to warn me about the widow Bellatin. And when she'd known Kolo's last words to me.

The Dowager wandered over to the glass cabinet again,

her back to the room. I could have sworn she was trying not to look at us.

A pair of twin doors leading into the study slid open. Talian stepped through, hands folded at his waist.

"I apologize for the delay," Talian said softly, sharing a humble smile with everyone. "I needed to contact the Lordcourt."

Talian had changed since he'd helped me and Callie thwart Edilman Jaxter and fend off the balanx attack in Vengekeep. He looked thinner, his scarlet-and-black robes clinging to his lithe frame. And he seemed much older than twenty. In these past few months, he'd become so reserved, so measured . . .

So adult. It was frightening.

"Mr. and Mrs. Grimjinx," Talian said, "I must apologize. I'm sure this was incredibly stressful. Please let me assure you the Palatinate doesn't make a practice of seizing children from their parents without any warning."

Da exhaled loudly, expelling enough air that he almost doubled over. Ma blinked twice and her smile widened. "I knew this was a mistake," she said. "Thank you, Talian. Yes, we've had quite a scare. But if you can just see that Aubrin is brought back to us safely, we'll say 'No harm, no foul' about the whole matter."

Ma and Da stood as if to leave. But Talian made no move to see them to the door.

The mage frowned. "I'm afraid I haven't made myself clear. We apologize for the abrupt way your daughter was taken. But—"

"She won't be returning to Vengekeep."

At the sound of this new voice, we all turned to the open study doors to find a tall woman wearing the majestic robes of the Palatinate Lordcourt. A gold-rimmed monocle covered her left eye. The smile on her lips could have frosted the windows with ice. We all stood. Not to be respectful but because of what my great-great-uncle Gellimore Grimjinx always said: *Sit with your enemy, never stand again.*

"My name is Nalia," she said. But we knew who she was. It's hard to forget someone who, just two months ago, tried to have your entire family imprisoned as part of a plot to destroy the Palatinate.

"What are *you* doing here?" I asked.

Nalia ignored me and swept across the room to address my parents. "I came as soon as Master Talian told me there was a problem. The Palatinate deeply regrets this inconvenience."

Inconvenience? Prison was inconvenient. This was inexcusable.

Da looked ready to explode, but Ma put a steadying hand on his shoulder and did what she always did when facing down an adversary: she smiled. "And why won't my daughter be coming home?"

Nalia took a chair across from the sofa and motioned for my parents to sit. They didn't. "You know, of course, that we believe your daughter is a seer. Even as we speak, the Palatinate is testing Aubrin. The tests are safe and harmless. If it proves true, she'll be taken to the Creche."

"The Creche?" I asked. "What's that?"

"It's a special facility," Talian explained. "All seers live there from the moment their abilities are discovered. It's secure and nurturing, a place for them to learn more about what they can do. It's all done in the interest of security."

"Whose security?" I asked. "Aubrin's or yours?"

The more hostile we got, the calmer Nalia became. "The security of the Five Provinces, of course. Seers are wondrous people . . . but we can't allow their talents to be abused. Suppose a seer was kidnapped by an enemy of the High

Laird. That seer's prophecies could reveal information about the Provinces' defenses. The Creche was built hundreds of years ago as a safe house and, by royal decree, all seers must live there."

At the words *royal decree*, all eyes moved to the Dowager. She looked down, almost guiltily. "It's a very old law," she said meekly. "Not many people know about it."

Ma's smile didn't fade but her harsh tone showed she was growing less patient. "This is all very fascinating but we can't allow our daughter to be taken away and raised elsewhere."

"Mrs. Grimjinx," Talian said gently, "this isn't done to be cruel. The Creche really is the best place for her. Dealing with visions of the future can be very upsetting. It's why seers don't speak for years. At the Creche, she'll receive the very best care. She'll be taught how to make sense of her visions."

"More important," Nalia continued, "your daughter will receive the very best of everything: food, clothing, education. Every need will be addressed. And when she turns eighteen, she'll be appointed to a position of respect in the High Laird's service. She'll want for absolutely nothing the rest of her life."

If there was anything Nalia could have said to take the

fight out of my parents, she'd just said it. Ma and Da had always claimed that, no matter what, they wanted me and Aubrin to be happy and content. That was why they let me turn my back on thieving and do research with the Dowager. In the Creche, Aubrin would have the best life possible.

I could see defeat in Ma's eyes. She turned to the Dowager. "Is there anything you can do, Annestra?"

The Dowager shook her head. "I can't go against royal law. But you have my assurances that what Nalia says is true. Aubrin will be happy and safe at the Creche."

Ma nodded sadly. "Yes. I can see it now. You're right. Ona and I only want what's best for Aubrin."

Nalia folded her arms and looked smugly triumphant. "Very wise, Mrs. Grimjinx. Now, if you'll excuse me . . ."

She stood and walked back to the study doors. Before exiting, Nalia turned back and threw us her most wicked smile yet. "Enjoy the Jubilee."

Talian followed her into the study, asking Callie to show us out. Ma and Da shuffled to the door, heads bowed. As we filed out of the house, I brought up the rear. I felt a tug at my elbow.

"You know I didn't mean this to happen, Jaxter," Callie

said. "You understand, right?"

"Sure, Cal," I said. But I didn't really.

Heading home, I helped Maloch along on his injured leg. Ma and Da slowed down to allow the Dowager and her guards to pull ahead.

"All right, boys," Ma said softly. "I think they bought it. Now, let's go get our little seer."

5

Dark Times

"Time tames the wary heart."

—Ancient par-Goblin proverb

Stealing Aubrin from the Creche. Those words alone would inspire pages and pages in the Grimjinx family album, detailing what might possibly be one of the most daring heists in our family's history.

It was a pity we wouldn't be around to write it.

Rescuing Aubrin wasn't just about returning my sister to her family. In this instance, it was also about treason. We'd be defying royal decree. And everyone knew the punishment for treason was death. Granted, our family album was overflowing with stories of Grimjinxes who'd beaten death sentences. But that seemed unlikely this time, especially with the Palatinate involved. We had no choice but to leave the Five Provinces. Forever.

With Luda just outside the bedroom door, Maloch and I quietly started packing the few belongings we'd be taking on the trip.

"Exciting, isn't it?" I asked. "Breaking into the Creche. I mean, you and me breaking into the Palatinate Palace was pretty exciting too. But I don't think that was nearly as illegal as this."

Maloch was unusually quiet. He kept eyeing the magic crystal on the nightstand. I could tell he really wanted to talk to Reena.

"You want me to leave so you can—?"

"I'm not going with you."

I stopped packing. "What?"

Frowning, Maloch sank down on the bed. "You can't tell your parents. Once we get Aubrin back, I'm staying behind."

"Mal . . ."

"My da is still a prisoner in the Palatinate Palace. I can't leave as long as he's there. You'd do the same for your da."

It really was a momentous day. Maloch was making sense.

"I have an aunt in Merriton I can stay with. I'm trusting you with this, Jaxter. You can't say anything."

I nodded. "Not a word."

We'd started out as friends, then we were enemies, and now we were . . . I didn't know what. I didn't want Maloch to stay behind. But I knew I couldn't stop him either.

Maloch stood and started packing again. "This must be hard on you. Leaving the Dowager and all."

I'd been so worried about Aubrin that I hadn't even *thought* about the Dowager. My chest tightened. I was supposed to be her intellectual heir, take over research at Redvalor Castle someday. That couldn't happen now.

The choice was clear: if I stayed, the Palatinate could use me to get to Aubrin. I *had* to go with my family. But the more I thought about leaving the Dowager, the harder it was to think about anything else.

How do you say good-bye and thank you to the person

who completely changed your life without letting her know that's what you're doing?

"I feel bad for Aubrin," Maloch said, snapping me out of my thoughts.

"Hmm?"

"She's been having visions for years. Must be confusing. She knew all along that the Sentinels were coming for her. That's why she didn't try to fight it. Scary, really. To know exactly when it's time for someone to take you."

I shuddered. In a way, it was like knowing exactly when you'd die. She must have felt doomed. From the moment we woke up that morning, she knew—

A spark went off in my head. "Maloch, what did you just say?"

"I said it must have been scary for her to know it's time for—"

"'It's time . . . ,'" I repeated. "That's what she said, right before the Sentinels appeared."

"Right," Maloch agreed. "She can predict the future. She knew it was time for the Sentinels to appear."

I paced, thoughts firing off faster than words. "No, no,

no. Aubrin kept a journal. She never let me read it."

Maloch nodded. "Yeah. She wouldn't let me look at it either. So what?"

"And what did she say when anyone tried to look at the book?"

"She'd snatch it away and say it wasn't . . . time." Maloch stiffened. I could practically see the gears in his tiny little brain starting to smoke and spark the faster they churned. "When she said 'It's time,' she didn't mean that it's time for the Sentinels to take her. She meant—"

"—it's time to read the book!" I shouted.

Aubrin had visions. She *knew* she was going to be taken to the Creche. And maybe she left us a *clue about how to rescue her!*

We charged down the hall to Aubrin's room. The black book I'd given her almost a year ago sat conspicuously on the table near her bed. Usually, she hid it. This was the first time she'd left it out in the open.

She wanted us to find it, I thought.

I closed the door and snatched up the journal. Maloch and I sat on the edge of her bed, holding the book between us. Inside, I instantly recognized Aubrin's delicate handwriting on the first page. Maloch scanned the scrawls and shook his head. “It doesn’t make sense. It’s gibberish.”

I grinned. “Not at all. It’s in our family code.” Every thieving family had a unique alphabet only its members could decipher. This was meant for Grimjinx eyes only. “Pretty sneaky, Jinxface.”

“So what does it say? Does it tell us how to get into the Creche?”

I turned a page and skimmed. The more I read, the deeper I frowned. “No. It’s pieces of par-Goblin nursery rhymes and Aviard fairy tales. But all the fairy tales I know are set in made-up places. Aubrin’s stories are set in real cities. Bejina, Vesta . . . even Vengekeep.”

“What are the stories about?”

I looked at him grimly. “They’re all about monsters.”

But these weren’t the stories that children across the Five Provinces had been brought up on. Aubrin had changed them. Made them more real. And scarier.

She described monsters attacking town-states and villages. As if it had all really happened. The last quarter of the book was blank. But the final two pages she’d written on were very distinct.

A series of strange symbols I'd never seen covered the right-hand page. It was like no language I'd ever seen. She'd stopped writing in our family code.

The writing on the left-hand page was much more telling. It read:

JAXTER, IF YOU'RE READING THIS, THEN THE SENTINELS HAVE TAKEN ME. DON'T WORRY. I AM SAFE. DO NOT TRY TO FIND ME. YOU HAVE SOMETHING MORE IMPORTANT TO DO. YOU MUST TAKE THIS BOOK TO EAJ. YOU'RE THE ONLY ONE WHO CAN. THE MESSAGE MUST BE TRANSLATED. DARK TIMES ARE COMING. ONCE YOU KNOW WHAT THE MESSAGE READS, YOU MUST LEAVE THE PROVINCES.

I had no idea what Eaj was. A village? A person? A landmark? I'd never heard of it. How could I take the book there if I had no idea who/what/where Eaj was? And why leave a message that needed to be translated? Why not just tell me what it said?

"Have you heard of Eaj?" I asked Maloch, reading my sister's note again. "And what do you think she means by 'dark times'?"

"Uh, Jaxter," Maloch said, soft and low, "did you read the *whole* message?"

Of course I'd read the whole message. I was just practicing a time-honored Grimjinx tradition of ignoring bad news and pretending it didn't exist.

The last part of the message—five words—ran along the bottom of the page. The letters were just a bit bigger than the rest and each word was underlined twice. It said:

YOUR LIFE DEPENDS ON IT!

6

The Rescue Mission

"When you eliminate the impossible,
whatever remains, however improbable,
is probably worth stealing."

—*Krinilla Grimjinx, leader of the raid on the Soulship stockyards*

Timing was critical.

It would be much easier to snatch Aubrin and leave the Provinces if the Palatinate and the Provincial Guard were otherwise engaged. Thankfully, the Jubilee gave us the perfect distraction. If we did this right, we could pull it off while the whole of the Provinces was busy celebrating.

We spent the next few days preparing. It would take a week to travel northwest to the Creche, and another week to go to the capital city, Vesta, where we could hire a ship to take us away. That left us with a week to find Aubrin and get her out.

The night before our trip to the Creche, my family sat around the kitchen table. The Provincial Guards stood at their posts, watching vigilantly. Luda waited near the fireplace, her eyes never leaving me.

The Dowager sat in our living room, trying to enjoy a pot of singetea while the Castellan went on and on about how the Vengekeep Jubilee celebration would be talked about for centuries to come. He asked the Dowager what she knew of her brother's plans to celebrate in Vesta.

"I know very little," the Dowager conceded. "He plans to honor the Palatinate for their service. He'll be presenting Nalia and the Lordcourt with some magical relics that have been locked away for hundreds of years."

Which, I thought, *was exactly what they wanted.* The Palatinate had tried to steal those relics. Now the High Laird was just handing them over.

A black-and-white striped candle burned in the center of the kitchen table next to a map of the Five Provinces. We each had a small dab of melted wax from the candle stuck to our earlobes.

"Are you sure this will work?" Maloch asked, nodding at the candle. "I mean, Luda is standing right there."

Ma and Da touched their temples—the family sign for *everything's okay*—and turned their attention to Aubrin's journal.

Da squinted at the curious symbols. "I used to study ancient languages. Thought it would come in handy when raiding old tombs. But I've never seen anything like this. Translating it could be tricky."

"We could see if the scholars at the Great Library of Thorosar know it," Maloch suggested.

"Maybe," Ma said, "but if we want experts in long-lost languages, we want the assassin-monks of Blackvesper Abbey."

We all shivered and spit, a thief ritual to ward off bad luck. The assassin-monks were a mysterious order, known almost as well for their devotion to cataloging every known language in the Provinces as they were for their abilities as assassins. You didn't exactly walk up and introduce yourself. They were hard to find. No two accounts could agree on where Blackvesper Abbey was located. In fact, the par-Goblins had a saying: *You don't find the assassin-monks, the assassin-monks find you*. Not exactly welcoming.

"I have an important question," I said. "Why does my life depend on delivering this message?"

"Huh," Maloch said. "I thought it meant your life depended on leaving the Provinces."

"I can see how you'd read it that way," Ma said. "She could have been clearer. I've warned her about imprecise language—"

"Can we *focus*, please?" I said. "My life depends on *something* happening or not happening. Which is it?"

Da closed the journal. "Well, you can ask Aubrin yourself when we get her out of the Creche. Which is what we're here to discuss. Let's hear your thoughts."

Everyone spoke fast. We threw around ideas, good and bad. We were so busy talking, we hardly noticed a knock at the door. When one of the guards opened it, Callie charged into the house, clutching a scroll. "I've got an idea how—"

She froze when she saw the Dowager, the Castellan, and the guards. My family and Maloch silenced Callie with big, wide-eyed smiles. Callie's gaze fell on the candle and, without hesitation, she smeared a bit of freshly melted wax on her earlobe.

"What are you doing with a garblewax candle?" Callie asked.

"A what?" I replied innocently.

She pointed at the candle. "I'm a mage, Jaxter. I know a garblewax candle when I see one. It magically masks your conversation. Anyone with wax on their ears can hear what you're saying, while everyone else"—she pointed to the Dowager and Jorn—"hears something completely different."

"Sorry, Callie," the Dowager called over from the living room. "What was that about eating cargabeast steak for breakfast?"

Callie raised her eyebrows at us to say *See what I mean?*, then smiled sweetly at the Dowager. "Nothing!" She sat next to me at the table. "Only mages can legally possess garblewax."

"You do remember whose house you're in, right?" Da asked.

Callie shrugged it off. "I know how to get Aubrin."

We stared uncomfortably at Callie. Technically, she worked for the Palatinate. Sharing our plans with her wasn't a good idea.

She waved her hand. "Oh, please. You're planning to

break Aubrin out of the Creche. I know you too well. I'm here to help."

We remained quiet for a long time. Finally, Ma said, "We appreciate the offer, Callie. But I think, under the circumstances—"

"I won't tell anyone," Callie insisted.

Maloch grunted. "No chance, Strom. You're one of them."

"I'm an honorary Grimjinx," Callie said, looking at Da to back her up.

"That she is," Da said. Callie had been given the title after she helped us destroy the fateskein tapestry. It wasn't a title we bestowed lightly on non-family.

Callie nodded once. "I've been reading up on the Creche in Talian's library—"

"Unless you've got a map that shows how to sneak in—" Maloch said.

"You don't need one. You can walk right in the front door and no one will think twice about it."

It didn't seem possible. With the Palatinate running the Creche, it had to be highly secure.

Callie leaned in. "Did you know there's not a single adult

there? Just the seers and a staff of caretakers . . . and they're all kids."

Ma perked up, suddenly curious. "Now why is that, do you suppose?"

"It's because adults tend to make the seers nervous," Callie said. "When they're surrounded by people their own age, the seers are much more productive and find it easier to master their skills. At least, that's what it said in *A History of Seers*."

"How is that in any way helpful?" Maloch asked.

Callie ignored him. "They don't use just *any* kids. The workers there are all criminals. They're sent to the Creche as a punishment."

I saw where Callie was going. "Bangers! So Maloch and I pose as prisoners—"

Callie nodded. "I'm coming too. The Creche has magical defenses. You'll need a mage to help."

Da wasn't convinced. "How will you explain it to Talian?"

"He's leaving for the Palatinate Palace tomorrow," Callie said. "All the mages in the Provinces are planning a special celebration for the High Laird during the Jubilee. I'm to stay with my uncle until Talian returns. But I'll just tell my uncle that Talian changed his mind and is taking me with him. So all we really need now is to forge some documents that say we've been sentenced to work in the Creche. . . ."

Callie batted her eyes at Ma, the family's forgery expert. "Oh, I think that's entirely possible," Ma said.

We finalized our plans. Callie would meet us tomorrow morning at the Vengekeep portcullis. Ma and Da would take us to the Creche, then go ahead to Vesta to arrange passage away from the Provinces. By the time we got Aubrin out of the Creche and met up with my folks at Vesta's Bellraven Inn (a secret safehouse for thieves), the Jubilee would be in full swing. People would be so busy celebrating that we could be halfway out to sea before anyone realized we were gone.

Callie went home. Ma and Da went upstairs to bed. Maloch muttered something about taking a last walk around Vengekeep and left. I sat alone at the table, while the Dowager wrapped up her meeting. When Jorn finally left, I took a deep breath. This was it.

Time to say good-bye.

The Dowager heaved a loud sigh as soon as the front door was between her and the Castellan. "You've lived in town with that man for twelve years?" she asked, wide-eyed.

"I can barely stand twelve hours with him."

I laughed and took a seat at her side. "You get used to the smell. Besides, you only have to wait until the end of the Jubilee."

"Exactly," she said. "Then we'll be back at Redvalor."

My stomach lurched. I tried to speak but nothing came out. *Tell her the truth,* I thought. *Tell her that unless she breaks the law and sets Aubrin free, you can never go back to Redvalor.*

But I couldn't. The Dowager would never ask me to turn on my family. I couldn't ask her to turn on hers. So I went with the story we created.

"Listen," I said, "we're taking a trip to visit Nanni in Angel Cove."

"Will you be back in time for the Jubilee?"

"Absolutely," I said, maybe a little too quickly.

"Oh, good," the Dowager said. "As soon as the Jubilee's over, we're going on vacation. I'm thinking a trip to the Firebrand Falls. Or maybe . . ."

She listed several exotic destinations throughout the Provinces. I smiled, but it was killing me inside. When she finished, she rose.

"We should get some sleep," the Dowager announced.

"You've got a long trip ahead of you and I have another day . . . with the Castellan."

As we moved to go up the stairs, Luda fell in behind us. "I'll miss you, Luda," I said, perhaps the biggest lie of the night. "But I'll see you when I get back."

The Dowager chuckled. "Don't be silly, Jaxter. Luda's going with you on your trip. You'll be in even more danger on the open road."

I hadn't planned on that.

"Right," I said, casting a quick look at the Satyran. I could have sworn she raised her eyebrow just enough to say, *And you thought you could get rid of me easily.*

"Good night, Jaxter," the Dowager said. She stepped into her room and closed the door. I watched her disappear from sight, knowing it would be the last time I'd ever see her.

Heading to my own room, I bumped into Luda. *Her* I'd have to see again. At least one more time.

The next morning, Ma, Da, and Maloch packed our covered wagon while I ran to the market to get food for our trip. Or, at least, that's what I told Luda. I wove my way through the streets of Vengekeep, and my Satyran shadow never strayed more than an arm's length away.

As we neared the market, I threw myself to the cobblestone pavement and screamed in agony. "The pain! The pain!"

Luda looked stymied. She wasn't very good with an opponent she couldn't bludgeon. "What happened?"

"It's my ankle," I whined. "I need you to bring the healers here."

"I will carry you," she said, bending over to scoop me up.

I swatted away her outstretched hands. "Are you naffnut?" I asked. "Don't you know anything about human bodies? This is a serious, life-threatening wound. If you move an injured ankle . . . my *head* could fall off!"

Not one of my better lies. But I was pressed for time.

Luda looked from my ankle to my head and back to my ankle, as if trying to decide how one could possibly be related to the other. I cried out again, hoping to speed her along. She glanced around at the passersby.

"If anyone kidnaps you, do not fear. I am a Satyran Grand Master at tracking. I can find you anywhere."

"Master tracker, right, great. Go track down a healer!"

Luda galloped away at full pace. As soon as she was out of sight, I bolted toward the city gates where Ma, Da, and Maloch were waiting with our mang-drawn wagon. A moment later, Callie appeared with a backpack, and together, we climbed aboard.

As Da drove the wagon under the portcullis, Callie produced a piece of paper. The edge was jagged, like it had been torn from a book.

"From Talian's secret library," she said. "It details the Creche's magical defenses. Between my spellsphere and your pouches, Jaxter, we should have no problem getting to Aubrin."

"Bangers, Callie," I said. "This'll be easy."

It was *not* easy.

7

Gobek and Mavra

"Need is a fickle taskmaster."

—par-Goblin proverb

"Now remember," I said, "kids sent to work at the Creche are hardened criminals. Only the lowest of the low are punished like this. Callie, stop smiling. Look meaner. Scowl a bit. Maloch, you . . . No, never mind, you're fine the way you are. Ready?"

The three of us stood, staring at the Creche looming before us. A perfect sphere of shimmering gold, it was nearly the size of a mountain. Beautiful whorls, wide as rivers, covered the surface. Occasionally, streams of magical energy would race through the whorl gullies, making the entire sphere flicker.

Nearby, Ma and Da were putting on their stateguard disguises. "Remember," Ma said, donning her helmet, "you've got a week to find Aubrin and then a week to reach Vesta. We'll be waiting there."

Maloch hadn't stopped gawping at the massive structure. "Is that enough time? This place is huge. If there are only a handful of seers every generation, why is it so big?"

"I guess we'll find out," I said.

Directly in front of us, a small alcove at the base of the sphere hid the only door we could find. Lowering the visors on their helmets, Ma and Da stood on either side of us. Da reached out, gripped the long rope that dangled near the door, and gave a hard tug. A muffled bell clanged.

Several minutes later, we heard clicks and rattling from within, like locks being unhitched. Then, the round door slid to the side, just enough to reveal a small figure within.

The creature was unlike anything I'd ever seen. He stood upright like a human, but that's where the resemblance ended. His eyes took up most of his face, with just a tiny nose and mouth below. Stubby arms hung from the sides of his bulbous body. Broad, gelatinous legs brought him up to my chest. His greasy, mottled gray skin looked like wet clay.

Those huge eyes glistened when he spotted us. "Is visitors!" he declared joyously with a thick accent. Then he frowned and said, "Is not allowed." With a tug, he slammed the door shut.

We stood there, unsure what to do. So Da rang the bell again. When the door slid open, the creature acted like he hadn't just seen us.

"Is visitors!" he cried again.

"No!" Ma said, before he could slam the door shut. "We're not visitors. We've been ordered to bring these prisoners to you."

Da held up the documents bearing both Talian's and Castellan Jorn's forged signatures. The creature waddled outside, grimacing with each step. He examined the papers closely.

"Is not first of month," the creature muttered, poking at Talian's wax seal. "Is first of month, is time for new workers."

"Ah, yes," Ma said, "but you see, these ruffians have been very bad. They're really quite terrible. Couldn't wait for the first of the month to get rid of them."

The creature shrugged. "Is making no difference to Gobek. Is always needing new workers. Is following me."

He turned and went inside, pushing the door wider so we could all come in. Holding tight to Tree Bag, I stepped over the threshold and caught a glimpse of a plaque that hung over the doorway.

The plaque read: YESTERDAY IS TODAY.

My heart skipped a beat at seeing Kolo's last words engraved over the door. I'd never been one to believe in coincidence. *This is what Kolo meant,* I thought. *He wanted me to come here.* I had a feeling I'd find more than Aubrin in these halls.

Iron pots filled with magical green-blue fire floated above our heads. A single corridor led us deeper into the sphere. Instead of walls made from stone or wood, the passages were formed by sheer yellow curtains that hung from above. The creature stopped in the middle of the room and groaned.

"Are you okay?" Callie asked.

"Is very difficult being Gobek," the creature said, pain pinching his voice.

"Can we help?"

Maloch cleared his throat and glared at Callie. We were supposed to be outlaws. Callie's concern wasn't helping our story.

But Gobek didn't seem to notice. He waved his hand and smiled. "Is nice of you, young criminal lady. Gobek is not able to help being Gobek. Is to be Gobek, is to be hurting. Is way of things."

Now even *I* was feeling bad for him. Every gesture, every step seemed to hurt. Still, he kept smiling at us.

"Is Gobek. Is caretaker. Is welcoming you to Creche. Is being good? Is treated good. Is being bad? Is not treated good. Is simple."

The curtains gave way to stone walls that curved widely to the right. All the while, Gobek chattered amiably about how he hoped we would enjoy working at the Creche. Truth be told, I got the idea that working under Gobek wouldn't be much punishment at all. He seemed rather nice. Talkative, but nice.

The corridor opened up into an expansive library. Kids our age and slightly older scuttled around with feather dusters, cleaning the bookshelves. The caretaker took us across the room to a tall, Aviard girl with short black feathers. She was throwing logs into the fireplace and prodding the embers with a poker. Actually, the way she did it was more like stabbing. And each stab made her frown more deeply.

"Is looking at this, Mavra," Gobek said to the girl. "Is new workers!"

Gobek had said they could always use new workers. The look on this girl's face suggested otherwise. She swung the poker around furiously, narrowly missing Gobek.

"It's not the first of the month!" she shouted. Nearly every worker in the room jumped when she spoke. "I just trained the last batch."

"Is in charge of workers," Gobek explained to us brightly, pointing at Mavra as if he hadn't even noticed how angry the girl was. Which was hard to miss. Dead people could have seen how angry she was.

"Is special circumstance," Gobek continued. "Is just three more." Before Mavra could protest again, Gobek said to us, "Gobek is leaving you in Mavra's care. Is listening to her carefully. Is being good." With that, he turned and waddled away.

Mavra's beak clicked furiously. She growled, then she spun to face away from us.

"So, Mavra," I said brightly. "I know this is *really* inconvenient for you. Believe me, it puts us out too. But we won't cause any trouble. My name is Tyrius, by the way. In case, you know, you ever want to say, 'Hey, Tyrius, go sweep out the seers' quarters—'"

Mavra squeezed a large bellows into the fireplace. "For now, just shut up and do what you're told. Stand in the hall, out of the way. When we're done here, I'll show you to the worker barracks. And stay away from the seers until *I* tell you it's okay."

We did as we were told and waited.

"Well," Callie whispered, "she's *lovely*."

"She's the one in charge," I said.

"So?" Maloch asked.

"So, it's like my great-aunt Rodina Grimjinx always says, 'A friend in charge means rewards large.'"

"Ugh," Maloch said. "It sounds like Rodina's been talking to Holm."

I peered at Mavra, who darted around the library, shouting orders at the other servants like a general in the Provincial

Guard. "If Mavra's in charge, she must know everything about the Creche. We get her on our side, and we can have Aubrin out of here in a day. Two days, tops."

Callie wasn't convinced. "I'm getting the idea she doesn't make friends easily. How are you going to do this?"

I pushed my glasses up to the bridge of my nose. "Grimjinx charm is a force to be reckoned with. You wait and see: by the end of the night, Mavra and I will be best friends."

8

A Baking Accident

"To steal a purse, first steal the heart."

—Ganjar Grimjinx, master thief of Yonick Province

Apparently, I was a mite out of practice using Grimjinx charm.

By the end of that night, Mavra and I were *not* best friends. In fact, days went by and the harder I tried to charm the Aviard, the more she seemed to hate me. When the week was nearly out, not only was Aubrin still nowhere to be seen but also Mavra's talons were wrapped around my throat and she was trying to kill me.

To be fair, I could see why she was angry. Her feathery

eyebrows had just been singed off when the scorchcake I'd placed in the oven exploded. But I didn't do it on purpose. Singe her eyebrows, I mean.

The explosion, though, was very much planned.

Every surface in the kitchen was covered in hot, gooey cake batter. Servants slipped across the floor, trying to put out the oven fire. In the middle of the chaos, Mavra had pinned me up against a wall. Thankfully, the batter on her hands made it hard to get a good grip. I slid from her clutches and ducked under a table.

"Now, Mavra," I said, scrambling away, "killing me won't solve anything."

"Wrong!" She dug her talons into the stone floor. "It will solve the biggest problem I have. You!"

Mavra was only four years older than me but she was as huge as any adult Aviard. Her beak dropped open, emitting a terrible screech, and she lurched at me. She tried to spread her wings and come at me from above, but the cake batter prevented her from flying. I pushed off the table, sliding across the room.

She began hurling everything she could get her talons

on: rolling pins, ladles, egg whisks. I did a good job dodging them until a well-aimed wooden spoon hit me right between the eyes and sent me down into the muck on the floor. Before I could recover, Mavra was on top of me.

My fellow servants were not exactly helpful. Once they put the oven fire out, they surrounded us, cheering on whoever they thought was winning. In other words, they were rooting for Mavra.

She slapped at me while I flailed around, pitching handfuls of batter into her eyes. This, of course, made her howl louder and pummel harder.

"Is too loud!"

Mavra froze, just as she grabbed my smock. Gobek tread carefully through the batter on the floor, wincing with every step. He took in the mess and shook his head. "Is not going to be good cake," he announced. Several of the kitchen staff laughed.

Mavra jumped to her feet and pointed at me. "Tyrius did this, Gobek."

"It w-was an accident," I stammered, doing my best to look sorry. "It's not as bad as you think. You look good with batter in your feathers."

The Aviard cried out and leaped at me, but Gobek gently pulled her away.

"Is not good being angry, Mavra," Gobek said. Then, his tiny mouth pursed into what looked like a vertical smile. "Gobek is knowing what is to be making Mavra happy."

He took a step back and bowed his head. As he did, his greasy flesh began to slide and swirl. His short, fat legs grew long and thin, while talons sprang from his feet. Multicolored feathers popped out all over a torso that had become lean and triangular. His head melted and was replaced with two long and springy necks, each sporting a new, single-eyed head with a beak that curved upward.

Gobek had become a garfluk, widely known as the stupidest bird in all the Five Provinces. One of Gobek's two heads warbled while the other head laughed. He ran in place, flapping his green-feathered wings and kicking his legs in a bizarre dance.

The other servants laughed as the Gobek garfluk pranced around the kitchen, bumping into tables and behaving like a buffoon. In the past few days, I'd seen Gobek change shape maybe a dozen times. He did it to entertain the servants. It only added to his mystery. In all my studies with the

Dowager, I'd never heard of a creature that could change from one thing into another.

While the other servants were enjoying the show, Mavra was not. She shoved a small girl toward a basket filled with vegetables. "Get back to work!"

The laughter died as everyone returned to their tasks. Gobek stopped, his heads dropping. The garfluk folded in on itself. The feathers dissolved and stretched out to become Gobek's claylike flesh. Soon, the small chubby creature was back to his normal form.

"Gobek is usually making Mavra happy with garfluk. Is maybe happier if Gobek becomes sprybird?"

Mavra's taloned fingers balled into a pair of nasty-looking fists. "He's been nothing but trouble since he got here!"

I scrunched my face up in the most repentant look possible. It worked. Gobek took pity on me. "Is new here. Is still learning. Is careful to remember Mavra was new once too."

Even as Gobek tried to calm her, Mavra continued to rant. I looked past Gobek in time to see Maloch and Callie slip into the kitchen from the hall and blend in with the assembled crowd. They caught my eye and touched their temples. I gave a small nod.

"Let me tell you," I said loudly, interrupting Mavra, "that I have really learned my lesson. Yes, sir, no more baking for Tyrius, that's for sure. How about I just clean up this mess and we'll call it good?"

I didn't give Mavra a chance to argue. I pushed past her and headed to the supply closet.

"Is seeing?" Gobek asked, patting her hand. "Is cleaning up. Is all better now, yes?"

Mavra spun on the other servants, who gaped from the far side of the kitchen. "What are you all looking at?" she demanded, sending everyone scurrying.

I took my time at the supply closet, selecting just the right mop for the job. Maloch and Callie strolled over, pretending they didn't know I was there.

"Did you get it?" I asked softly.

Maloch turned his cupped hand toward me. A small tarnished key sat nestled in his palm. "Swiped it the minute Gobek heard the commotion and came here." He surveyed the batter-spattered kitchen. "Nice diversion."

"Jaxter, what did you do?" Callie asked, trying to look horrified, but all she could manage was highly amused.

"Bit of baking," I said. I pulled up the smock that covered

my front, revealing my pouches. "For future reference, jellyweed does *not* bake well. But then, I already knew that." I touched my temple and nodded at Callie. "You know where to meet us. Midnight."

Callie touched her temple and walked away.

"Tyrius!" Mavra bellowed.

I grabbed a mop and bucket and shambled over to the Aviard. She began directing me where to mop, as if I couldn't tell that the batter was literally everywhere. But I didn't question it. I played my part, the faithful servant, and did as I was told. For now.

It had all worked exactly as planned. The cake explosion, Gobek leaving his quarters in a hurry so Maloch could steal the key.

Tonight, after nearly a week of trying to find Aubrin, we'd finally have some answers.

9

The Purple Prophecy

"Silver gilds the lie that opens the deepest vault."

—*Ancient par-Goblin proverb*

As a rule, I don't go around blowing up cakes or singeing Aviard eyebrows for fun. It *was* fun, but that's not why I did it.

I did it because I was desperate. Mavra worked the servants from sunup until long after sundown. We cleaned latrines. We cooked meals. We made beds. But we hardly ever saw the seers we were here to serve. And when we did, Aubrin was never with them.

Once everyone had gone to bed, Maloch and I, candles

in hand, sneaked out of the boys' barracks and made our way to the seer classroom. The seers spent their mornings in this room with Gobek, who taught them how to use their abilities. The room was far enough away from the servant barracks to keep our midnight meetings private.

"Do you think it's weird?" Maloch asked, while we waited for Callie.

"What?"

"This place. The seers are really valuable to the High Laird. And the staff is made up of criminals. What's to stop anyone from leaving?"

"I dunno," I said. "The Overlord, maybe?"

We both chuckled. Since our arrival, the other servants enjoyed telling us stories of the Overlord. Allegedly, Gobek *wasn't* the only one in charge of the Creche. Rumor had it that a mysterious figure—the Overlord—resided here as well, keeping an eye on everyone and everything. No one knew who it was or even if he or she really existed. I'd chosen to ignore the stories. Clearly they'd been concocted to keep the servants in line with the threat of an unknown, all-seeing gaoler.

At least, that's what I hoped.

Callie joined us a moment later, sitting at a round table with a sigh.

"I almost didn't make it," Callie said. "Mavra wouldn't take her eyes off me all night. I think she suspects we're up to something."

"I don't care about Mavra," I snapped, and immediately regretted it. "Sorry. I'm just . . ."

Callie squeezed my shoulder. "We'll find Aubrin, Jaxter. I can feel it. We're getting closer."

We'd seen seven of the eight seers, a group of children as young as ten and as old as sixteen. They rarely spoke to the servants, or each other for that matter. Honestly, they were all a bit . . . weird. Always gave you a look like they knew something you didn't.

We quickly figured out that our best chance of finding Aubrin was to learn everything we could about the Creche. But after almost a week of searching, we were no closer to finding her. Time was running out. Ma and Da were waiting for us in Vesta. If we were to meet them on time, we had to leave the Creche in two days.

"Okay," Callie said, "what have we learned today?"

Mavra kept us so busy during the day, these midnight

meetings were our only chance to share what we'd learned. We were always on alert, noting any clues that might lead us to Aubrin.

I cupped my chin in my hand. "Only thing I learned today is that they're very thorough in collecting all the seers' prophecies. Why is that, do you think?"

"Ah," Maloch said, "I know that one. I was cleaning the hall outside the classroom when Gobek was teaching the seers and I overheard the lesson."

He reached to the center of the table where a glass bowl filled with colored marbles sat. He plucked out a bright purple marble. "Okay, pretend this represents a vision of the future. Let's say . . . the High Laird chokes on a bone while eating roast gekbeak." He set the marble down near the table's edge.

"Now," Maloch continued, "that event didn't just happen on its own. Before he ate the gekbeak, it was prepared by his cook." He pulled a blue marble from the bowl and laid it next to the purple one in a line that pointed to the middle of the table. "Before the cook could prepare it, a servant bought the gekbeak from a butcher." He pulled a green marble out and laid it next to the blue.

"The butcher bought the gekbeak from a huntsman"—next, a yellow marble—"who killed the gekbeak along a ridge"—an orange marble—"all because the huntsman got up at sunrise because he knows that's the best time to hunt gekbeaks." Finally, Maloch placed a dark red marble in the center of the table. All the marbles lined up perfectly, red to purple. Maloch ran his finger along the line. "All of these *must* happen to get us here," he said, tapping the purple marble.

"But," he added quickly, returning his hand to the red marble, "let's say the huntsman didn't wake at dawn like he planned." He flicked the red marble and it rolled away. "Which means the gekbeak got away"—he flicked the orange marble—"so the butcher had no gekbeak to sell that day"—there went the yellow marble—"and, without any gekbeak at the market, the High Laird's servant decided to buy a carga-beast steak instead"—flick went the green marble—"and the cook prepared a boneless steak"—the blue marble spun off, and Maloch snatched up the purple one—"leaving the High Laird healthy."

I peered at the scattered marbles. "So," I said slowly, "a vision is just *one possible future.* And the more marbles—I mean visions—you can record that lead up to the purple prophecy, the more likely it is to occur."

Callie nodded. "And that means, if you know everything that leads up to the big event before it happens, you could knock out one of the marbles to make sure the purple prophecy doesn't happen. You don't just have to stop the red marble. Affecting any event in the chain disrupts the pattern, right?"

Maloch shrugged. "Maybe. I think that's why they gather every prediction, no matter how small. You never know what role it might play in future events."

Another thought occurred to me but I kept it to myself. Gathering *all* the predictions was also a good way of making sure no one else knew of all the small events that led to a big one.

Callie shifted uncomfortably in her chair. "That explains . . . ," she whispered softly.

"What?" I asked.

"I overheard two seers say that Aubrin is an augur. That's the most powerful kind of seer. Their visions give the most accurate view of things to come. Maybe that's why they keep her separate. She can be used to verify the other predictions."

"Did they say where she's kept?" I asked.

"We *know* where she is," Maloch said. He held up the key he'd stolen. "Your diversion was all about getting this."

There were three places in the Creche that servants were forbidden to go. The seer dormitory was one. But it didn't make sense for them to keep Aubrin somewhere so obvious. That left . . .

"This will get us into the Athenaeum?" Callie asked.

The Athenaeum was behind a locked, golden door. The seers spent their afternoons in there, doing who knew what. Servants weren't even allowed in to clean. Since we knew the seers spent a lot of time behind the door, it made sense we'd find Aubrin there. The only other option was . . .

"Unless you want to see what's behind the Black Door," Maloch said gravely.

We knew a little about the Athenaeum. We knew absolutely nothing about the Black Door. It stood at the dead end of a corridor near the seer dormitory. Some servants believed the mysterious Overlord lived there. Others thought it was a place they tortured servants who misbehaved. The only thing all the servants agreed on: it was a place to fear.

Sometimes, late at night, you could hear screaming

behind it. Inhuman, pain-filled wailing. If Aubrin was as important as Callie said, chances were she wasn't back there. Checking behind the Black Door was our very *last* option.

I snatched the key from Maloch. "All right, then. What are we waiting for? Let's go to the Athenaeum."

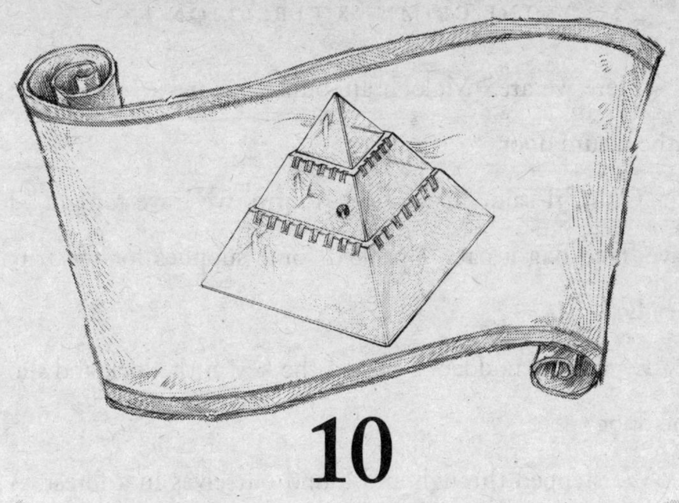

10

Into the Athenaeum

"Secrets buried in a six-foot hole
are seven feet from discovery."

—*The Lymmaris Creed*

As we made our way through the shadowy halls of the Creche, I couldn't stop thinking about the warning in Aubrin's journal and what Maloch had said about the marbles. If it was true, the future wasn't set. Things could change. I just had to figure out how to flick away the marbles that led to me dying.

Which sounded right. The more I thought about it all, the more convinced I was that I was losing my marbles anyway.

"Here we are," Maloch announced as we arrived at the Athenaeum door.

"Okay," I said, "if we find Aubrin, we leave tonight." I gave Tree Bag a pat. "I packed some supplies for the trip. Ready?"

Everybody nodded. I turned the key in the lock and slid the door open.

We stepped through and found ourselves in a forest. A huge, dense, moonlit forest.

"Didn't see this coming," I admitted.

We padded softly across the grassy ground, ducking under low-hanging branches covered in leaves as big as my body. At the top of the Creche, a glass dome let in light from both moons hovering high overhead.

"I'm just going to ask," Maloch said, "why is there a forest *inside* the Creche?"

"I think the Creche was built *around* the forest," Callie said. "These trees seem very old. Maybe hundreds of years. Now we know why the building is so big. It could take us hours to search the whole thing. Or days."

"Fine. Next question: why build the Creche around a forest?"

I ran my fingers across the rough bark of the nearest tree. “They must be special somehow.” Reaching up, I took one of the mammoth leaves in hand and held it up to the moonlight. The leaf appeared to glow, revealing a map of veins under the leaf’s surface. “Maybe the Palatinate wanted to protect—”

I stopped. The dark veins within the leaf began to shift. The leaf wriggled gently between my fingers. Within seconds, the veins had repositioned. Instead of reaching out in random directions, they now spelled out near the top of the leaf:

“Whisperoak!”

"Huh?" Maloch asked.

"It's whisperoak. An entire forest of whisperoak trees. They were supposed to have died out a long time ago. Look . . ." I took another leaf in hand and said softly, "Jaxter was here."

I held the leaf to the light and the veins read:

"The Dowager told me that Aviards used these centuries ago to record family histories," I said.

"That doesn't explain why the Creche is built around an entire forest," Maloch mumbled.

Carefully, I climbed up to the lowest branch of the nearest

tree and grabbed some leaves. Words covered the surface. I checked leaf after leaf—each carried comments more cryptic than the last. Many detailed commonplace events at the Jubilee, which was just a week away.

"This must be how they record prophecies," I said. "Safer than writing them in books, which could get stolen."

"Jaxter . . . ," Callie said softly.

"But if the prophecies are so valuable," I continued, "you'd think they'd be better protected."

"Jaxter . . . ," she said again.

"I mean, building the Creche around the forest was effective but if someone really wanted to get in here—like we did—it wouldn't take very much. Didn't Talian's book say this place was enchanted? Where are the magical protections—?"

Callie reached up and slapped my foot. "Jaxter!"

"What?"

She nodded toward the heart of the forest. Maloch and I followed her fear-stricken gaze. In the distance, a pale blue sphere of light floated between the trees. A moment later, a second and third appeared. Each pulsed and flickered . . . and moved in our direction.

"Ah," I said, "that would be the protection."

"What are they?" Maloch asked.

"Gaolglobes," Callie whispered as she consulted the page she'd stolen from Talian's library. "Magical sentries. They zero in on movement and sound. Nobody move."

We held our breath as the radiance from the gaolglobes lit the trees around us. The globes were twice our size. We waited as they floated past and disappeared into the forest behind us.

"All right then," I said, shimmying down the tree carefully. "We know to avoid the big floaty glow balls. Let's spread out and look for Aubrin."

We split up, each creeping carefully into the darkness. With every step, I felt more confident that we'd find her. If Callie's theory was correct, they probably kept Aubrin here where she could easily read and verify the other predictions. I just hoped they'd given her a decent bed.

An hour flew past as I searched. It seemed like the forest would never end. I carefully scaled the biggest tree I could find so I could get my bearings.

A faint humming below told me the gaolglobes were patrolling again. I held my breath, waiting for them to pass. The moons above lit the leaves all around me. My eyes passed over the tiny words spelled out in the veins.

Kleptocracy . . . Aviard Nestvault plunder . . . Sanguibeasts . . .

I reached out for the nearest leaf and raised it to the light.

War . . . Sourcefire . . . Par-dwarves . . .

These trees were ancient. The Creche had been built around a grove of whisperoak trees that had been used to record the prophecies of seers for hundreds and hundreds of years. The forest was one giant history book.

I grabbed a handful of leaves and read as fast as I could. A lot of it was rubbish. Some leaves held mundane prophecies, discussing what blacksmiths had for breakfast centuries ago. Others described visions of children dressing up in Grundilus Day costumes. They really did chronicle *every* prophecy, no matter how small.

I returned to the ground and moved deeper into the forest, scanning leaves all the way. The farther I went, the older the history. The story of the creation of the Sourcefire, a ball of eternal magical energy from which the land was supposedly created. A detailed account of the fall of the par-Goblin Rogue Triumvirate two hundred years ago. Blow-by-blow details of the Satyran Civil War.

The history of the Uprisings *had* to be here. Somewhere.

I thought of how Aubrin had told me to remember Kolo's last words. It's like they were *both* telling me I needed to learn about the Uprisings.

Then I found the tree I was looking for.

Mannis Soranna . . . Scions . . . Uprisings . . .

I nestled with my back to the whisperoak's trunk and started reading.

"Jaxter?"

I sat on a high branch. My eyes ached. I had no idea how long I'd been reading. Glancing up through the glass dome, I spied hints of daybreak turning the sky deep purple.

We'd been in here all night.

"Jaxter?" Callie's whisper broke my concentration. I could just make out her and Maloch at the base of the tree, looking around.

"Be right down!" I slid gingerly down the trunk and joined them on the ground.

Callie grinned. "If you'd told me a year ago that I'd see Jaxter Grimjinx climb out of a tree instead of fall out of it—"

"Listen," I said. "We have to find Aubrin. *Now.*"

My mind raced. I knew now why Kolo had wanted me to learn about the past. I needed to find Aubrin, not just to get her out but to ask her if what I read was true.

Callie grabbed me by the shoulders, her eyes narrowing. "Jaxter, what's wrong? You're white as a snowsloth."

My stomach ached. I could feel sweat beading my brow.

"We're in terrible danger," I said.

"When aren't we?" Maloch asked.

I whirled on him. "You don't get it. I'm not talking about us. I'm not talking about Aubrin. I mean *everyone*. If we don't get Aubrin out of here tonight, the Five Provinces will fall."

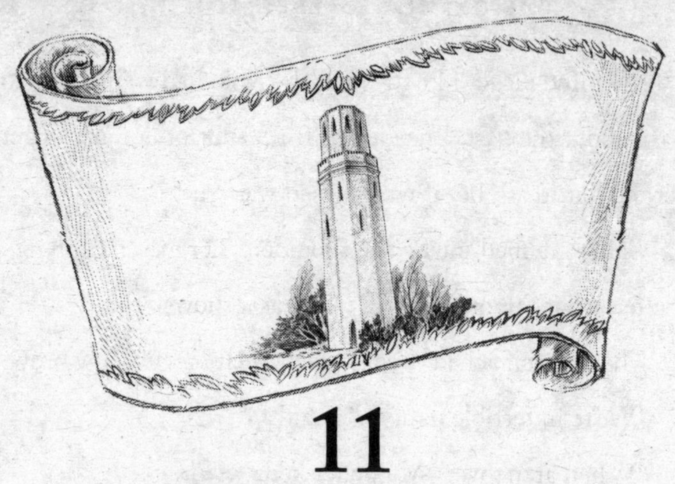

11

The Great Uprisings

"There are no secrets.
Only knowledge in search of a buyer."

—*Selldar Grimjinx, omni-rogue*

Somewhere, far away, the gaolglobes hummed as they continued their patrol. It was the only sound.

Maloch broke the near silence with a nervous chuckle. "Don't be so dramatic."

"I'm not," I said. "Kolo warned me. I spent months trying to figure it out. And now—"

Callie held up her hand. "Hold on. Kolo *warned* you?"

"Kolo was obsessed with the Uprisings," I explained. "He told me I should research them. He hinted that something bad was going to happen and understanding the Uprisings would help prevent it."

"Kolo was also crazy, remember?" Callie said. "He tried to blow up the Palatinate Palace."

"I know," I said, "but I think he had good reason to be worried. Look, centuries ago, before there even *were* Five Provinces, a group called the Scions tried to enslave the land."

Callie's brow furrowed. "The Scions? I thought they were just a story. Powerful mages who wanted to enforce magical rule."

"They were real," I said. "They enslaved thousands of sanguibeasts and vessapedes and spiked orvathorns and turned them into an army."

"Why animals? Why not just recruit soldiers?" Maloch asked.

"The Scions created control medallions that make the wearer obedient to a mage's will. But the medallions don't work on intelligent creatures. By using animals, the Scions had complete control over them."

Callie gasped. "Control medallions? Like the ones we saw Xerrus using at the Onyx Fortress?"

I nodded. "Maloch and I saw thousands of medallions being made in the Palatinate's forge. When you and I found Xerrus last year, I don't think he'd gone rogue. I think the Palatinate had sent him there to figure out how to make the medallions. And those experiments with animals—"

"So what happened with the Scions?" Maloch interrupted.

"The Scions enslaved town-state after town-state. They killed all the par-Dwarves, who were immune to magic. They built the Onyx Fortresses to store huge amounts of magical energy for combat. They were just about to take over completely when one man organized an insurrection. Mannis Soranna."

"The first High Laird," Maloch said.

"They say the war that followed was the bloodiest the land has ever known," I said. "But in the end, Soranna vanquished the Scions, destroyed the Onyx Fortresses, and created the Five Provinces. He made it illegal to learn about the Uprisings. He thought that if no one knew the history, it could never happen again. But because the stories were outlawed, no one could see history repeating itself."

"What does this have to do with anything?" Maloch asked.

"This is why Kolo was telling me to learn about the Uprisings." The words rushed breathlessly from my mouth. "'*Volo ser voli.* Yesterday is today.' Things that are happening now happened back then. The Palatinate is trying to take over the Provinces."

Maloch's face went blank. "Look, you know I trust mages as far as I can throw them. But you're talking about the Palatinate going up against the High Laird and the Provincial Guard. Magic or not, how is that even possible?"

"They learned from the Scions' mistakes," I said. "The Scions made an army out of ordinary creatures. Too easy to kill. So the Palatinate needed a new army. A *different* army . . ."

Maloch understood. "The monsters! Bloodreavers and nightmanx and all the ones you saw in the Palatinate Palace."

I nodded. "The Palatinate is using creatures of legend, made from pure magic. Not so easily killed. I think that's what Xerrus was working on. At first he tried combining real creatures to make them stronger. And when that didn't work . . ."

"They have an entire army hiding in their palace,"

Maloch said. "So, why haven't they used them? What are they waiting for?"

"The right time."

Callie looked ill as she whispered. This couldn't have been easy for her to take. She'd dedicated her life to studying magic. Now it seemed like her masters—even her own cousin—weren't at all who she thought they were.

"They've been waiting for the right time," she repeated. "Think about it. The spiderbats were hunted nearly to extinction. Just like the par-Dwarves. *Anything* that can naturally resist magic has been disappearing. Jaxter, even you've noticed that magic-resistant plants have been dying for years. They've been eliminating anything that can stop them."

"And that's why they had the Sarosans exiled," Maloch said. "Anyone who hates magic—and knows how to counter it—is a threat to them."

"Remember the relics stolen from the High Laird's vault?" I asked. "They were forged by a group of mages who worked for Soranna *against* the Scions. They didn't believe mages should rule absolutely. Those relics were vital in turning the tide of the war for the High Laird."

"How?" Callie asked.

"The relics had the ability to manipulate the Sourcefire. They used it as a weapon against the Scions. After the war, Soranna created the Palatinate to make sure magic was never abused the way the Scions had done."

"Yeah," Maloch said with a grunt, "that worked *really* well."

"To make sure no mage got too powerful, the first members of the Palatinate enlisted the High Laird to guard the four relics they'd created to manipulate the Sourcefire."

"Wait a minute," Callie said. "You said 'four.' *Five* relics were stolen from the vaults."

"The last relic, the Vanguard, wasn't made to fight the Scions. No one knows for sure where it came from. But it proved to be the ultimate weapon against the Scions. The Vanguard has the ability to *destroy magical energy.* If there's any chance of stopping the Palatinate, it means finding that relic."

Callie frowned. "We don't know where it is or what it looks like."

Maloch leaned against the tree. "We know Kolo stole it. That's a start."

"We've got something better than a start," I said. "We've

got *an augur*. If we can find her."

"We've looked everywhere," Maloch said. "Aubrin's not in the Athenaeum."

"Okay," I said, "that means there's only one other place she can be."

Callie nodded grimly. "The Black Door."

I pointed to the dome and the faint sunlight. "The others will be awake soon. We can't risk them finding us near the Black Door. We need another diversion."

"Please," Maloch said, "no more exploding cakes."

"No time," I said, rummaging through my pouches. "Cal, you said you could beat the magical defenses here. Think you can take on a gaolglobe?"

I mixed ground paggis root and jellyweed in my palm. The harder I stirred with my finger, the more the concoction started to crackle and fizz. Callie's eyes widened as she realized what I was going to do. "Do I have a choice?"

"You two keep them busy," I said, "and I'll get Aubrin. Meet me outside the servants' barracks. And try not to get caught."

I threw the concoction in the air. It sparkled and hissed like fireworks, lighting up the dark and echoing off the trees.

Far away, the gaolglobes responded, turning from blue to red. The pulsing spheres shot through the forest, headed right for us, howling loudly enough to wake the entire Creche. Soon, everyone—the servants, Gobek—would be here.

"This is the part where we run," I said.

The three of us shot through the forest, pushing aside branches and tall grass. The spheres had grown brighter, lighting our path with deep crimson. We split up, zigzagging to lose the spheres as they drew nearer.

I lost sight of the others and charged blindly ahead. It was purely by accident that I came across the clearing where we'd first entered. There, just ahead, was the exit. If I could get there before Mavra and the others showed up . . .

Holding tight to Tree Bag, I ran. I glanced over my shoulder, looking for the sphere. Nothing. I was going to make it. And just as I thought I was safe, it dropped from above.

Pop!

Crimson light exploded around me. The gaolglobe vanished and I was left in darkness. There was no way the herbs in my pouches were strong enough to counteract it. So why—?

I didn't have time to worry about it. I slipped through the door, back into the Creche.

"It's coming from the Athenaeum!" Mavra's shrill voice filled the corridor. I turned and ran in the opposite direction, disappearing around a corner just as the servants arrived on the scene. The Aviard girl pushed her way to the Athenaeum door, ordering everyone to back off until Gobek arrived.

Under my breath, I wished Callie and Maloch good luck, then I tiptoed down the hall and made my way to the Black Door.

12

Beyond the Black Door

"A liar with a poor memory
leaves a trail of unfortunate truths."

—Ancient par-Goblin proverb

For as ominous as everyone had made it out to be, the Black Door wasn't so scary up close. It didn't even have a lock. I guess it didn't really need one. Who wanted to go in there, what with all the unholy screaming?

I pressed my ear to the cold, black wood. No howling. No sounds of torture. This was getting better by the minute. Checking to make sure my pouches were at the ready, I ducked inside.

Tiny orbs of green-blue fire floated above, dimly lighting

a slender passage. I crept along the wall, hugging the shadows. Even behind the door, I could hear the wailing of the gaolglobes. Good. That meant they hadn't caught Maloch and Callie.

I walked until the narrow hall opened up into an oval room filled with lit candles. The smell of animal fur and sweat nearly knocked me over. Cages filled with mythical monsters—very much like the ones I'd seen in the Palatinate Palace months ago—sat stacked atop one another, creating a small maze across the room.

Hunched over, I moved among the cages. The creatures snarled and cooed menacingly as I passed. Each wore a control medallion that sparkled with magic.

"Is please to be eating, Bright Eyes."

Ahead, Gobek's pained voice rose above the sounds of the creatures. Kneeling, I squinted and looked around until I spotted Gobek near the center of the room. He was holding a tray of food, standing in front of a cage smaller than the rest.

"Is good food," he said. "Is healthy food. Is not healthy not to eat."

No response.

"Is upset. Gobek is knowing how to fix that. Is watching Gobek, Bright Eyes."

Gobek set the tray down. His greasy flesh folded in on itself and, a moment later, he was a dweek—a giant, furry worm with a single eye at one end. The dweek wrapped itself into a coil, like a spring, and began bouncing back and forth between the ceiling and floor.

That did the trick. I heard a soft giggle. A *familiar* giggle. I moved closer and finally saw Aubrin sitting in the cage. She leaned against the bars as the dweek changed back into Gobek.

"Is smiling," Gobek said, his teeth clenched. He moaned.

Aubrin reached out to him. "You're hurt."

Gobek waved his hand. "Is always hurting. Is not to worry, Bright Eyes."

"Please let me out, Gobek," Aubrin whispered, flashing him her smile weapon.

Gobek looked unsure. "Is difficult, Bright Eyes. Is up to Overlord."

Overlord?

"Gobek!"

A chill tickled my back. The voice had come from the far

side of the room. I curled up into a ball, keeping one eye on Gobek. A tall figure stepped into the shadows and towered over the Creche's caretaker.

"The gaolglobes are howling," the Overlord said. "Find out why."

I *knew* the voice. But I couldn't place where I'd heard it before. I squinted at the tall silhouette in the darkness, trying to get a better look.

Gobek sighed. "Is always howling. Is set off by tiny things. Gobek is thinking gaolglobe magic is not very good."

The Overlord roared. "Go!"

Gobek turned his large, sorrowful eyes toward Aubrin. "Is having learned her lesson, Overlord. Is maybe time to return her to other seers, yes?"

"She should have thought of that before she tried to start a rebellion with the other seers."

I had to stifle a laugh. So *that's* why Aubrin had been removed from the seer dormitory. She'd done what any Grimjinx would have done: rallied the oppressed and tricd to revolt. I'd never been more proud of my sister.

"And she still refuses to share her prophecies with us," the Overlord continued. The silhouette shifted, stepping forward into the light to reveal a man. The candlelight reflected off his bald pate and a twisted face I'd tried very hard to forget over the last year.

It was Xerrus.

I could still picture his sanctum at the top of the Onyx Fortress in Splitscar Gorge. Bubbling cauldrons, balanx skeletons, and cages filled with creatures he'd fused together using forbidden magic. The fact he was here meant I'd been right. He'd been working for the Palatinate the whole time.

Xerrus walked slowly around Aubrin's cage. "But I think I've found a solution. One that will make her much more cooperative. You see, child, I once tried melding two creatures into one. It proved more difficult than I first thought. Then I turned my attention to making creatures out of pure magical energy. Gobek was my first real success. He made me realize that anything is possible."

Xerrus dropped to one knee quickly and pressed his face up against the bars. Aubrin didn't even blink. "And I've been thinking: maybe I gave up on my initial experiments too quickly. Maybe there is still a benefit in fusing two creatures. How docile you'd be if I combined you with, say, a hedgewump."

Gobek's slimy hands shook. "Is not necessary, Overlord. Gobek is knowing that Bright Eyes will be good girl."

Xerrus lashed out, striking Gobek across the face. "I told you to go to the Athenaeum. Leave the augur to me."

My hands balled into fists at my sides. I'd seen the results of Xerrus's experiments. The combined creatures were in constant misery. I couldn't let him touch Aubrin.

Xerrus stalked through a door on the far side of the room. I suddenly understood the *real* reason no adults were allowed in the Creche. It wasn't because adults made the seers nervous. It was because they'd be more likely to resist Xerrus. The servants were kids and easy to intimidate.

Gobek, looking ashamed, nudged the plate at Aubrin. "Is to be eating, Bright Eyes," he said, before leaving.

Once she thought she was alone, Aubrin exhaled. She crawled over to the cage's lock and started to fiddle with it.

"He's right, Jinxface," I said, emerging from hiding. "You really should eat something."

Aubrin yelped. Then her face lit up as I approached. "Jaxter!"

We reached through the bars and hugged, but when she pulled back, her face had gone from happy to horrified.

“What are you doing here?” she demanded.

“You thought we’d just let you stay here?” I asked. I took the vintage lockpicks from my wristband and slipped them into the lock on the cage door. I could feel the tumblers inside the lock move away from my picks. The lock snickered.

Zoc. It was a Moxnar.

“I hate sentient locks,” I muttered. At least it was only a Class 2. They had the ability to twist their innards around, making it hard for lockpicks to stay in place. A Class 4 could actually call out to warn its owner. Undaunted, I thrust my picks down the lock’s barrel and wrestled for control of the Moxnar’s tumblers.

Aubrin shook her head and gripped the bars. “Jaxter, you have to leave right now.”

“Hey, calm down, Jinxface,” I said. “I’ve got Maloch and Callie with me and we’ve got a plan.”

“You have to go!” She was full-on sobbing. “Don’t you understand? By coming here, it means you’re going to die!”

13

The Greater Gain

"Even a last-minute plan is still a plan."

—*Rimordius Grimjinx, chief builder of Umbramore Tower*

Well, there it was. Out in the open. Laid bare for all to see. With that, the mysterious warning "your life depends on it" had transformed into "you're going to die."

As far as rescues go, this one could have been going much, *much* better.

Aubrin's lip trembled. "I've seen it, Jaxter. I've had a vision where you die."

I did my best to stay calm. If I panicked, it would only upset her. I needed to be a big brother. I needed to ignore the fact that she had foreseen my death. And, in ways I didn't want to admit, I needed my mommy.

"Look, Jinxface—"

"Coming here to rescue me is one of the things that leads to your death and— Oh, never mind. You couldn't understand."

"Hey," I said, "I'm not totally useless. I get it. Maloch explained the whole thing with the marbles. One event leads to another and eventually, you get to the purple marble." In this case, the purple marble was me dying.

Aubrin nodded. "And this? Here and now? This is the yellow marble. The red and orange marbles already happened. If you don't leave me here, you'll keep going until you die. We have to stop the chain of events."

"Well, what are the other events? Maybe we can stop one of them."

Her shoulders slumped. "I don't know. My visions weren't complete. I was trying to find out from the other seers if they'd seen anything about you, but I got locked up in here before—" She suddenly reached out and grabbed my tunic. "Please tell me you took my journal to Eaj."

"I don't know who or what Eaj is."

"What do you mean?" she demanded, slapping my arm. "You're supposed to know." Another slap. "You're supposed to take the journal and— Jaxter, this is bad. This is very bad."

"What are you talking about?"

She rolled her eyes. "The visions I've had . . . So much relies on you taking that message to Eaj. But—but I assumed you knew what Eaj was."

"Sorry to say, I don't. Look, we'll get you out of here and— Ow!" I yanked my finger back and the Moxnar snickered. I think it nipped me. I held up the picks, ready to dive back in, when Aubrin's hand appeared, holding a small key.

"This will be easier," she said, slipping the key into the lock and turning it smartly. The door clicked open and she was free.

"Where did you—?"

She grinned. "Picked Xerrus's pocket when he leaned in. Come on, we've got a revolution to stop."

I held her arm. "Wait, you know about that?"

She clicked her tongue. "I'm an *augur,* Jaxter. I've known for a while what the Palatinate was planning. But I couldn't say anything."

"Why not?"

"Seers don't see the future so much as we see *possible* futures. That's why Gobek teaches us the marble lesson. What the Palatinate is doing has opened up several *possible* futures, none of them very good. If I'd tried to warn anyone about the Palatinate, it could have started a whole new chain of events. And something worse could have happened."

"But if you *don't* warn anyone, they *will* take over."

"Not necessarily," she said, an odd smirk on her lips. "There might be another way. . . ."

I shook my head. "My job is to get you to Vesta so we can hop on a ship out of here."

Aubrin suddenly looked very serious. "Jaxter, to take over the Provinces, the Palatinate will wipe out their enemies. That means the royal family. Which includes . . ."

My heart fell.

The Dowager.

★

By the time Aubrin and I emerged from behind the Black Door, the gaolglobes had stopped howling. I wasn't sure if that meant Callie and Maloch had been caught or if

Gobek had declared it all a false alarm.

We made straight for the servant barracks and found Maloch and Callie waiting. Aubrin threw herself at the pair, hugging them tightly. Callie explained how she used her spellsphere to camouflage Maloch and herself so they blended in with the forest. Eventually, Gobek called off the gaolglobes and the servants dispersed. I quickly filled Callie and Maloch in on what Aubrin and I had discussed.

"So how do we figure out what 'Eaj' is?" Callie asked.

I shrugged. "Aubrin thinks we may not need to . . . if we can stop the Palatinate."

"Oh, right," Maloch said. "Stop a legion of highly trained mages with an army of unbeatable monsters. Nothing to it."

Aubrin led us through the corridors. "It's all going to happen in Vesta at the Jubilee," she said. "The High Laird is going to present the Palatinate with the relics. That one event changes everything."

"Right," I said. "So, we stop the High Laird from handing over the relics."

"How?" Callie asked.

"I'm still working on that part," I said. "I thought about asking him nicely."

We came to an intersection and Aubrin headed right.

"Hang on, Jinxface. *That's* the way out." I pointed to the left.

"We're going to the seer dormitory," she said, not even pausing. The rest of us ran to catch up with her. "The Palatinate needs two things to succeed: the relics and the seers. We get both of those, we win."

"Why both?" Callie asked. "Can't we just steal the relics?"

Aubrin shook her head. "Both are potential weapons to the Palatinate. They see the seers as the greater gain. Only the seers can tell their enemies what the Palatinate is planning."

Maloch snapped his fingers. "That's why they keep all the seers here in the first place: to prevent anyone from hearing the prophecies that involve their plans."

"We need to get the seers as far away as possible," Aubrin said.

I didn't like what she was suggesting. "You mean . . . take them with us? Aubrin, we don't have a lot of time to get to Vesta. That many people will slow us down."

Maloch stopped suddenly, forcing us all to halt. "No, it

won't," he said. "You get Aubrin to Vesta. I'll take the seers to the Dagger."

Once he'd signed the Shadowhand Covenant, Maloch had gained access to the Dagger, the Shadowhands' secret bunker. I stopped in midstride. "Maloch—"

He raised a hand. "I told you I won't leave the Provinces without my da. The Palatinate doesn't know where the Dagger is. I can keep the seers safe there for a long time, if needed."

"It's perfect," Aubrin said, beaming at Maloch.

As we got to the dormitory door, I wondered aloud, "How are we going to explain to the seers what we're—?"

But we didn't need to explain anything. Entering the dormitory, we found all seven seers awake, alert, and standing with bags packed.

That's when it occurred to me: breaking into a magically enchanted facility filled with people who could see the future probably wouldn't go down in the Grimjinx family album as one of our more brilliant plans. The seers smiled, as if they'd been waiting for us.

Which, of course, they had.

Single file, with seers in tow, our caravan crept through

the halls toward the exit of the Creche. With Maloch leading the way, Callie and I brought up the rear.

"Jaxter, something's wrong," she said. "Even if they can get the relics from the High Laird, how will the Palatinate control an army of monsters? Using magic makes a mage weak."

She was right. It was strange. But I was willing to bet the Palatinate had a solution to this obvious problem.

"Don't worry about that now," I said. "If we hide the seers, we've won half the battle."

"It's the other half I'm worried about," she said. "The half that involves an army of monsters. How can we win against something like that?"

A voice rasped in the dark. "You can't."

We spun around to find Xerrus standing right behind us.

"You'll never win," the mage continued. "The seers will return to their dormitory immediately"—he leaned forward, squinting at Callie and me—"while I deal with the pair who thwarted me at Splitscar Gorge."

14

Escape from the Creche

"The greater your destiny, the greater the price."

—*Ancient par-Goblin proverb*

Oh, zoc. He remembered us.

"You're not still holding a grudge about that, are you?" I asked as Callie and I backed away. "It all worked out for you in the end, right? Look at you! The Overlord. Very impressive. That sounds like a promotion."

"Don't make him mad," Callie said quietly.

"Allodar Grimjinx said, 'Anger breeds mistakes.'"

"Sometimes I wish your ancestors would just *shut up*!"

Xerrus pulled out his spellsphere. His gaze fell on Callie.

"I smell magic on you. Yes, I heard you became your cousin's apprentice. If I recall, I was going to combine him with a gexa. Seems fitting I should try that with you instead."

The spellsphere danced between his fingers as though he had trouble holding it. I remembered that Xerrus was old-fashioned. He'd been using a spellbook when we first met. Chances are he hadn't gotten the hang of a spellsphere. So how easy would it be . . . ?

"Don't worry, Cal," I said. "We've seen his work combining animals. He's not very good." Frustrated, Xerrus's fist closed around the spellsphere. I shrugged at Callie. "See what I mean? Mistake."

With the spellsphere hidden and therefore unusable, I pulled a handful of smoke pellets from my pouches and threw them to the floor. A cloud of dense white smoke instantly filled the corridor.

"Run!" I yelled.

Callie and I took off, herding the seers along with us. Behind us, Xerrus fired bolts of energy, dispelling the smoke. We rounded a corner and emerged from the haze. Maloch took the lead as we bounded down the hall.

We raced through the Creche, aiming for the exit. The walls turned to sheer cloth, which meant we were near the door.

"Get behind me!"

Ahead, I heard Maloch cry out near the Creche exit. Sheer yellow curtains draped from the ceiling, covering the walls and framing the door that led outside. Maloch stood, one arm protecting the seers behind him, the other wielding a candlestick like a sword. Between him and the exit was the biggest sanguibeast I'd ever seen. Covered in poisonous barbs, the serpentine creature snarled, baring rows upon rows of pointed teeth.

Sanguibeasts were the deadliest creatures known throughout the Provinces. There was no way the candlestick in Maloch's hand could stop one. I reached for my pouches, but Aubrin pushed her way through and walked right up to the salivating creature.

"Jinxface!"

Aubrin raised her hand to keep me away. Calmly, she approached the sanguibeast.

"Gobek," Aubrin said softly. The creature immediately stopped snarling.

"That's *Gobek*?" Maloch asked.

Aubrin stroked the sanguibeast's scaly cheek. "Gobek, you *know* what the Palatinate is doing is wrong. They've caused you so much pain. You don't owe them your loyalty. Please, Gobek. Let us go."

The sanguibeast quivered. It almost looked . . . ashamed. Suddenly, it started folding in on itself. The barbs and teeth vanished as the creature shrank and became Gobek again. He looked up sadly at Aubrin.

"Is trouble coming," Gobek said. He looked past Aubrin, directly at me.

Aubrin followed his gaze. "I know."

Gobek bowed his head and stood aside. As he did, a bolt of green lightning seared the air and struck the caretaker, who flew across the room.

Xerrus entered behind us. "I told you to stop them!" he screamed at Gobek. The strange creature whimpered, barely able to move.

I ran to help him but Gobek raised an arm. "Is to be leaving," he said faintly.

"Never!" Xerrus cried, raising his spellsphere in the air.

The floor buckled as stone pillars sprang up, sending

us all flying. The mage shouted in the magical tongue, and giant hands made of earth and rock reached up from the floor and closed around the seers one by one. I dropped Tree Bag and ran to Aubrin as a set of stony fingers sprouted up around her. Before I could help, one of the silky drapes flew across the room and wrapped itself around me.

I fell to the floor, struggling as the sheer cocoon constricted tighter and tighter. I tried to call out for help but my bonds were so tight I couldn't breathe. Squirming, I found Callie and Maloch fighting off other curtains, their faces clenched in pain.

Xerrus stepped forward, spellsphere pulsing in his hand. "I need only the seers alive."

My vision started to blur and my limbs went numb. I was convinced the last thing I was ever going to see was Xerrus's sneering face.

Ffft! Something pierced the air above me. Through a haze, I saw Xerrus step back once, then twice. Then he collapsed. As he did, the spellsphere fell from his hand and went dark. The living draperies loosened their grip and I shook myself free. Struggling to my feet, I wiped my eyes and found Xerrus lying on his back, a spear sticking out of his shoulder.

"I told you I could track you anywhere."

Luda, her mammoth Satyran frame filling the exit, glared at me.

"And it only took you two weeks!" I said, still gasping for breath. "This calls for a hug!"

The sneer on her face suggested that such a hug might end with bits of Jaxter being flung everywhere. So I settled for giving her a thank-you wave from across the room.

I went to help Gobek but Aubrin held me back. "Gobek can't come with us," she said. "Not yet."

I was starting to hate her cryptic little warnings. I wished she would just *say* what she had seen. But I knew she couldn't. It could make everything worse.

The stone fingers that held the seers crumbled to dust. As Maloch gathered the seers, Callie grabbed Xerrus's spell-sphere. "If he can't warn the Palatinate, we'll have a better chance of stopping them."

"Stop the Palatinate?" Luda stepped into the room. "What is going on here?"

I ignored Luda, threw Tree Bag's strap around my neck, and led everyone from the Creche into the woods beyond.

"Stick together and try to keep up," Maloch instructed

the seers. A young girl, as small and wide-eyed as Aubrin, went right up and hugged him. Maloch rolled his eyes. "I'm going to hate this, aren't I?"

I shook his hand. "Good luck. If all goes well, we'll send word to the Dagger."

Maloch nodded but he didn't look convinced that all would go well. He hugged Aubrin good-bye and, with one last look at us, he led the seers east.

Luda's hand closed around my forearm. "When we return to Vengekeep—"

"You can do anything you want to me," I assured her. "But we're going to Vesta first."

"Yes, to stop the Palatinate. From doing what?"

I took Aubrin by the hand, got my bearings, and pointed the four of us north.

"We've got a long walk," I said to Luda. "More than enough time to tell you everything you need to know . . ."

15

Jubilee

"Better a lie be told by one before all,
than by all before one."

—The Lymmaris Creed

A week later, when we arrived in Vesta, the Jubilee was already in full swing. The entire population of the capital city had turned out into the streets, eating their fill of scorchcake and roast hemmon. Strings of purple and black pennants wove a web high overhead, connecting every rooftop. Mobs of people choked every pathway, making travel across the city difficult at best.

Except when the Sentinels approached. Then people suddenly found space to move.

Even though we had his spellsphere, Xerrus had somehow warned the Palatinate. Sentinels were everywhere, peering through their blank-faced masks for any sign that the Creche escapees had arrived in Vesta. Luda ripped the awning from outside an alchemist's shop and tore us each a square of the fabric. We wrapped ourselves in the makeshift shawls and, eyes down, scurried through the crowd.

We found Ma and Da's third-floor room at the Bellraven Inn. When Ma opened the door, she squealed with delight. Aubrin jumped into her arms while Da pulled me into a hug. But the joyful reunion was very short. Ma's smile quickly soured. "Luda?" she asked, spotting the Satyran next to Callie. "And where's Maloch?"

We stepped inside and I launched into the story of everything that had happened at the Creche. Ma and Da listened closely to every detail, nodding at each revelation. They didn't seem the least bit surprised to learn that the Palatinate was planning to overthrow the High Laird. When I finished, they considered carefully.

"On the one hand," Da said, "a ship leaves in half an hour. We could all be on it and safely away before any of this nastiness occurs."

"On the other hand," Ma said, a mischievous smile twisting her lips, "we could stop the Palatinate and put the High Laird in our debt for the rest of our lives."

It was hard to say which idea appealed more. The Grimjinx instinct for self-preservation was a powerful force, and leaving was certainly the easiest option.

"It's a tough decision," I said. "Running is a noble Grimjinx tradition. But I've found that using cleverness to get out of impossible scrapes can be just as fulfilling."

Aubrin cast the deciding vote. "If the Palatinate takes over," she said quietly, "everyone will suffer. Thousands will die. I've seen it. But it doesn't have to happen that way. If we end this here and now . . ." She paused, casting a small glance in my direction. "We can save lives."

It was all Ma and Da needed to hear.

"So, are we going to catch that ship before the onslaught begins?" Callie asked teasingly.

"And miss the chance to put 'saved the Five Provinces' in the family album?" Ma asked. "Never."

Da put his arm around Ma's waist and pulled her close. "I was hoping you'd say that."

"So, what's the plan?" I asked.

Ma tsked. "Need I remind you what Hallimor Grimjinx always said?"

Aubrin grinned. "'Who steals first, steals best.'"

"Exactly!" Da said. "We've got the seers. Now let's get those relics."

We left the inn and wove our way through the busy streets. Da stopped to pull a flyer from a nearby wall. We gathered around as Da held up the schedule of today's events.

"Pity, we missed the hammer throw," Ma said. "I bet Luda would have scored top marks there. Let's see. . . . The High Laird's speech is in ten minutes. Then the Veiled Sisterhood of All Things Eternal will do a celebratory dance. Oh, that could go on forever. . . . Then the High Laird will present the relics to Nalia." She looked at Da and smiled.

Da tapped the schedule. "It's like they've gone out of their way to make it easy."

"Easy?" Callie asked. She pointed down the road to the stage. Spectators lined the lip of the tall wooden platform, shoulder to shoulder and impossible to bypass. All along the edge of the stage, Provincial Guards and Sentinels stood watch. "How will *that* be easy?"

But Ma's attention was on a dress shop across the way. A

sign hung in the window reading CLOSED FOR THE JUBILEE. "Tell me, Callie, didn't you train in dance with the widow Bellatin . . . ?"

I've always been proud of Ma. As a thief at the top of her game, she'd assisted in the ransacking of the par-Dwarf fire mausoleums. Her forgeries of Satyran money nearly bankrupted the island of Rexin. But even though I'd have given anything for her skills, there was no way I would have traded places with her inside the dress shop.

"Just close your eyes, Luda," Ma said in a soothing voice. "And take a deep breath . . . now!"

Luda gripped a pillar, squeezed her eyes shut, and inhaled. Behind her, Ma yanked on the strings of Luda's new corset. The mighty Satyran warrior's eyes bulged as her midsection shrank. Together, Ma and I struggled to tie the strings. When it was all done, we stepped back and Ma beamed.

"There!" she cried. "Now aren't you . . . a sight."

Her armor in a nearby heap, Luda was wrapped from horn to hoof in great swaths of sheer orange gossamer. The dress shop didn't have anything large enough to fit a towering Satyran, so Ma had improvised and wrapped bolt after bolt of fabric around Luda like an Aviard mummy.

"This will not do!" Luda said. "I cannot protect you if I am *dainty*!"

"You don't need to protect anyone," Ma reminded her. "You just have to help us get to the relics."

"Hey, Luda!" I twirled to show off my flowing blue gown. I pulled a matching piece of gossamer across my face. "Think I make a great Veiled Sister?"

"Indeed," Luda said.

The door to the shop opened. Callie, Da, and Aubrin entered, already wearing the dresses and veils Ma had gotten them. Da passed me two of the pouches from my belt.

"You really know your sleeping draughts, son," Da said as I reattached the pouches to my belt.

Aubrin nodded. "I slipped the herbs into their tea just like you told me. The Sisterhood will be asleep for hours."

"I found the relics," Callie said. "At the back of the stage, there's a round dais with a box on top. There are two Provincial Guards in front of the box."

She glanced at me nervously. Ma, Da, and Luda were

crucial to our plan. They were big enough to mask the view to the relics box. Ma and Da weren't about to let Aubrin out of their sight, so she was staying close to them. And Callie's dancing ability was the reason we had a diversion at all. That left *me* responsible for nicking the relics. Callie had a right to be nervous, given my . . . history.

"Have a little faith," I said, trying to sound far more confident than I felt. If it all worked out, we could be halfway to the city limits by the time anyone realized the relics were gone. And then we'd force the High Laird to listen to us. We'd show him what was going on at the Creche. And we'd be heroes.

Again.

Really, if we didn't stop doing this sort of thing, it was going to ruin our reputation as scoundrels.

A brassy fanfare rent the air outside. We peeked out from the shop's window and watched as the Lordcourt, led by Nalia, sauntered onto the stage and took their seats. A feeble mage who walked with the assistance of a staff took a seat behind the Lordcourt. His left arm hung in a sling; a large white bandage clung to his shoulder.

Xerrus. That made things trickier.

With the crowd's attention on the stage, we exited the shop just as Chancellor Karadin strode down the middle of the platform, waving to the crowd.

"Good citizens of Vesta," the Chancellor called out. "Where once there was chaos, now there is order. Where once there was sadness, now there is joy. All that we are, we owe to the Soranna family. It is thanks to their wisdom and guidance that we are here today. We are Five Provinces but we are one in spirit."

The crowd didn't seem impressed. I couldn't blame them. Karadin's treacle-like admiration was a mite much.

"Today, we celebrate five hundred years of rule under the House of Soranna. Good people, I present your sovereign, the High Laird Gadris Soranna!"

As the High Laird took the stage, the applause was polite at best. I even heard a few boos. But when members of the Provincial Guard moved to the edge of the stage, the crowd offered respectful, if grudging, quiet. Unhappy as they were with the High Laird, people still feared him. And given how erratic his behavior had been recently, no one was willing to protest *too* much and end up in Umbramore Tower.

"My people," the High Laird said, "when my ancestor

Mannis Soranna formed the Five Provinces, he sought to unify a land divided. But he did not do it alone. Wise as he was, hc knew he would need even wiser counsel to advise him. To this end, he consulted the most sagacious mages he knew and they formed the Palatinate. This Jubilee, we honor not only my family's legacy of benevolence but also the service of the Palatinate, which has governed the use of magic with fairness and intelligence. Without these mages . . ."

The High Laird droned on and on, singing Nalia's praises to the point where I thought I might actually be sick. The head of the Lordcourt did her best to accept the praise with the appearance of modesty, but her eyes rarely strayed from the relics box.

Ma led us quietly toward the tent where the Sisterhood slumbered. We crept around the side, waiting to be summoned. Subdued applause told us the High Laird had finished. The Chancellor nodded in our direction.

"That's our cue," Da whispered.

The six of us took the stage, faces veiled. Thousands of eyes watched from the sea of people before us. Callie moved to the center. "Just follow me," she said quietly.

The band launched into a lively reel with tin flutes piping

and oxinas strumming at a breakneck pace. Callie's jaw dropped and I realized: the widow had trained her to dance like a lady. Ladies danced *slowly.* Nothing in her training had prepared her for this.

But if it fazed her, it was only for a second. With a joyous whoop, Callie leaped straight up, arms out and legs spread. The rest of us followed a split second later, a far less graceful echo.

As the music took off, Callie twirled and hopped around the stage, spinning and bending in a completely made-up dance. But she sold it.

Aubrin took after Callie. She stood on her tiptoes and frolicked around, mirroring Callie to perfection. I wish I could say the same for Ma and Da. At first, they did their best to imitate Callie. But when she proved far more flexible, they gave up and just started to flail about like they were going through the spasm stage of blackbone fever.

Luda surprised us all. She remained in the dead center, her arms slicing the air with graceful precision. Every so often, she would jump, her legs shooting out in magnificent arcs. Soon all eyes were on her as she whirled about like she had a grudge against the emptiness around her.

I stayed near the back, gyrating my hips and swishing my arms side to side as I inched closer to the relics box. The guards were too busy watching Luda, who'd scooped up Aubrin and starting twirling her, one-handed, high in the air. Casually, I sneaked behind them to the back of the box.

Odd as we looked, the crowd seemed to appreciate us. The wilder the dance got, the more they whistled and tossed coins on the stage. I kept one eye on the Lordcourt, who'd begun muttering to one another. They were anxious to get their hands on the relics. I had to be quick.

I pulled out my picks. *Please,* I thought to any deity willing to listen, *let me do this just this once. I swear I'll never try to pick another lock again.*

Just then, the music stopped. The crowd burst into applause as my family froze in place. I could see Da looking around for me. When he spotted me near the box, I wiggled my thumb to tell him I needed more time. He threw back his head and called out in a high-pitched voice, "One more time!"

The band immediately started playing again and my family launched into their demented jig. When Nalia stood as if to call an end to the festivities, Da sashayed over, hooked his arm in hers, and spun the mage around vigorously. The crowd went naff-nut, cheering Nalia on.

With everyone distracted again, I inserted my picks into the lock. I felt the tumblers inside shift. Zoc. Another Moxnar. I jammed my picks in deep, hoping to catch the lock off guard.

"What are you doing?"

The tinny voice reverberated as the barrel of the lock moved like a pair of lips.

Oh, zoc. A Class *4* Moxnar. The kind that could speak.

"Guards!" The lock shouted to be heard over the music and rhythmic stomping. *"Thief! Thief!"*

As the box's guards stirred, I ducked and scurried on all fours, hoping they wouldn't see me.

"Hey!" one of the guards shouted. "What are you—?"

I pretended that I'd been dancing all along. I sprang up, bounced around, threw my hands in the air . . .

. . . and tripped on my own two feet.

Sprawling forward, I crashed into Aubrin. We went down together. As I reached out to break our fall, my fingers snagged Aubrin's veil, yanking it from her face.

"The augur!"

Xerrus sprang up from his seat behind the Lordcourt, pointing at Aubrin. On hands and knees, Aubrin and I backed away. I eyed the box, trying to decide if I could make it to the relics. A trio of Sentinels moved forward, not even sparing the box a glance. Nalia smiled.

Behind me, Ma gasped. Then Da groaned. And one by one, we all realized the same thing. The seers were important to the Palatinate. But not nearly as important as the most powerful seer. The augur.

My sister.

With the relics nearby and Aubrin at their feet, we'd accidentally delivered everything the Palatinate needed to rule the Five Provinces.

16

The Fall of the House of Soranna

"The foolish thief looks to tomorrow.
The wise rogue uses tonight."

—Ona Grimjinx, master thief of Korrin Province

The High Laird rose from his chair. "What is going on here?"

I yanked off my veil. "Your Highness, Nalia and the Lordcourt want to depose you. If you give them the relics—"

"This little game has been fun," Nalia said, her monocle glistening in the sun. "But it's time we brought it to a close."

With a flick of her wrist, she produced her spellsphere and sent a bolt of energy toward the dais. The guards dove for safety as the top of the box exploded, revealing a pair of gauntlets, a scepter, an orb, and a coronet.

Nalia led the Lordcourt to the relics. She pulled the gauntlets over her long fingers. Hissing in the magical tongue, she lifted her arms to the sky. Shafts of green light shot from her fingertips. Screams rang out from the crowd.

"Hear me!"

Nalia's voice shook in my chest and seemed to come from everyone at once: down the road, around the corner, right behind me.

"Benevolence? Wisdom? The Soranna family claims to have served the Five Provinces. That may have been true in the past. But *this* High Laird serves only himself."

Nalia pointed to the High Laird, who looked bewildered by the sudden betrayal. I almost felt sorry for him.

"The time has come for a new law of the land. The Palatinate will guide you now. Under magical rule, there will be new order."

The crowd murmured. Some people seemed to think this was an entertainment, like the dance. Others looked unsure, as if trying to decide which leader they wanted to follow.

"Gadris Soranna," Nalia said, "I charge you with treason against the people of the Five Provinces. Guards, arrest him. And take that child"—she pointed to Aubrin—"into custody."

The Provincial Guards on the stage drew their weapons. My family moved to surround Aubrin, putting themselves between her and the guards. But instead of arresting the High Laird or even glancing at Aubrin, the guards advanced on Nalia and the Lordcourt.

Nalia's lips curled. "You serve a new sovereign now. Stand down and obey me."

When the Provincial Guard refused to back away, all the members of the Lordcourt took out their spellspheres and spoke as one. The air over Vesta rippled as dozens of quick-jump rings materialized overhead. Everything grew still. Then, like the opening of a floodgate, hundreds of monsters began pouring through. Some flew on leathery wings. Others dropped right onto the crowd, screeching as they descended. Each wore a golden control medallion.

A host of bloodreavers fell upon the guards closest to the Lordcourt, driving them back. Spindly creatures with four arms and two sets of jaws, the bloodreavers clawed and bit as they attacked. The soldiers closed ranks around the High Laird. While a wall of guards fought off the bloodreavers, the Chancellor and the High Laird's confidants rushed the monarch away down the back of the stage.

When Nalia saw this, she slashed the air with her gauntlets. A wave of power knocked the guards off their feet.

"Find him!" Nalia shouted at the nearest Sentinels. "The High Laird cannot be allowed to escape."

But the Provincial Guards weren't done. They got up and took arms against the Sentinels, doing everything they could to buy the High Laird more time. And maybe it was seeing that—the unwavering support of the Provincial Guard—that turned the crowd against the Palatinate.

It also hadn't helped that the Lordcourt had just summoned a legion of monsters.

A wave of patriotism took over the crowd. Whatever concerns they'd had about the High Laird, everyone apparently had even *more* concerns about putting the mages in charge. People rushed the stage, pitching vegetables, food on sticks, and anything else they could find at the Lordcourt.

That's when it occurred to me. Despite all the High Laird had done, people still supported the House of Soranna. If he was free, the Provinces would never be loyal to the Palatinate.

And the same was true of the Dowager. I had no doubt

that a mix of Sentinels and monsters was on its way to Vengekeep to apprehend her. I couldn't let that happen.

By now, the streets were in chaos. The Palatinate monsters that weren't attacking Provincial Guards were corralling the rowdy glut of spectators. The citizens of Vesta scattered, trying to get as far from the monsters as possible. With the Lordcourt distracted, my family joined hands and hid in the river of people trying to escape.

"We should head to the docks," Ma said. "Quickly, before the ships realize there's trouble and set sail."

"But, Ma," I said, "we can't leave the Dowager. We have to get to Vengekeep."

Da nodded at Aubrin. "Right now, your sister is a bigger threat to Nalia. We'll get her hidden first, then go find the Dowager. She's a smart woman. She'll know to hide."

Luda led the way, clearing a path as we headed west toward the docks. Callie and I flanked Aubrin, squeezing her between us. Ma and Da brought up the rear, casting nervous looks over their shoulders to be sure the Sentinels weren't following us.

Suddenly, a vine of magical light sprang up from the ground, wrapping itself around Ma and pulling her arms tight to her sides. Nalia stormed toward us, her spellsphere crackling in the palm of her gauntlet.

When Ma cried out, Luda stopped. A twinkle lit up Nalia's monocle and before Luda could attack, another magical rope appeared and ensnared the Satyran.

Callie hugged Aubrin close as Da and I blocked Nalia's path. Nalia laughed.

"You're coming with me, augur," Nalia said sweetly.

"The zoc she is!" Ma said. Bending at the waist, she charged into the mage, sending them both to the ground. As Nalia's concentration broke, the magical ropes around Ma and Luda vanished. Da and I ran to help Ma but stopped when a pair of Sentinels spotted us.

"Get the girl!" Nalia cried to the Sentinels as she and Ma wrestled on the street.

"Go!" Ma yelled at us. "Ona, get them out of here!"

"No!" I said, reaching for my pouches. I could distract the Sentinels with a smoke cloud. But Da didn't even give me a chance. He snatched my wrist, picked up Aubrin, and led us away. The last thing I saw before we rounded the corner was the Sentinels casting a spell that made Ma fall limp.

The people of Vesta had lost their taste for battle. It had

become obvious quickly that fighting the Palatinate's monsters was useless. The creatures began to herd the crowds down alleyways in an effort to clear the streets. In the confusion, we ducked into the dress shop.

As Luda put her armor on, I pulled away from Da and grabbed Tree Bag. "How could we just leave Ma?"

"Your ma and I have a rule," Da said. "We do whatever it takes to protect you two. She let herself be captured so you and Aubrin could be free. If we get caught now, she did it for nothing."

Callie peeked out the window. "We can't stay here. Something big and spiky is getting closer."

Da scratched his chin. "You might be right, Jaxter. Getting to Vengekeep and rescuing the Dowager might be our best bet now. I'm just not sure how we get out of the city. They've probably already started sealing off the exits."

"The fastest way to Vengekeep is a quickjump spell," Callie said, pulling Xerrus's spellsphere from a pocket in her dress.

"Wish you'd thought of that at the Creche," I said. "We could have gotten here faster."

"It's very advanced magic," she said. "I'm almost positive

I can't pull it off. But given the circumstances, I have to try."

Callie peered into the spellsphere and started chanting. It took a couple of tries before a quickjump ring appeared on the ground. The ring twisted and didn't look exactly stable. But we could see the streets of Vengekeep through it. Callie's face strained at the effort of keeping it open.

"Hurry," she whispered. Da tested it by tossing Luda's discarded corset through. A second later, it landed in Vengekeep.

Da poked Aubrin in the nose. "You first. I'll be right behind you."

Aubrin stepped to the edge of the ring and jumped in. She reappeared above the streets of Vengekeep, landed, and tumbled to safety.

"Bangers, Callie!" I said. "It worked. You next, Da."

Da kissed my forehead. "If we get separated, Jaxter, you know what to do."

I nodded. A moment later, Da landed softly next to Aubrin in Vengekeep. He waved, letting us know it was safe to follow.

"I need to go last to keep the ring open," Callie said. "You go."

I pulled Tree Bag tight and leaped into the air. But the second I touched the ring, it disappeared in a flash.

Callie stomped her foot. "But it was *working*!"

My stomach fell. The image of Vengekeep was gone. Da and Aubrin were on their own to find the Dowager and get her to safety. And *we* were stranded in the heart of the revolution.

Callie opened her mouth, as if to try the spell again. But the building shook and a nearby wall collapsed as a nightmanx, battling a squadron of Provincial Guards, fell through the gaping hole and into the dress shop.

Acting quickly, Luda hoisted Callie and me up under her arms. She charged out into the streets. As we got closer to Vesta's perimeter wall, we could see that Da was right: Sentinels and monsters were already blocking many of the exits. Whirling about, Luda spotted an unguarded gate. Moments later, we were running through the wilderness just outside the capital city.

My mind swam. Ma . . . Da . . . Aubrin . . . All gone.

If we get separated, Jaxter, you know what to do.

"South, Luda," I said. "We need to go south."

"To Vengekeep?" Callie asked.

"Too dangerous," I said. "We need to go somewhere safer."

"Where?" Callie asked.

Behind us, Vesta fell to the Palatinate. By now, I imagined, Sentinels were on their way across the Five Provinces, monsters in tow, to secure the Palatinate's victory. I couldn't be sure how long it would be before all the Provinces were under their control. A week? A month? One thing was certain: soon, nowhere would be safe.

My sister was the key to everything now. I had to make sure they didn't touch her. No matter what. But first, that meant finding her. Luckily, I knew just how to do that.

"South," I repeated.

And we ran.

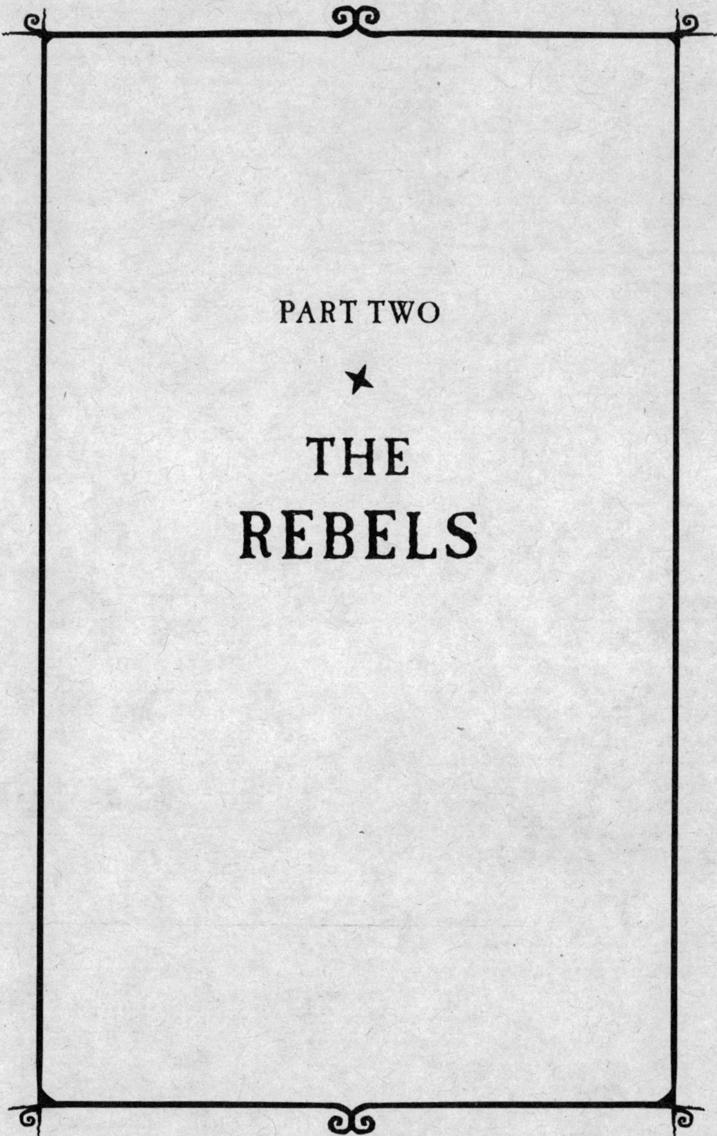

PART TWO

★

THE REBELS

17

Oberax

"Confession may be good for the soul,
but passing the blame is good for the purse."

—par-Goblin proverb

Seers see possible futures, Aubrin had told me.

Apparently, none of these possible futures involved me working side by side with the Dowager again at Redvalor Castle like I wanted. Those days seemed like a dream, unlikely to come again.

Aubrin had also said that if you acted to stop one possible future, you could accidentally bring about an altogether worse one. That thought made me afraid to do anything. With my luck, I'd put on my shoes in the morning and make a volcano erupt.

But the longer we stayed in hiding, the clearer it became. Being afraid of making a worse future meant you never did anything to make a *better* future.

I started every day by telling myself, "I do *not* believe in destiny. I make my own future."

The hope being, of course, that if I said it enough, I'd start to believe it.

"Fifteen minutes."

Slime seeped through my trouser legs as I knelt at the edge of the swamp. The mist that rose off the filthy water took on the scarlet glow of sundown. I dipped my sieve into the mire, scraped the pond's bottom, and pulled it out again. Silt drained through the tiny holes, leaving a handful of rocks that shimmered in the dim light.

"I told you the swamp would be a great place to find glowstones," I said, chucking the rocks into Tree Bag with the others we'd collected.

"Fourteen minutes."

I was starting to regret giving Callie my fob watch to

keep an eye on the time. She did it a little too well. My ninth cousin, Sillrick Grimjinx, always said, "The fewer the minutes, the greater the inspiration." Well, I had *plenty* of inspiration. I'd have traded six buckets of it for just a few more minutes.

I jumped to my feet and grabbed Tree Bag. Callie pocketed my watch and eyed the sack warily.

"Will it be enough?" she asked.

"It'll have to be," I said. "We're almost out of time. Come on."

We sloshed our way through the morass and took off. Clouds choked the night sky, hiding both moons somewhere beyond the treetops. As wide as a house and endlessly tall, the everember trees provided the only light to guide us on. Beneath their mottled bark, the trunks radiated a pale orange glow like a dying fire.

"Thirteen minutes," Callie announced as we raced forward.

"You don't even have the watch out anymore," I said.

"I was guessing."

Ahead, we could hear commotion—people rushing about, shouting orders back and forth. A bell, deep and hollow, sounded ten times.

"Ten minutes," I muttered.

As the trees cleared, torchlight led us to the outskirts of Slagbog. We slowed as we passed the mud huts of the par-Goblin village. A motley assortment of par-Goblins, humans, and Aviards scurried about. Some lugged huge barrels down the tiny village's single long street. Others pushed carts filled with root vegetables toward the center of the town. Nearly everyone in the village—all fifty of us—was busy. A typical scene for the end of the month.

Callie and I headed straight for the town square. There, a massive cauldron hung over a roiling fire. Standing over the cauldron, a hooded figure used a wooden plank to stir the pot's bubbling, viscous contents. I peeked over the cauldron's edge.

"Six months in hiding," I muttered softly with a smile, "and your cooking hasn't improved."

The figure drew back her hood and I got the nastiest look ever from the Dowager. She wore a black wig, its long strands woven into a braid. Fake sagpox pustules dotted her face, an important part of her disguise. It kept most people from getting too close and realizing her true identity.

"Six months in hiding," the Dowager retorted, "and I've yet to see you cook!"

Nearby, Aubrin climbed onto a wooden scaffold next to the cauldron. Her once-long red hair had been cut short, disguising her as a boy. Fake scars crisscrossed her face, making her hardly recognizable. She leaned over the pot and added a bucket of chopped herbs to the mixture within.

"Everything okay, Jinxface?" I asked.

"I'm fine," Aubrin said cheerily. "Farkada is the one *making a stir*." She pointed to the Dowager.

Callie and I groaned. We were on the run, in mortal danger every second of our lives, and my sister was still making bad jokes.

The Dowager *humph*ed at her fake name. When we first went into hiding and chose false identities, the Dowager thought she was being clever by picking the name Farkada. She thought it meant "wisdom" in ancient par-Goblin. She was so proud, we didn't have the heart to tell her that it meant "ancient." By the time she found out the truth, too many people knew her as Farkada and we couldn't change it.

The bell sounded five times. "Zoc," I cursed, grabbing a fistful of glowstones from Tree Bag. Then I shouted, "I need that mortar. And a pestle. Now!"

"Tyrius!"

My neck muscles tensed as I heard my false name bellowed by a painfully familiar voice. I turned to find a pudgy, short par-Goblin marching toward me. Her green-gray skin glistened with sweat. The white hair that shot from her long, slender ears practically covered the sides of her head like a rug.

"Oberax!" I said. "Madam Mayor. Good to see you. Have you trimmed your nose hairs? They're looking very—"

Oberax growled. "Where is your father? *He's* supposed to prepare the tribute."

"Da is . . . elsewhere at the moment."

The par-Goblin's lip twitched like a stickworm. "You don't mean he's—"

"Afraid so," I said.

Oberax gurgled. For a moment, I worried she was choking on her own anger.

"Now? He's doing it *now*?"

I put my arm around her shoulders. "Everything's under control."

She shook off my arm. "Under control? We're one cask short." She pointed to the scaffold. Three wheelbarrows filled with vegetables sat atop the wooden platform. Nine wooden casks as tall as me sat next to the wheelbarrows, a dull orange glow emanating from under the lids.

"The tribute is to include *ten* casks of everember sap," Oberax said, reminding me of something I already knew too well.

"Yes, but we've been draining the forest dry of sap for months," I said. "We came up a mite shy this time."

"If we don't have ten casks—"

"You'll have the last cask," I said, "as soon as I get a mortar and pestle."

A slim par-Goblin hobbled over and handed me the equipment. Aubrin dumped the glowstones into the mortar. With the pestle, I broke the rocks apart, grinding them to dust. The powder twinkled with a soft light that grew brighter the harder I pressed.

Oberax groaned as she understood what I was doing. "You wouldn't. You can't!"

"The Palatinate will never know one cask is fake," I said. "They'll think it was a bad batch from a sick tree."

At least, that's what I'd hoped when I'd concocted the plan an hour earlier. I continued grinding and looked confident. As my great-great-aunt Turrina Grimjinx always said, "Fake or real, the currency of confidence spends the same." If that was true, I was *rich*.

Aubrin poured the glowstone dust into the cauldron. Inside, the sap from a regular mokka tree burbled and fizzed. As the dust mixed in, the sap started to pulsate with an orange radiance. As the bell sounded twice, we had our fake everember sap.

"Ready to go," I said. A group of burly men transferred the sap into a tenth cask.

I'd just saved the village by completing the tribute, but Oberax looked unimpressed. "If this doesn't work, we're finished," she said.

"Oberax," I said with a smile, "trust me. This has never not worked."

The par-Goblin grumbled and strode over to the scaffold where the men were placing the tenth cask with the others. Aubrin jumped down from her chair and poked me.

"But, Jaxter," she whispered, "we've never tried this before."

"Exactly," I said. "This has never not worked."

The bell rang out with a single, lonely sound. Oberax

cupped her hands around her mouth. "It's time!" she shouted.

The village's sparse population lined the square. Aubrin squeezed my arm and looked up at me pleadingly.

"Jaxter . . . ," she whispered. In the past six months since Vesta had fallen and we'd all met up in Slagbog, we'd made it through several inspections. And each time, Aubrin got nervous.

"It's okay, Jinxface," I said.

The Dowager took Aubrin and Callie by the hand and moved near the abandoned cheese shop. Those three pretended to be a family to throw off suspicion. I checked to make sure my false nose was in place and pulled a tattered cap down over my hair, long since dyed blond.

A hush fell over the village. The fire beneath the cauldron crackled and snapped. The only two things I could feel were the cool night breeze and my heart pounding like it wanted out of my chest.

The air above burst open. A ring of blue light appeared. Two cowled mages descended, landing softly near the scaffold. A moment later, three magravores flew from the circle. These days, mages never traveled without magical creatures for protection. Winged lizards twice the size of my da, magravores feasted on liars, according to par-Dwarf legend. If that was true, Slagbog was on the menu.

One mage stepped forward and threw back his cowl. Xerrus. After all the inspections he'd done in Slagbog, it was pure, dumb luck that he hadn't recognized us. Yet.

"Is the tribute ready?" Xerrus's voice boomed.

Once the Palatinate had asserted their control, anyone who'd professed loyalty to the High Laird had been imprisoned. Castellans and magistrates alike had been deposed in favor of the five mage-thanes who ruled their respective Provinces. The Lordcourt replaced yearly taxes with monthly tributes of food, money, and anything else they desired.

Xerrus served as mage-thane of Jarron Province. Since assuming the job, he'd gotten a reputation for his cruelty. A *well-earned* reputation.

Arms behind his back, Xerrus walked slowly down the street, inspecting each and every person. Everyone lowered their eyes obediently as he passed.

"For a par-Goblin village," Xerrus shouted, "you don't have many par-Goblins. I find this strange, Oberax."

The mayoress sneered at Xerrus. "After we give you our food, we barely have enough to live on. Half my people left for the town-states, thinking they'd find more to eat. Slagbog would have died if we hadn't taken in refugees."

What she said was true. When the Palatinate began seizing land and assets, many people had found themselves homeless. They wandered the Provinces, seeking charity. But few were allowed to settle in Slagbog. We were *very* selective about who lived here.

As Xerrus approached, I let my eyes drift to the ground. I waited for him to pass. Instead, he stopped right in front of me, grabbed my chin, and forced me to look up.

My throat clenched. He'd finally recognized me.

"Boy," he said gruffly, "your hands are glowing."

I looked down. My palms, covered in a light coat of glowstone dust, pulsed with light. I almost collapsed with relief.

"You know," I said, wiping my hands on my trousers, "I think you're right. Let me take care of that."

Xerrus snatched my hand and pulled it so close to his face I could feel his hot breath on my palm. He leaned in, inspecting the dust.

I stammered, trying to come up with a good explanation. Oberax leaped from the scaffold and stomped toward Xerrus, arms swinging at her sides.

"You're working us to death," Oberax shouted. "In trying to collect the sap, this boy fell into a cask and nearly drowned. It's a wonder he's not glowing all over. What does it even matter? You've got your tribute. Now leave us be."

The villagers traded nervous glances. From time to time, Oberax challenged Xerrus. It never ended well.

The other mage, a portly woman with short brown hair, brandished her spellsphere and spoke a single word. Yellow tendrils of light struck the par-Goblin, sending her to the ground with a scream.

"You will show the mage-thane respect," the female mage said.

Oberax writhed in pain a moment, then brought herself to all fours. Xerrus dropped my hand and laughed. "Must every conversation we have end like this, Oberax?"

I stepped back quietly now that his attention was elsewhere. Oberax had saved me from being taken away and interrogated.

"Let's go, Mirris," Xerrus said to the other mage. "I can hardly stand the stench anymore."

Xerrus summoned a quickjump ring at his feet. Mirris cast a spell that made the wheelbarrows and casks float down into the ring. Next, she jumped into the circle, followed by the magravores. Xerrus took a final look around and stepped into the ring. With a crack, the spell ended.

As one, the people of Slagbog exhaled. Heads down, they returned to their homes. I went to Oberax and offered my hand. With a grunt, she pulled herself to her feet.

"Thank you," I said.

She shook her head. "Your little switch worked this time. I doubt it'll work again in a month for the next tribute. Time is running out. If your father's got a plan, he needs to do it soon. It won't be long before Xerrus learns the truth about Slagbog."

She waddled off and I returned to the mud hut I shared with Da. Lighting a candle, I waited for his return.

Oberax was right. The everember trees had been drained dry. There could be no more tributes. But that didn't matter. If everything went well, the only thing Xerrus would find in Slagbog next month was an abandoned village.

We'd finally be long, long gone.

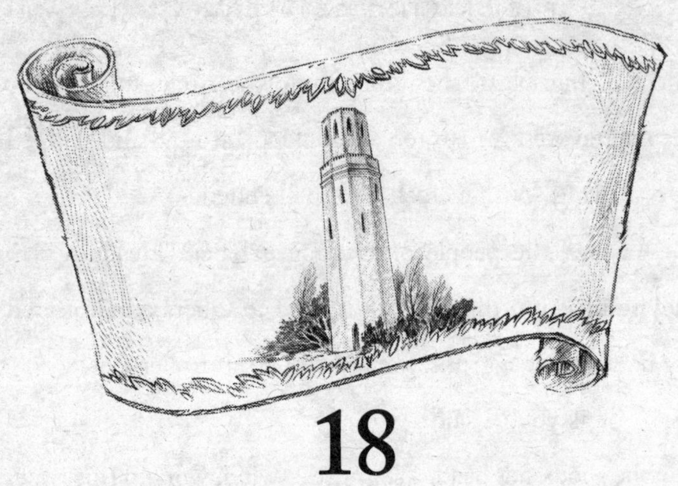

18

The Truth About Slagbog

"Luck is a fiendish lender, never a patron."

—Ancient par-Goblin proverb

Our mud hut was a far cry from our two-story house in Vengekeep. Built for much smaller par-Goblins, the single, domed room was just barely enough space for Da and me. But as my great-great-aunt Lumira Grimjinx said, "A hovel's a palace to a thief in flight."

I'd almost finished brewing a pot of tea when the door opened and Da entered, bent over and smiling.

"Mite late, don't you think?" I asked. "Oberax wasn't happy you missed the tribute."

"When is Oberax ever happy?" Da asked with a wink. Just behind him, two women squeezed their way through the door. The taller woman's long hair, striped black and white, spilled down over her shoulders. The shorter woman clutched a shawl around her head and looked down. Neither seemed impressed with our abode.

"At least you had a good reason for being gone," I said, nodding at our guests.

"Son, these are the Scalander sisters, Sarquin and Minss. Ladies, this is my son, Tyrius."

I'd heard of them: two of the best pickpockets this side of the river Karre. I waved at the women, then poured two cups of tea. Each regarded her cup suspiciously.

"I told you," Da said patiently, "you're safe here. And in good company."

The taller sister, Sarquin, downed the tea, only gagging on it slightly. Minss ignored the cup before her.

"You have relatives in Umbramore?" I asked.

Sarquin nodded once. "How did you know?"

I pointed to her sleeve. "Those scratch marks look like you narrowly escaped a bloodreaver. They're using the blood you share with your relatives to sniff you out. But that tea will mask the scent." I pushed Minss's cup toward her. "You should drink."

"My sister is very tired," Sarquin said. "I'll make sure she drinks it later."

"*Everybody* here has relatives in Umbramore," Da said. "That's the point."

Forgetting the swamp and the stench and the fact that the village was decrepit, Slagbog had proved to be an excellent hiding place. It was far from the town-states, where the Palatinate held the most power. It was of no real value to the Palatinate (except for its proximity to the everember trees). And, most important, it was half a day's journey to Umbramore Tower, the prison where the Palatinate held their enemies.

Including Ma.

When the par-Goblins began abandoning the doomed village, Da quickly struck a deal with the mayoress. He would help her repopulate the village to keep it from dying if she turned a blind eye to *how* he was doing it. She agreed and part one of Da's plan was complete.

Slagbog became a haven for thieves.

Everyone here was wanted by the Palatinate. Everyone here had relatives incarcerated in Umbramore. And everyone here was willing and ready to help with the second part of Da's plan: the storming of Umbramore and the release of its prisoners.

So Da had spent the last six months tracking down thieves in hiding and bringing them here. Whenever we weren't pretending to be an innocent village, we were gathering all the information we could about the prison and its defenses. Once we had our families back, anyone who wanted to was welcome to join us on a ship that would leave the Provinces forever.

"We don't get a lot of news," I said, trying to make conversation with Minss, the shorter sister. "Tell us, what's the latest?"

Minss said nothing. She just kept looking at the ground.

"The news hasn't changed in six months," Sarquin answered. "The Palatinate's rule is absolute. And now that the Provinces have fallen in line, the Palatinate is focusing their energy on one thing: finding the Grimjinxes."

"No doubt," Da said. "It's a miracle that family has stayed hidden so well."

Miracle was exactly right. After we fled Vesta, Callie, Luda, and I spent two weeks hiding in every forest, swamp, and mountain pass we could find. Long ago, my parents had taught Aubrin and me that if our family was ever separated by a disaster—for example, a mob of unruly villagers wielding pitchforks and torches—we would meet up in Slagbog. I knew that if Da and Aubrin had succeeded in rescuing the Dowager, that's where they'd go.

Sure enough, we found the three of them waiting for us. Da had recounted how he and Aubrin arrived in Vengekeep just before a legion of mages and monsters came to apprehend the Dowager. Her Provincial Guards had been killed during the escape. But clever old Da managed to smuggle her out of the city before Vengekeep was sealed.

Even as stories of the Lordcourt tracking down their enemies reached Slagbog, we remained safely hidden. The only time we heard from the Palatinate was when they came to collect the everember sap tribute or when Sentinels plastered the town with wanted posters bearing sketches of the Dowager and Aubrin. The High Laird, it was rumored, had fled the Provinces on a ship. That left the Dowager and Aubrin as the Palatinate's greatest enemies.

"Those lucky Grimjinxes," I said. "Clever folks, aren't they? I've heard that boy, Jaxter, is as smart as they come."

Although we had gathered the greatest collection of thieves, scoundrels, and rogues the Provinces had ever seen, we'd been careful not to let anyone know our true identities. Chances were good there wasn't a thief here who wouldn't turn us over to the Palatinate, thinking it would earn them a pardon.

Sarquin sniffed. "We also heard that the Palatinate discovered the location of the Shadowhands' secret headquarters and destroyed it."

"The Dagger?" I couldn't hide my alarm and cast a look at Da. He stayed calm and shook his head sadly at this news.

We still had no idea where Maloch and the seers were. We'd assumed they were still hiding out in the hidden Shadowhand compound. Shortly after we first arrived in Slagbog, the Dowager sent Luda to retrieve Maloch and the seers. None of them had returned.

Maybe now we knew why.

"We live in curious times," Da said. "It's hard to know which rumors are true and which are things the Palatinate *wants* us to believe to make themselves seem more powerful."

He addressed Sarquin but he was really talking to me. He was saying: *Don't believe it quite yet.*

"It's getting late," Da announced. "Let's find you two a place to stay and tomorrow we'll get you set up with some disguises."

"They could move into the cheese shop," I suggested.

"We don't know how to make cheese," Sarquin said.

"Well," Da answered cheerily, "won't it be fun to learn?"

Sarquin didn't seem pleased. Minss, as always, said nothing. But clearly Da had explained that one of the conditions of being allowed to hide out in Slagbog was that everyone pitched in.

Da escorted the women from our hut while I washed the teacups. I couldn't stop thinking about what Sarquin had said about the Dagger. Even if it explained what happened to Maloch and the seers—and I was *really* hoping it didn't—what had happened to Luda?

Depressed, I blew out the candles and got ready for bed. Just as I kicked off my boots, the ground shook. One short, sharp jolt. A moment later, another shake, this one strong enough to rattle the walls. "What the zoc?"

Bits of mud fell from the roof and mugs on our only shelf

tumbled to the ground, shattering. I'd been in earthquakes before and this didn't feel like one.

Outside, a shrill howl, dissonant and powerful, filled the air. I plugged my ears. Another shake, more powerful than the rest. Whatever was making the noise and shaking the ground was getting closer.

19

The Braxilar

"Never let your fleeting foot
be faster than your boot."

—*The Lymmaris Creed*

I ran barefoot into the street, where I found most of the village waiting. Nearly everyone was in their nightclothes, looking around confused. The village's collective murmur fell silent when another earsplitting shriek sounded, sending chills up and down my arms.

From somewhere deep in the moonlit swamp, a shadow passed over the village. It was hard to make out where it came from. The only thing for sure was that whatever was casting the shadow had a long, spiky neck.

Several people cried out in panic, ducking back into their mud huts. Da, returning from the cheese shop, put his hand on my arm to steady me. The ground shook twice more, we heard another howl, and far off, a plume of blue flames rose into the sky.

"That's not good," Da muttered.

"Home Guard!"

Oberax waddled quickly down the main street, wearing a helmet and holding a spear twice her size. Da and an assortment of men and women of every race stepped forward. The Home Guard volunteers protected the village from rare monster attacks. The Palatinate had unleashed so many beasts into the world that they barely noticed when one shook off its control medallion and went on a rampage. There'd only been two attacks since we'd arrived—but they'd been scary.

"To the armory!" Oberax shouted, leading the Home Guard to a locked hut.

Another roar, closer than ever, sent a chorus of screams through the village. The Home Guard armed themselves and Da gave me one last nod as he marched off into the misty woods.

I entered the Dowager's house without knocking. Her

hut was slightly larger than ours and a bit nicer. Callie sat on a lopsided sofa, a comforting arm around Aubrin. The Dowager stood at a small table, cutting up strips of cloth to use as bandages. She'd made herself responsible for aiding any Guard members who came back injured.

I dipped into my pouches and started making a supply of burn ointment. If whatever was out there could belch blue flame, we might be treating a few scorch injuries.

Three quick jolts rippled the ground. Aubrin buried her face in Callie's shoulder. "I think it's almost here!" Aubrin said.

I suddenly realized the problem with sending the Home Guard out into the forest to track down the beast. It left the village undefended.

Seeing Aubrin cower, I knew what I had to do. Stomach clenched, I took one of the Dowager's cloth strips and used it to tie a wooden serving fork to the top of a broomstick.

"What do you think?" I asked Callie, brandishing my weapon. "Does it say 'mighty warrior'?"

She clicked her tongue. "With you holding it? It says 'highly crazy person.' What are you doing?"

I scooped up a wash bucket from the corner and put it on

my head as a makeshift helmet. "Proving you right," I said, and walked out the door before they could protest.

The village was still. Anyone who hadn't gone with the Home Guard had retreated inside. I tread softly down the dirty street. I listened carefully, hoping to hear the Home Guard in the woods. Nothing. Were they quietly stalking the beast . . . or had it already choked them down as dinner? And was it now preparing to raid Slagbog for dessert?

I walked to the edge of the village and peered into the mist-filled forest. Cool tendrils of fog licked at my toes. "Da?" I whispered into the darkness. "Oberax?" I paused. "Hungry monster?"

I turned and cried out to find three silhouettes directly behind me. I fell back onto the ground. Like me, the Dowager wore a protective bucket on her head. In her right hand, she twirled one of her cloth bandages wrapped around a stone mug like a sling. Aubrin held a small stool over her head. Callie held her spellsphere. The iron marble was dark. She knew the Palatinate could trace her if she actually cast a spell, so she wouldn't dare use it unless it was absolutely necessary.

"What are you doing here?" I asked.

"Please," Callie said. "Like we'd let you have all the fun."

A howl from the monster, the closest yet, echoed through the village. Each of us raised our weapon. Another shadow slithered across the mud hut rooftops.

"Huh," I said.

"What?" Aubrin asked.

"Is it just me or did the howl come from the left . . . and then the shadow came from the right?"

The Dowager looked around. "I . . . I think you're right."

"How could something as big as this move from one side of the village to the other in an instant?" I asked.

Near the village square, we heard stirring. The Dowager, Callie, and me crowded around Aubrin and approached cautiously. As we rounded a corner, a dark figure leaped out at us.

The Dowager reacted first. She swung the sling over her head and sent the stone mug flying. It struck the figure's head, connecting with the thunk of stone meeting metal. The stranger's head snapped back before he hit the ground. We quickly surrounded him, weapons at the ready.

The man at our feet was dressed head to toe in thick leather armor. Magnifying glasses of varying sizes hung from a chain of copper rings that dangled down his chest. Straggly gray hair poked out from under a patchwork metal helm. He held a rusty-bladed halberd in one hand and a small lantern in the other.

"That doesn't look like a monster," Aubrin said.

"But he doesn't live here in Slagbog either," I said.

The man sat up on one elbow and shook his head so hard his bushy mustache flittered. "Ga'zounds!" he said in a deep, grumbly voice. "What are you doing? I nearly had the beast!"

The four of us looked at one another. We stepped back as the odd man got to his feet.

"Who are you?" I asked, gripping my broom spear.

"Azborah Bleakhex," the man said, with a slight bow at his waist.

I studied his face. The name sounded familiar to me. Had I seen it on a wanted poster? I couldn't remember.

We all jumped as the beast in the woods screamed again. Bleakhex hoisted his halberd to a ready position. "I've been tracking this braxilar for days. Finally cornered the wily beast in these woods."

Bleakhex crouched and moved toward the edge of the village on tiptoes. The rest of us followed in similar manner.

"Excuse me," the Dowager said, adjusting the bucket on her head so she could see better, "but did you say you've been tracking this beast?"

"Indeed, madam," Bleakhex said. "That's my job. I track down creatures that stray from the Palatinate's control. Don't you kind folks worry. I won't let the beast harm anyone here."

The others were listening to everything he was saying with rapt attention. I rolled my eyes. Something didn't seem quite right. And I *knew* I'd heard the name before.

But a braxilar was serious business. A fire-breathing monster from par-Dwarf mythology. If this man was here to help, we'd take it.

The ground shook so hard we nearly fell over. Then a roar, strangely distant. Surely, the beast had to be right on top of us. Why did it sound so far away? Then, just ahead, a plume of blue flame seared through the orange fog.

"Prepare to die, foul beast!" Bleakhex shouted. Leveling his halberd, he charged into the forest.

The Dowager held on to Callie and Aubrin. "We should let him do his job."

But I stepped around and ran after Bleakhex as the others called after me. I disappeared into the swamp, running farther and farther from the village until I tripped on the uneven ground. Rising, I found myself standing in a colossal footprint: as wide as I was tall and twicc as long. The braxilar was *very* close.

Suddenly, the Home Guard burst from hiding. They ran directly toward the last fire burst, weapons raised. Disoriented, Bleakhex stumbled into the Guard's path and collided with Da, sending both of them to the ground. The Home Guard continued running toward the unseen beast.

I ran to help Da as the braxilar howled again in the night, this time far behind us. Da pushed himself up to his knees, shaking his head in a daze. We both looked over to Bleakhex. His fake mustache drooped perpendicular to his mouth. His helmet had fallen off and with it, the shaggy gray wig he wore. Without the wig, he was nearly bald, with tufts of wiry white hair just over his ears.

Da leaned forward. "Garax?"

"Ona?" the monster hunter asked.

I groaned. Of course. My uncle—Da's brother—Garax Grimjinx.

As the braxilar roared to our right, Uncle Garax groped frantically at his belt. He grabbed a small bone horn, raised it to his lips, and blew. The horn's cry bounced off the ever-ember trees in three short bursts. With the exception of the Home Guard, sallying wildly forth, the forest grew quiet. All sounds of the braxilar vanished.

Uncle Garax lowered the horn and gave us a sheepish look. "Well," he said, "that about does it for the braxilar. So, how have you been?"

20

Ghostfire

"Don't spend your bronzemerk
until you nick the silvernib."

—Rannox Grimjinx, warrior-bard of Merriton

We lay low, keeping a watchful eye on the Home Guard as they patrolled the forest. When the "braxilar" failed to show itself, they gave up and returned to the village. Alone again, the three of us rose and Uncle Garax led us deeper into the swamp, lighting our path with his lantern.

"Imagine running into you here," Garax said jovially. "By the Seven! What are the odds? The Palatinate has all its resources aimed at tracking you down and it's little ole me who finds you."

"Indeed," Da said.

Uncle Garax poked me in the ribs. "Look at you, little Jaxter. Zoc, it's been how long since I've seen you? You were just a wee thing. I didn't recognize you. Hey, you're one of them brainy kids, right? You'll appreciate the modifications I've made on the old homestead."

We came to a dip in the terrain. A tall, moss-covered rock, as big as a house, sat at the bottom of the slope. Over the last four months, I'd spent days prowling the woods around Slagbog, collecting herbs to replenish my pouches. I knew the area well. This rock had never been here before.

Uncle Garax gave a low whistle that trilled up and down. A second later, a similar whistle answered. The moss near the base of the rock rustled and a pair of tall, brutish-looking men—one bearded, the other bald—stepped out from behind.

"My, er . . . assistants," Garax said. He leaned in and said more quietly, "Not the brightest pair, but they get the job done."

Da looked the rock up and down. "I take it business is booming."

"Is it ever!" Uncle Garax bellowed. My uncle's assistants

moved to opposite sides of the rock's base. They reached through the moss and grabbed hidden discs. As they cranked at the discs, a series of ropes pulled at the curtain of moss, drawing it up. Camouflage burlap, painted to look like stone, rose higher and higher to reveal a large house mounted on massive wheels. A sign over the house's door, carved in wood, read GHOSTFIRE.

The Ghostfire Proxy. It was embarrassing that I hadn't figured it out sooner. The Ghostfire Proxy was an old family business, handed down through the Grimjinx clan for nearly three centuries. From this mobile house, Garax ran one of the oldest scams in Grimjinx history.

Step One: simulate the threat of an attacking monster in the middle of the night near a remote village. Step Two: show up and offer to exterminate the monster . . . for a price. Step Three: rid the village of the "monster" in a flashy battle of smoke and mirrors and leave with the villagers' payment.

"How's this then?" Garax asked, snapping his fingers at the bearded henchman. Beard held up a small piece of parchment cut to look like the outline of a braxilar. He passed it in front of Uncle Garax's lantern. A giant, menacing shadow slid across the trees.

"Big monster gonna come get you, Jaxy-Waxy," Garax said with a titter.

I faked a smile. Somehow, it had escaped my dear uncle that I wasn't five years old anymore. Still, it could have been worse. At least Alsa and Olsa weren't with him. Garax's daughters—my cousins—were horrid. They used to sneak up behind me when I was five and yank my undergarments up out of my trousers. Thankfully, they'd been exiled years ago for crimes Garax never wanted to discuss.

"The stomping was a nice touch," Da admitted.

Uncle Garax pointed proudly to the back of the house. A wooden crane hung off the roof, suspending a large boulder by a thick rope and several pulleys. "One of my modifications. The higher we drop the boulder, the bigger the stomp."

"So, when you blew that horn," I said, "that was the signal something's gone wrong and you should stop with all the braxilar stuff, right?"

Uncle Garax tapped his nose. "And another new feature . . ." He pointed to the bald man, who scaled a ladder on the side of the house. Stomping across the shingles, Bald went to the chimney, which was unlike any I'd seen. Elbow-shaped glass tubes ran in and out of the brickwork. Rusty gears and pistons covered nearly every surface.

Bald grabbed an L-shaped crank and gave it several turns. The gears and pistons came to life, ticking and clicking quietly. A river of black dust ran through the glass tubes and shot out the top of the chimney. I immediately recognized the smell of tinderjack powder. Bald pulled a cord. We heard flint strike metal. A spark shot up, igniting the tinderjack powder into a ball of blue flame.

"Bangers!" Da said. Even I had to admit it was a clever way to simulate the braxilar's fire breath.

"It's good to know you're well, big brother. Ma's been worried about you," Uncle Garax said.

"You've seen Nanni?" I asked. We'd tried to find my grandmother, but she'd already gone into hiding.

Uncle Garax nodded. "Few months back. Smart old bird our ma is, Ona. She was lying low near Cindervale, last time I saw her."

I saw Da relax. This was the first bit of good news we'd had in a long, long while.

Uncle Garax pulled Da close. "So, what do you think, Ona? Wanna help us pull the scam once more for old time's sake? Mind you, that little pit of a village you're in doesn't look like it can afford our services. But they must have *something* of value, right?"

Da shook his head. "Too dangerous, Garax. We can't run the risk of the Palatinate getting involved."

Uncle Garax frowned, his greedy gaze fixed on Slagbog. "Are you sure? I could really use the cash."

"I thought you said business was good," I said.

Garax waved his hand at the chimney contraption. "It's not cheap, faking monster attacks. Equipment like this costs a few silvernibs."

It was more likely that my uncle burned through his money faster than he could "earn" it. If he was hurting for cash with a successful scam going, it was his own fault.

"Come into the village in the morning," Da said. "You can claim to have chased the braxilar away. You might get a decent meal out of it."

I noticed Da was careful not to mention that the meal would probably consist of the only plentiful food in the village: grubslush, a sort of gray ooze made of ground-up slugs and grubs that the par-Goblins considered a delicacy. For the record, it tastes exactly as delightful as it sounds.

Beard and Bald, who had yet to say a word, perked up.

I got the idea they might not have had real food in a while.

Uncle Garax sighed. "Fine. You used to be a lot more fun before you became the Palatinate's worst enemy. We'll see you in the morning."

Da shook his brother's hand. When Uncle Garax disappeared into the Ghostfire house, Da and I started the trek back to Slagbog.

"So," I said. "Uncle Garax."

"I know," Da said. Garax was the black gronx of the family . . . if a family of thieves could have a black gronx. He had a history of looking out for himself only. Not exactly trustworthy, my uncle. "Still, we might be able to use the Ghostfire house in our plan."

"True."

"And it's nice to hear that Nanni's doing well."

"And I suppose it's good to see your brother again," I admitted grudgingly.

Da smiled and put his arm across my back. "Let's not get carried away, son."

21

The Seeds of Rebellion

"A thief's greatest enemy
isn't the law, it's distraction."

—Baloras Grimjinx, architect of the First Aviard Nestvault Pillage

We awoke to a loud rumble the next morning. Groggy from the previous night, Da and I stumbled over and pulled back the curtain.

Our window filled with the sight of Uncle Garax's house on wheels as it lumbered slowly into town. People outside pressed up against their mud huts as the rolling house passed. My uncle sat on a perch at the front, his legs cranking on the pedals that moved the house forward. Two long, wooden levers allowed him to steer. He wasn't very good. When his hand slipped and veered slightly right, the house's mighty wheels crushed a row of rain barrels.

"Sorry 'bout that!" Garax called out to the Aviard woman who owned the shattered barrels.

The house came to a stop in the square, igniting loud chatter from everyone. But the noisy discontent of the crowd was instantly extinguished by the thunderous shouts of Oberax.

"She's got quite a mastery of par-Goblin profanity, our mayoress," I said.

Da got dressed. "I should run interference," he said, ducking outside.

Oberax's cursing grew quieter as Da quickly explained that it was "Mr. Bleakhex" and his associates who had saved the village from the braxilar last night. Oberax grudgingly offered them Slagbog's hospitality. As Oberax led Uncle Garax and his henchmen away to claim their meal, the rest of the village, now roused, went about their daily business.

After breakfast, Callie left with Da for their weekly trip to Umbramore. The prison's magical defenses were so powerful that they prevented the Palatinate from detecting Callie's spellsphere as she probed the tower, looking for weaknesses.

Da wrote down everything Callie learned. Really, I think Da went because it brought him close to Ma. Callie once told me that sometimes he spoke quietly in the prison's direction, as though Ma could hear him.

The Dowager, Aubrin, and I went to the town square to make enough blood-masking tea for the entire village in the massive cauldron. Over the past six months, we'd perfected the formula. The Dowager had even made a few adjustments that took the bitter edge off. It was now only *mildly* disgusting to swallow. More important, it kept the bloodreavers away.

As the Dowager and I added the necessary herbs, Aubrin sat on the nearby scaffold, engrossed in her journal. I kept sneaking glances her way and every time I did, her eyes rose to meet mine.

After the tenth time, she said, "Just ask me and get it over with."

I pretended she hadn't caught me spying. "Sorry?"

"We both know you want to ask what's on your mind. It's been eating you up for months. Just ask."

The Dowager snickered. She enjoyed seeing me fail at being sneaky.

I stared into the cauldron. "I don't know what you—"

"About the prophecy. Your death," she prompted.

Oh. *That* question.

The truth was that I didn't want to know. Six months of running and I'd never brought it up. Those few times the knowledge of my demise crept into my mind, I thought about the marbles. No single prophecy was inevitable. Several events had to align perfectly before a predicted future event came true. Prophecies were delicate things. Anything could disrupt them.

And I had a talent for disrupting things.

"I figured that since you hadn't said anything, it wasn't an issue anymore. Maybe we'd avoided it."

She looked down guiltily. "I—I thought we had too. But lately . . ."

She didn't have to say any more. Since we went on the run, Aubrin's visions had been few and far between. Most didn't make sense, and *couldn't* make sense unless we had the other pieces of the puzzle: namely, the visions from the other seers. But the fact that she was nervous meant she'd seen my death again. And that meant it was still a good possibility.

Despite my resolve not to think about it, I'd be lying to

say I wasn't a tiny bit curious. "Okay," I said, "what did you see?"

Aubrin fell quiet, her face twisting as she gave it some thought. "I saw you. You were dirty and injured. And there was a pillar of light. Tall and powerful. You walked right up to it, paused, then stepped inside. You were consumed immediately."

I felt sick to my stomach. "Consumed immediately" was *not* promising. "So, the lesson here is: avoid pillars of light. Got it."

"It's not that simple," she insisted, a tremor in her voice. "If we don't change things, you're going to *die*."

"You said yourself it's a *possible* future. And if we try to change things, we could make something worse happen."

She held her journal tight to her chest and said softly, "Jaxter, what could be worse than your death?"

I swallowed. For six months, we'd spent every minute of every day in fear. It was rare when sentiment broke through and made me remember how much I loved my sister.

Aubrin moved closer. "I've been thinking about it. Maybe the way to stop your death is *here*." She thumped the pages of her journal. "Maybe that's what the message is.

Maybe it tells us how to save you."

"Then why did you write it in a language no one can translate?" I asked.

"It's what I saw in my vision, you garfluk," she said, exasperated. "I saw a hand write this. The same hand wrote 'Jaxter—deliver to Eaj.' I bet that's what it is. I bet it's the secret to saving you."

"Well, Ma once said the only people who might be able to translate it are the assassin-monks of Blackvesper Abbey. And we can't exactly ask them, can we?"

Besides being notoriously difficult to find, rumors everywhere suggested that the monks had joined forces with the Palatinate, enforcing the new law side by side with the Sentinels.

Aubrin sighed. "This would be easier if we had the other seers here. I hope Luda returns with them and Maloch soon."

I didn't mention what Sarquin Scalander had told us about the Dagger. It was better for Aubrin to think there was still a chance they could return.

"Anything else I should know about my death?" I asked.

"Yes," she said. "You die in the rebellion's attempt to overthrow the Palatinate."

"Well, that's it then, isn't it? We already tried to stop them. And I lived."

Aubrin hit me with her most serious look. "There's another rebellion coming."

"Did you see it in a vision?"

She shook her head. "I know because of her." She pointed to the Dowager.

All the while we'd been speaking, the Dowager had been quiet. In the old days, it would have been strange for her to remain silent for so long. Not anymore.

It had been a long time since I'd seen the Dowager. I mean, she was standing right there and I could *see* her. But she wasn't *my* Dowager. She was no longer my mentor, with fire in her belly. Months on the run had changed her. Symptoms of her childhood illness—mag-plague—had flared up recently, making her tired and weak. She rarely spoke these days and kept to herself.

But now, with Aubrin pointing right at her, she could no longer stay quiet. "Rebellion? What are you talking about?"

Aubrin nodded across the square to an empty notice board. Just last week, a Sentinel had come to the village to replace one of the many wanted posters—with sketches of the Dowager and Aubrin—that always seemed to mysteriously vanish from Slagbog. Despite what the Scalanders had said, one thing was clear: it *wasn't* just the Grimjinxes the Palatinate wanted.

"If they're still looking for the Dowager," Aubrin reasoned, "then that means people are still loyal to her family. The Palatinate knows she's still a threat. They know people would rise up if she asked."

I searched the Dowager's weary face for a sign that Aubrin had struck a nerve. Instead, a ghost of a smile crossed her lips and she said, "Aubrin, you are far more of a threat to the Palatinate than I'll ever be. An augur could undo all their plans. Our job is to protect you. Of the two of us, *you* are the greater loss. We can't allow that to happen."

Aubrin opened her mouth to argue but I silenced her with a look. I knew when to argue with the Dowager and when not. Now was definitely a not.

Steam rose off the cauldron. The tea was nearly done. Aubrin reached over the edge, dipped a small cup, and handed it to me. "Drink your tea," she said, before filling another cup for herself. I spent so much time brewing the tea for the whole village and making sure everyone drank it daily that I sometimes forgot to take my own dose.

I watched the Dowager carefully as she rang a bell, beckoning the rest of Slagbog to come drink. Even though she rarely spoke, I knew the Palatinate's power play had hurt her deeply. She'd refused the job of High Laird to devote her life to studying the natural world. But deep down, she felt a duty to her family's legacy.

All our efforts in the past months had been devoted to getting Ma out of Umbramore so we could leave the Provinces. We'd never once talked about fighting back. Maybe because it seemed so impossible. Would we even stand a chance?

People formed a line in front of the Dowager as she handed out cups of tea. I caught her sneaking glances at me more than once. Aubrin's words *had* gotten to her. The seeds of rebellion had been planted. The only question that remained: What would it take to make them grow?

22

Betrayed

> "Beware the lesson that nets a copperbit
> but costs a silvernib."
>
> —*Allia Grimjinx, master forger of Korrin Province*

Over the next few days, Da barely got any sleep. He knew the raid on Umbramore had to occur by month's end when the next tribute was due. Late into the night, he consulted feverishly with anyone in the village who'd ever spent time in the prison. Together, they drew up crude blueprints and formed a plan of attack. It wouldn't be long now.

Uncle Garax and his assistants still hadn't left town. Long after they'd received their free meal, the Ghostfire house remained parked in the square. Although food was in short supply, most of the villagers didn't mind sharing with the "monster hunters." Ghostfire's presence made people feel safe. Uncle Garax soaked it all up. He loved being the center of attention.

I kept a closer eye on the Dowager. Part of me hoped that Aubrin's talk of rebellion had sunk in and that whenever she sat quietly, she was really thinking of ways to lead a revolt. I had a feeling that once we got Ma out of prison, the Dowager wouldn't leave the Provinces with us. The land was her birthright. But any plans she had, she kept quiet.

Knowing we'd be facing Umbramore's magical defenses, I stocked up on magic-resistant plants. It was hard to say if they'd help, but they certainly couldn't hurt. On our way to collect plants one day, Aubrin and I found Da pounding on the door of the Ghostfire house.

"Something wrong, Da?" I asked.

Da put his hands on his hips. "Have you seen your uncle? It occurred to me that we could use the Ghostfire house to transport any sick prisoners away from Umbramore. I wanted to run the idea by him."

Aubrin shrugged. "Maybe he's off hunting monsters."

Da snorted. "Somebody told me he borrowed a mang and

rode it out of the village. Where do you suppose he got to?"

"He's probably just getting ready for his next scam," I said. "Come on, Jinxface, let's have a look around."

Slagbog could be walked in under fifteen minutes and we covered it well. Uncle Garax wasn't in the village. We were about report back to Da when we spotted two familiar, hulking frames lumber their way into the tavern.

"Let's see if Uncle Garax's assistants know where he is," I said.

"I thought they didn't have any money," Aubrin said.

"Yeah," I agreed. There was that to look into as well. I hoped they weren't planning on stealing their drinks. Normally, as a Grimjinx, this would be completely acceptable. But we had too much to lose these days. A brouhaha could attract the Palatinate.

It was a wonder the tavern was even open. Times were so hard that the only beverages came from two bottles on the back counter filled with more water than ashwine. As we walked in, Gandrick, the par-Goblin tavern owner, was arguing with Beard and Bald.

"Credit?" Gandrick shrieked. "I don't give anyone credit. Cash only."

"Reward come soon," Beard said in a low, slow voice. "Drinks now."

Gandrick frowned. "Reward? What reward? Look, you pay *now* or no drinks."

"Everything okay, Gandrick?" I asked. Seeing me, Beard and Bald quickly turned to face the other way. I got the idea they thought that if they couldn't see me, I couldn't see them.

"Nothing I can't handle," the par-Goblin said before returning to watering down the ashwine.

"Hey," I said, "you two seen Uncle Garax?"

They didn't say a word. They just pulled their arms in tighter to their bodies, like they were trying to make themselves smaller.

"Look, he's not in trouble. We just want to ask him if we can use—"

I stopped. *Reward*. They'd said they were going to pay for the drinks once their reward came. Suddenly, I knew where Uncle Garax had gone.

I ran from the tavern. Outside, Aubrin flashed me a quizzical look.

"Jaxter, what's—?"

I snatched her by the wrist and pulled her with me as we

ran home. Inside, we found Da chopping vegetables in the kitchen, preparing for dinner.

"There you are," Da said. "I'm making grubslush casserole. Go grab the Dowager and Callie and we'll—"

"We have to go!" I said. "Uncle Garax sold us out. He's telling the Palatinate where we are for the reward."

Da looked up sharply. "What?"

"His goons are out spending money they don't have yet," I said. "They said they're expecting a reward. We don't have much time."

We didn't have *any* time. Just then, we heard the familiar *crack* of a quickjump spell. I peeked outside and saw two bloodreavers descend from the glowing circle above the town square. Next, two figures floated gently down onto the scaffolding below. The first was Uncle Garax, head bowed humbly. The second was a tall, lean Sentinel. His masked face scanned the village as those nearby cowered. The Sentinel raised his hand, holding a glowing spellsphere, and got right to the point.

"Bring me the Grimjinxes!"

23

Danger in the Swamp

"An ugly nose breathes just the same."

—*Ancient par-Goblin proverb*

Da didn't think twice. He dropped his knife and opened a cupboard. From within, he pulled two of the emergency packs he kept in case we needed to make a fast getaway. Before I could utter a word, he thrust the packs into my hands.

"Take your sister," he said, pointing to the back door.

"What about you?" Aubrin asked.

"I have to get the Dowager and Callie," Da said. "But you need to leave now. Go north. Wait at the far edge of the swamp near the valley. If we haven't joined you in one hour—"

"—we'll head to Cindervale to find Nanni," I finished.

Da nodded, then ducked outside, hiding behind the row of mud huts on his way to the Dowager's house.

I grabbed a map. "I just hope Nanni hasn't left Cindervale yet," I said.

"No," Aubrin said, "we need to find the assassin-monks." Before I could protest, she added, "They're the only ones who can tell us what the message means. And we'll never know if they work for the Palatinate unless we try. Trust me."

I didn't have much choice. For all I knew, the arrival of the Sentinel was one more sign that my death was imminent. The sooner we got that message translated and delivered to Eaj, the better.

I gripped Tree Bag tightly and ushered Aubrin through the back door. We could hear people turning out into the streets as the Sentinel summoned all Slagbog to the square. Unfortunately, the square stood between us and the way out of town. Holding hands, we crouched behind an empty wagon, waiting for our chance to bolt.

"You are harboring fugitives," the Sentinel's deep voice boomed. "You will immediately turn the Grimjinx family over to me."

A murmur rippled through the assembled villagers. People looked around, as if expecting to see someone wearing a sign around their neck saying "I am a Grimjinx." Oberax pushed her way to the front of the crowd. "I'm very careful about the people I let live in Slagbog. If the Grimjinxes were here, I'd know about it."

A bolt of lightning shot from the spellsphere, splitting a nearby everember tree.

"You will *all* be arrested if the Grimjinx family isn't brought to me . . . now!" The Sentinel's masked face scanned the crowd. He nudged Uncle Garax. "Where are they?"

"They were here this morning, your most powerful magicalness," Garax said. "I can take you to their house."

But before Uncle Garax could move, one of the bloodreavers threw back its head and bellowed in that all-too-familiar screech. The second bloodreaver mirrored the first and soon both were growling and thrashing about. Finally, the eyes of both bloodreavers rested on the wagon where Aubrin and I were hiding.

Aubrin gripped my arm. "Jaxter, did you drink your tea today?"

Oh, zoc.

"It's too late for me," I told her. "They've got my scent. Get to the valley. Da will be waiting there."

I stepped from our hiding place, arms raised in the air, and walked slowly toward the square.

"Oya!" I called out. "Looking for a Grimjinx?"

Slagbog issued a collective gasp. Uncle Garax looked relieved. "Yep. That's one of 'em. Want me to nab him for you?"

"Good luck with that," I muttered to myself. Head down, I ran through Slagbog toward the swamp.

Pop! Behind me, I heard the bloodreavers vanish. A second later, they appeared in a cloud of smoke on the roof of an adjacent mud hut. I dashed side to side, trying to throw them off. The bloodreavers kept pace, leaping from roof to roof in pursuit. Chunks of thatch rained down as their claws dug in for purchase.

Ahead, the village opened up into the thick swamp beyond. If I could make it there, I had a chance of losing them in the scumpits. I also had a chance of being swallowed by the scumpits, but I couldn't worry about that. I had to evade them just long enough for Aubrin to get away.

But the bloodreavers were even faster than I remembered. No matter how hard I ran or changed directions, they were closing in. I charged past the last mud hut on the village's border. The ground beneath my feet became marsh. Swamp water filled my boots.

True to form, that's when my foot snagged a tree root.

I fell face-first into the muck, just as one of the bloodreavers jumped. The beast overshot and got tangled in the slimy vines that hung between the swamp trees.

I grabbed at the tree to pull myself up. Pain shot through my hand. Wiping the mud from my eyes, I found pinpricks of blood all over my palm. I'd wrapped my hand around a thatch of vexbriar. My head spun. The poison from the vexbriar's thorns was already going to work. I'd be unconscious within minutes. Depending on how much poison I'd absorbed, I could be dead shortly thereafter.

The second bloodreaver, seeing me struggle to move, leaped in the air and came down on top of me.

But the instant we made contact, the bloodreaver vanished. There was a puff of black smoke as multicolored sparks fell into the swamp water and sizzled away.

I craned my neck. I knew bloodreavers could disappear in one place and reappear close by to surprise their prey. But why do that when it had me? And why wasn't it reappearing?

I hauled myself out of the mud, stumbled forward on wobbly legs, and hid behind an everember tree. If I could find a bit of lorris—a fungus that was fairly plentiful in the swamp—it would counteract the poison. I just needed time.

Which I didn't have.

The first bloodreaver finally freed itself from the mossy vines and stalked about loudly. I held my breath, waiting for the scent of my blood to betray me.

"Over here!"

Aubrin's squeaky voice carried on a gentle breeze. I peeked out and saw her in the distance, waving at the bloodreaver. The creature looked her way, raised each of its four arms, and screeched. Aubrin turned and ran, the bloodreaver quickly following.

I jumped up and nearly fell over, dizzy from the poison. But I couldn't let the bloodreaver get her. "It's me you want!" I yelled, stepping out.

The bloodreaver stopped. I held up my bloody hand.

"Yeah, you can smell me, right? I'm the one."

"Jaxter—"

"Go!" I yelled as the bloodreaver made up its mind and charged me. "Find the assassin-monks!" She hesitated, then ran. I turned and headed for my last hope: the scumpits.

But I'd underestimated how much the poison was slowing me down. I could barely move and, in seconds, the bloodreaver was on me. I felt its talons grip my arm and—*poof!* Black smoke and rainbow-colored sparks rained down.

My ears filled with my own heaving breaths and pounding blood. What was going on? The bloodreavers had me. Why would they pounce and then vanish?

The vexbriar's poison coursed through my veins. My breath grew short. I stumbled feverishly, searching for lorris.

When my legs finally gave out, I fell against a mound of rocks, not far from the swamp's edge. I looked down into the valley just beyond. Sitting there, among the mokka trees, was a tall, octagon-shaped tower of white stone. It had never been there before.

I drew a feeble breath. Delirious, I thought I saw several shadowy figures running up the side of the valley toward me. I heard what I thought was Aubrin's voice but when I turned to look, I saw the blurry outline of someone tall. Did this person have horns?

I thought I heard Aubrin say, "We're here, Jaxter."

There were a lot of things I thought I saw and heard. Hard to say which were real and which were imagined. Darkness took me just then.

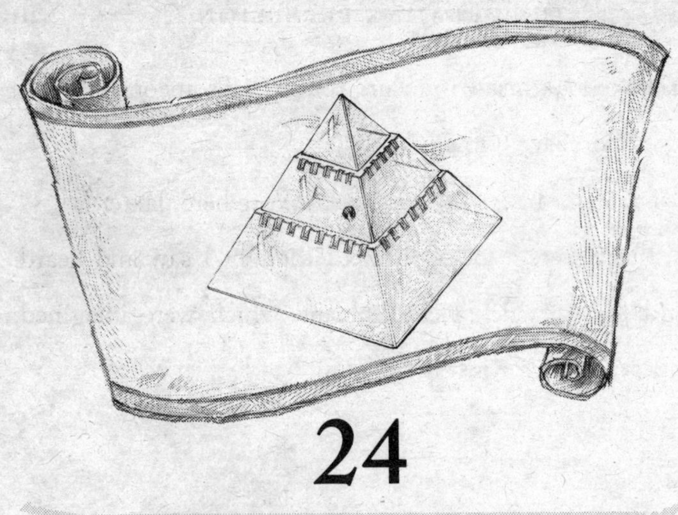

24

Blackvesper Abbey

"The greedy eye starves as the itchy palm feasts."

—*The Lymmaris Creed*

The first thing I noticed was the soothing aroma of starkholly. Eyes closed, I inhaled deeply and allowed the herb's healing properties to fill my lungs. I felt myself cocooned in a warm, heavy blanket. Wherever I was lying was soft and comfortable. As memories of being attacked in the swamp reappeared, I tried to go back to sleep. Surely I'd earned a little rest.

But then I remembered Aubrin. Rest would have to wait.

I sat up. The cot on which I was lying ran the length

of the small, square room. A black candle, little more than a mound of melted wax and a stubborn wick, burned on a rickety table next to the dish of smoldering starkholly. My possessions—pouches, vallix skin gloves, and Tree Bag—hung from the bedpost. Sitting up, I found a cup and metal pitcher, filled with water, near the foot of the bed.

It was official. I'd been kidnapped by gracious innkeepers.

I reached for the water pitcher and found the hand with which I'd grabbed the vexbriar thorns neatly bandaged. I peeked under the cloth. My wounds were covered in an oily green salve that smelled of amberberries. Between the starkholly incense and the lotion, whoever lived here clearly knew something about healing.

After downing several cups of water, I tried the door. Locked. Should have guessed, really.

"Hello?" I called. "I'm awake. Not to presume anything but I'm kinda hungry and could use some food. Hello?"

Silence. So much for the gracious innkeepers.

Some time later, keys rattled in the lock. A tall boy with smooth, dark skin, carrying a glass tray, gently pushed the door open with his foot. He looked about my age. The extra fabric of his ill-fitting brown robes pooled near his ankles. The very model of confidence, he stepped over the threshold, tripped on his robes, and fell flat on his face.

The tray shattered, sending slices of cheese and bits of fruit flying. As I knelt down to help, the boy sat up quickly, driving the top of his head into my chin. With a grunt, I fell back against the cot. The boy, holding his head, tried to get to his feet . . . but slipped on the cheese and ended up flat on his back. We both lay there, rubbing our injuries. There was something very familiar about this.

It was like I'd met my long-lost twin.

"You know how to make an entrance," I joked. But he wouldn't look me in the eye. Slowly, we both got down on all fours and gathered the spilled food.

"It's okay," I said. "I wasn't that hungry." It was a lie but he seemed so ashamed, I had to say *something* to make him feel better. "Not quite the welcome I was expecting at Blackvesper Abbey."

The boy stopped gathering food and eyed me sharply. "How could you know this is Blackvesper Abbey?"

I glanced slyly at his robes. "Bit of white powder near your collar, smells of ground yarmick seeds. I caught a whiff when

I bent over to help you. It's often used in holy rituals. Your ink-stained fingers suggest you spend a lot of time gripping a quill. There are three religious orders in the Provinces where extensive writing exercises are mandatory. The Brotherhood of the Glistening Aura don't wear robes—they don't wear any clothes at all, in fact—so that's one down. You have to be at least sixty years old to join the Order of the Withering Days Monastery. That leaves Blackvesper Abbey."

The boy sat slack-jawed at my deduction. Then, all traces of embarrassment bled away. He looked as confident as when he first opened the door. He offered his hand. "I'm Bennock. Pleased to meet you, Jaxter Grimjinx."

We shook. "You know who I am?"

"Your roots are brown. You dyed your hair blond, probably to hide. These days, people only hide from the Palatinate. There are currently ten children being hunted by the Lordcourt. Four of them are girls. Two of the boys are par-Goblins, two are older than you, and one of the boys lives here in the Abbey. That leaves one boy: you. Jaxter Grimjinx."

I can honestly say I'd never been more impressed or excited to meet someone in my entire life.

"Also, your sister told me."

"Ah."

"But I had you going."

"Yes, you did."

We stared at each other, neither willing to budge, each wearing the same knowing smile. It really was like meeting another version of me. Very exciting.

Bennock cleared his throat. "Well, so much for my vow of silence. Made it a whole twenty-two days this time."

Now it was my turn to feel ashamed. "Sorry I made you break your vow. I've heard it's important to your order."

"All acolytes must remain silent for an entire year."

"Then you become an assassin-monk?"

"Then the monks decide if I'm worthy."

His stare told me that meant a lot. "Listen," I said, "I won't tell anyone you spoke to me. You can just wake up tomorrow and let it be day twenty-three of silence."

His dark eyes narrowed. "*I'd* know," he said softly. "No, once I drop you off with the abbot, it's back to Day Zero for me."

Pity. He was clumsy, good at verbal sparring. . . . Here I thought we were going to be best friends. But he was a bit too honest for me. Well, no one's perfect.

"I'm sorry, what was that? The abbot?"

Bennock stood and opened the door. "I'll escort you to him," he said. "And I'll, um, see if I can round up some more food for you."

I stood my ground. "I want to see my sister."

"The abbot will explain everything. Don't worry. He's fair and wise."

I wasn't sure what to think. It was Aubrin who'd suggested we seek out the monks to help translate the message in her journal. I should have been grateful they were this easy to find. But it felt just a little *convenient* that they'd found us just as the Palatinate had tracked us down. I had a feeling that the rumors of the monks' allegiance to the Lordcourt were about to be proven true.

With no other choice, I gathered my things and followed Bennock out into a long stone corridor lit with green-blue torches. Ascending a spiral staircase, I could hear the distant sound of chanting, melodious and hypnotic. We passed monks—both men and women—on the stairs. Unlike Bennock's robes—loose fitting and voluminous—the black robes of the monks were custom-made, clinging to their lithe bodies. They wore soft-soled boots that made no sound as they moved. Cowls covered the tops of their heads, while their faces were hidden behind black porcelain masks that cut off just below the nose.

Bennock led me into a dark niche just off the staircase to a door made of weathered gray wood. He bowed deeply and muttered what sounded like a prayer before opening the door and ushering me in.

The abbot's chamber was only slightly larger than the room I'd woken in. A similar cot sat against one wall. A square table, covered in maps of each Province, took up the center of the room. A modest desk pointed to an alcove through which I could see an outdoor balcony and what looked to be the first rays of sunlight on the horizon just beyond.

Seated at the desk was the abbot. His attention was directed down at a large open book on the desktop. He wore clothes identical to the other monks, but unlike theirs, his mask was dotted with tiny red jewels along the edges.

"Very good, Bennock. Please leave us."

The abbot's voice was deep and scratchy. I waited for him to look up but he continued to read from the book.

"Abbot," Bennock said, eyes lowered, "I spoke. I broke my vow. Again."

As he stared at his book, the abbot folded his index fingers into a steeple and brought them to his lips. He considered for several moments. Then he said, "The vow of silence is a tradition as old as the halls of this Abbey. Followers of the order undertake the task as a way to remind themselves that not all words are spoken. That, often, gestures are far more powerful.

"But you, acolyte, I feel you were born with this knowledge. Every day, your gestures of kindness inspire every monk in the order. There is much *you* could teach others, but I feel you've little else to learn from the lesson of silence. Therefore, I release you from the vow. You may speak freely from now on."

I thought Bennock was going to cry, he looked so happy. But he lifted his chin and bowed to the abbot he revered so greatly.

I reached out and shook Bennock's hand. "So, tell me, when do I get to meet the other boy on the Lordcourt's most wanted list? The one who lives here in the Abbey."

Bennock smiled. "You already have."

I had a feeling.

The acolyte bowed his head again and left me alone with the abbot.

"That was nice of you," I said. "Letting Bennock off the

hook with his vow. He said you were wise and fair."

The abbot stood very slowly. He stared at me, unblinking, for the longest time. "What do the par-Goblins say? *Uruhl derets sil bruk derets ta.* 'People believe what they want to believe.'"

Something had changed. The timbre of the abbot's voice was a bit higher. A Yonick Province accent slurred the words together. And why was he quoting par-Goblin proverbs? Only thieves did that.

"Any chance I could see my sister?" I asked. "She's probably worried."

The abbot's gloved hands moved slowly across the desk as he gripped the cover of the book and closed it. "There'll be time for that later. I think it's best that you and I speak first. It'll give us a chance to catch up on old times."

The edge in his voice triggered a memory, and a breath caught in my throat. The abbot slid his mask off. I instantly recognized those steely eyes, sunken deep into pockets of twisted, scarred flesh. I was staring into the disfigured face of Edilman Jaxter.

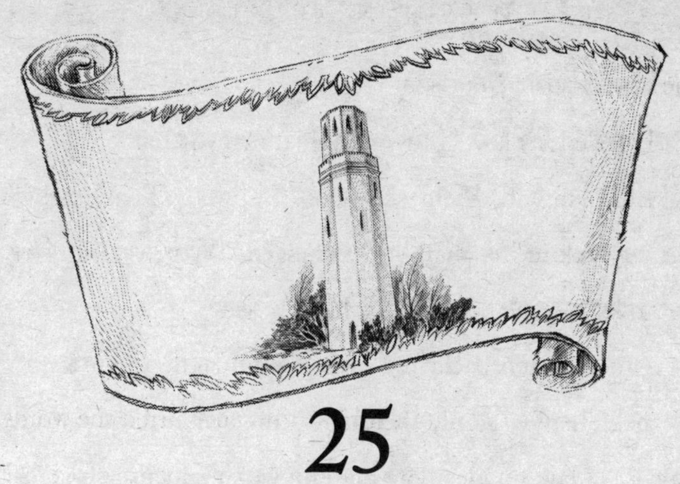

25

The Abbot and the Answer

"Hasty theft pleases only the Castellan."

—*Sareth Grimjinx, pillager of the tin mines of Rexin*

The right side of Edilman's face looked like a map: waxy pink scars ran like roads from his chin to just under his eye. The skin sagged a bit, like it was barely clinging to his skull. I vividly recalled the day he got burned. More accurately, I remembered burning his face. He'd tried to stop me from destroying a magic tapestry with an acidic solvent and got hit by accident.

I must have been gazing a little too hard at his injuries because he grunted and said, "Don't worry, Jaxter. I don't blame you for this any more than I blame your parents for the years I spent in prison."

I steeled my jaw. "But you *do* blame my parents."

Edilman laid the mask aside. "Oh, yeah. That's right." He sat back in his chair and shrugged. "Well, then I'll try not to let it come between us. Have a seat."

I took a step back, my eyes scanning the room for an escape. There was only the door to my rear and the outside balcony. I had no idea how high up we were. But I seriously considered flinging myself out the window and taking a chance. It seemed better than if I stayed within arm's reach of Edilman.

The "abbot" *tsk*ed. "Jaxter, if I wanted to hurt you, I had all night while you slept." His foot snaked out from under the desk and pushed a stool at me. "Sit."

Resigned, I did as he said. "If you touch Aubrin—"

"Aubrin's fine," Edilman said. "She's enjoying breakfast right now in the dining hall with my monks."

I laughed. "'Your' monks? How are they 'your' monks?"

Edilman smiled. "I'm the abbot of Blackvesper Abbey."

"Very impressive. Certainly one of your better cons."

He folded his hands and lay them atop the book on his desk. "Believe it or not, it's no con."

"I don't believe it." The idea of a garfluk like Edilman having command over a league of assassins was terrifying. But it appeared to be true.

He sighed. "Your arrival has placed the Abbey in grave danger."

"What do you mean?"

"It should have come as no surprise to anyone that the Palatinate was planning a takeover. The monks and I had seen the signs for months. The disappearance of the Shadowhands, the theft of magical relics from the High Laird's most secure vaults . . ."

"How do you know about that?"

"The assassin-monks have informants everywhere. Like I said, the takeover was no surprise to us. The fact that the Palatinate's first order of business was to hunt down *your* family . . . Well, now, that was a little surprising. I should have guessed that you and your parents would be mixed up in it all. Only a Grimjinx could incur the wrath of every mage in the Provinces." He leaned in. "Once I knew how badly the Palatinate wanted you, I knew I had to find you first."

I frowned. "To kill us before they can?"

Edilman rubbed his eyes tiredly. "You need more proof

you're safe?" he asked. "Take a look outside."

I stepped through the curtains and out onto the balcony. The swamp was gone. The Abbey stood on a precipice overlooking the ocean. To the right, past the stony cliff face, I saw vast open fields. Below, the ocean roared as it crashed against the rocks. The warm glow of sunrise shimmered off the morning tide.

Edilman joined me. "The Abbey likes this place. We come here a lot. A day and a half by mang from the nearest village or town-state. The Abbey likes isolation."

"I'm sorry but— What?"

Edilman smiled. "'You don't find the assassin-monks, the assassin-monks find you.' Sounds very spooky. But it's quite literal. The tower is enchanted. Very strong magic from before the Great Uprisings. If someone needs the monks, the Abbey goes where we're needed. When we're not needed, we find ourselves here, in this exact spot. I think the Abbey might have been built with stone from these very cliffs. Maybe it thinks of this place as home."

That explained my hazy vision before passing out. A magical, moving tower. Very helpful, especially when trying to hide from the Palatinate.

"So, you go where you're needed," I repeated, trying to grasp the idea. It explained how easy it was for the monks to find us. Aubrin and I had certainly needed them. "And a lot of people have need for holy men who also kill people?"

Edilman laughed. "We train in the art of assassination so that we might know the darkness of an evil mind, not to use the skills for harm. And, yes, you'd be surprised how many people need us."

He stepped back into his chambers. When I followed, I found him standing over the table covered in maps.

"Since the Palatinate came to power, we've hardly stopped moving," Edilman said, pointing out locations all over the maps. "The Abbey has taken us across the Five Provinces. We wake up in a new location practically every day. We've become a traveling refugee camp, taking in strays everywhere we go, staying one step ahead of the Sentinels. It's getting hard."

"Why would the Sentinels be after you?"

"Oh, the Palatinate knows we're a threat. We're something they can't control. That's why they spread a rumor that we were working for them. It made people stay away from us."

"So what happens now?"

Edilman's jaw tightened. "Things have changed. The Palatinate doesn't just want to lead the Provinces. They want absolute control. The monks are devoted to making sure that doesn't happen. But we can't do it alone. And isn't it your own grandmother who's fond of saying 'Common enemies create uncommon friends'? Come with me."

Edilman replaced his mask and led me from his chambers. We made our way down the staircase and through a set of double doors into a massive hall with rows of tables and benches. In their cowls and masks, monks moved from table to table, offering food and drink to a strange assortment of humans, Aviards, par-Goblins, and other creatures. These were the refugees Edilman had mentioned.

Bennock approached, carrying another tray of food, which he offered with a secret smile. I grabbed a juicy blackdrupe from the tray and bit into it. It was then I realized I was starving.

"Jaxter!"

A short, red blur grabbed me around the waist, nearly sending us both to the floor. I reached down and put my arm around Aubrin.

"You okay, Jinxface?"

She nodded. “I found the Abbey in the valley just outside the swamp. I knocked on the door and told them you were in trouble. And they came!”

“Of course they did. How could they resist this face? Because this face . . .”

“. . . is a *weapon!*” we finished together.

“And guess what else?” she said, eyes glistening.

“What?”

Aubrin pulled back, grinning at something just behind me. A meaty hand clamped down on the back of my neck. I turned and felt the air rush from my lungs.

It was Maloch. His eyes were red and baggy. It made him look a lot older. There was something seriously wrong with his face. It looked broken or distorted maybe.

Or maybe it was just that he was smiling.

I couldn’t help myself. I threw my arms around him and squeezed. The only thing more surprising was when Maloch hugged me back.

“We thought you were killed,” I said.

His wide shoulders slumped and his face grew ashen. “We almost were. It all happened so fast. One day, we were in the kitchen eating dinner, and the entire mountain started shaking. There were explosions everywhere. When the ceilings started falling, I tried to lead everyone out but the exit caved in. We were trapped inside."

"How did you get out?"

Maloch looked across the room to Luda, who sat at a table, surrounded by the other seers. If seeing Maloch smile was a shock, it was nothing compared to watching Luda with those kids. Her gruff exterior was gone as she joked around, making faces to get them to eat the vegetables on their plates.

"She arrived just as the attack started. Luda tunneled her way to us. She got us out just in time. We wandered for days. We would have died if the Abbey hadn't suddenly appeared."

Behind me, Edilman cleared his throat. Now that I'd seen proof he was telling the truth, now that I knew he'd saved Luda and the others, I had no choice but to listen to him.

"Can you excuse me?" I said to Aubrin and Maloch. I pulled Edilman into the corner where we couldn't be overheard.

"You said you were looking for my family," I said. "Why? To hide us? Protect us?"

"I told you," he said quietly. "The Palatinate wants you very badly. That means we can't let them have you. Or the Dowager. I assume she's with your family?"

"She's with Da," I said.

His burned lips mustered a frightening smile. "Good. He won't let anything happen to her. This brings me to my next question. We found you because you needed us. Why do you need the assassin-monks?"

I motioned for Aubrin. "Did you show him the journal?"

She handed the book to Edilman, opened to the mysterious message. "I was waiting for you."

"Aubrin saw this in a vision," I told the abbot. "We need to get it translated. It's . . . important."

Edilman squinted at the text for several moments, then waved to a passing monk. The woman came as beckoned, bowing to her abbot. "Jaxter, this is Sister Andris. The assassin-monks are the guardians of all known forms of communication, with archives containing the secrets of every known language. If anyone can translate it, she can."

Sister Andris ran her finger over the strange symbols and muttered to herself.

"Can you read it?" I asked.

"It's Xyrin," she confirmed. "Very old. One of the very first recorded languages. It may take some time, but I can translate it." The monk tucked the book into her robes, bowed, and hurried away.

By now, Luda had spotted me and crossed the hall. A fresh scar divided her right cheek. The horn on the left side of her head had been broken off halfway down, leaving a jagged nub. She pursed her lips and stood to her full height. I reached out but she stopped me with a hand on my forehead.

"We have discussed this," she said. "I do not hug."

"Just this once."

"If you try, I will be forced to break you."

"Well, we don't want that. It's good to see you, Luda. Thank you for saving my friends."

For a second, I thought she might accept the thanks. Instead, she stiffened and said, "A soldier requires no thanks for performing her duty."

I was wearing her down. I could tell.

I turned to Edilman. "Can you get us back to Slagbog? We need to see if anyone's left."

Edilman scowled. "What do you mean?"

I told him how the entire village was populated by thieves

and about the recent arrival of the Sentinel. It was possible that everyone in Slagbog had already been transported to Umbramore.

But Edilman didn't seem concerned about the appearance of the Sentinel. He was far more interested in the idea of Slagbog being a haven for thieves.

"That might be just what we need," he said, before striding quickly from the hall.

Small fingers laced with my own. I looked down to see Aubrin smiling up at me. We glanced around at the monks and the seers and our friends.

"Jaxter," she said, "how did you fight off the bloodreavers?"

I took a deep breath. "I have no idea."

The question had haunted me. The more I thought about it, the more I sensed there *was* an answer just beyond my reach. . . .

"Something weird is happening, Jinxface." I listed everything I could think of. When the Sentinels who came for Aubrin in Vengekeep failed to stop me with magic . . . when the gaolglobe failed to capture me . . . when the quickjump spell failed in Vesta . . . and finally, when the bloodreavers had exploded after touching me.

"I didn't think much of it each time," I said, "but now it's hard not to see. Magic keeps failing around me. You think working with magic-resistant plants has made me invincible?"

She guffawed. "Hardly."

"But it can't be a coincidence, right? So what's . . . ?"

I quickly gave myself a pat down and found nothing but the Twelve Essentials in my pouches. I opened up Tree Bag. Again, nothing.

But as I ran my fingers along the bottom of Tree Bag, I came to a lump in the corner that I'd never noticed before. The thick fabric made it easy to miss, but *something* had clearly been sewn into the bottom. I dug my fingers in, tearing at the thread that held the bag together. The bottom tore and something sparkly fell out.

I picked up a small crystal pyramid. Its four crenellated sides shone with a soft iridescence. Squinting, I could make out a tiny black sphere embedded inside. I held it up and rolled it around in my hand. It was beautiful but completely ordinary in every way.

Or was it? The Palatinate had used magic to search Tree Bag when Kolo was in their custody and found nothing. Kolo had tried hard to hide this from them. Why? Unless . . .

My hands grew cold. I knew what this was. To test my theory, I walked to one of the green-blue torches lit by magical fire on the wall. I touched the top of the pyramid to the flame. The fire vanished in a wink.

So it was true. This was the one thing the Palatinate could never find by magical means. The one and only thing that could have caused all the magical disruption.

The Vanguard.

26

The Rebel Mage

"No thief cries for wasters who want."

—Allamondas Grimjinx, architect of the Wrathborne Castle cenotaph plunder

I was *really* hoping that everyone in Slagbog was still there and safe. Mainly because I would have felt guilty if anything bad had happened to them because of me. Also, a small part of me wanted to see the looks on their faces when I walked down the street, accompanied by a half-dozen assassin-monks and a heavily armed Satyran warrior.

But we didn't know what to expect. As a precaution, the Abbey had materialized in the swamp, not far from the village. With Maloch and Luda at my side—not to mention

Edilman and the aforementioned monks—we crossed the town's border, prepared for the worst.

What we found was business as usual. The people of Slagbog tended their gardens and chatted in alleyways as if nothing had happened. The Scalander sisters even nodded casually to me, like I hadn't been gone for a day.

Here I'd inexplicably evaded two bloodreavers and brought the most notorious monks in the Provinces as our new allies and no one was even blinking. Some people were just impossible to impress.

It was when I tracked down Da and the Dowager that I finally got a decent reaction. Da picked up Aubrin and pulled Maloch and me tight. Luda threw herself at the Dowager, begging forgiveness for not returning sooner. The Dowager interrupted her, helped Luda to her feet, and shook the Satyran's hand warmly.

I was burning to tell Da about finding the Vanguard, but his reaction to spotting Edilman changed the topic very quickly.

"We can't trust him," he insisted. Edilman stood stone-faced as Da argued vigorously for casting the abbot from the village. It took me and Aubrin and Luda and Maloch to convince him otherwise. He finally allowed Edilman to stay but only because, he said, we had a bigger problem.

"I had to come clean and tell everyone we're Grimjinxes," Da said as he led us to the hut where the Home Guard stored their weapons. "Turns out, we're sort of heroes to the other thieves. People admire the way we've kept hidden so long."

We'd been heroes a lot lately. I'm not sure what our Grimjinx ancestors would think about that. It's not exactly something you race to add to the family album.

Da unlocked the armory. The weapons had been emptied out. Inside was just a chair . . . and the Sentinel tied firmly to it, his back to us. His head was slumped forward. His mask lay on the ground at his feet.

"It was all very . . . spontaneous," the Dowager explained. "Once the bloodreavers took off after you, the entire village charged the Sentinel. They overpowered him in no time."

"Jaxter!"

Callie ran down the street, nearly knocking me over as she arrived.

"Good to see you too, Cal."

She frowned and pointed to the Dowager and Da. "Jaxter, talk to them. Make them listen."

"To what?"

Callie stepped into the armory and spun the chair around. The Sentinel, it turned out, was Talian. A rag, stuffed deep in his mouth, hung down his chin. Scratches marred his cheeks and forehead.

"Look what they did to him," Callie said.

"To be fair, Callie," the Dowager said in her kind-but-firm voice, "when Talian was attacked, no one knew he was your cousin."

"We had to lock him up for his own safety," Da told me. "There was talk of drowning him in the swamp."

Callie placed herself between Talian and the group. "*No one* is touching him."

This was indeed a problem. We couldn't let Talian go. He'd report where we were to the Palatinate. But Grimjinxes weren't murderers and we couldn't let the villagers kill Talian.

"Let's just think," I said. "There's got to be a way—"

"Have you considered," Edilman said, yanking the rag from Talian's mouth, "*talking* to him?"

★

"I've been looking for you."

Callie tipped a wineskin to Talian's lips to help his hoarse voice. We all sat in the Dowager's house, Talian still tied to his chair. Maloch had drawn the curtains, but kept watch for prying eyes. The people of Slagbog wanted blood. It would be hard to explain why we were having a private meeting with the Sentinel.

"Every mage in the Provinces is looking for us," Da replied.

Talian nodded. "And how do you think you've evaded them for so long?"

The Dowager took a seat across from Talian. "Are you saying you had something to do with it?"

"After the insurrection, I became a Sentinel because I knew the Lordcourt would give them the job of finding you," Talian said. "We've had dozens of reports on your whereabouts for the last six months. I altered those reports and made sure the Palatinate was always looking in the wrong place. And I was doing a good job keeping it quiet until *that fool* showed up at the Palatinate Palace, shooting his mouth off."

That fool came with a glare to the far corner where Uncle Garax was tied to his own chair. Apparently, when the village overpowered Talian, Beard and Bald had fled. Since then, Uncle Garax had been bound here in the Dowager's house. That thought alone made me incredibly happy.

The Dowager could see Da was skeptical. "Ona," she said, "I think he's telling the truth."

Talian looked relieved. "I didn't come here to turn you over to the Lordcourt. If you'd just surrendered yesterday, I'd have taken you someplace safe and—"

"But why would you help us?" I asked.

"Not all mages agree with what the Lordcourt has done," Talian said. "All those terrible things the High Laird did—the taxes, the persecutions, the revoked freedoms—he did because Nalia and the Lordcourt advised him to do so. They made him believe the actions were necessary to prevent being overthrown. The High Laird was paranoid, so he agreed. The Lordcourt has been manipulating him for years. Nalia thought it would make it easier to get popular support for their takeover if the people hated him."

"But just in case," I said, "they made a monster army."

Talian sighed. "I didn't know about their plans until it was too late. A small group of mages are working from within to set things right again."

Volo ser voli, I thought. Just like the mages who fought the Scions.

"Pockets of resistance are forming everywhere," Talian continued. "They need our help."

"He's right." Edilman, who'd been leaning quietly against the door, moved next to Talian. "The monks have heard rumors about dissent among the mages."

Da scoffed. "And rumors also say the monks work for the Palatinate. We can't trust rumors."

"You mean you can't trust me," Edilman said softly. He and Da stared at each other, dropping the temperature in the room to near freezing.

"You need to let me go."

Talian's plea broke the tension. Maloch shook his head. "We let him go and two minutes later, the Sentinels will show up with an entire zoo of monsters and turn Slagbog to dust."

"That's what will happen if I *don't* return," Talian countered. "I can go back and say that you were here but escaped before I arrived. I'll tell them you're trying to get back to Vengekeep. They won't be interested in Slagbog and you can stay here to get organized."

"Organized?" Da asked. "For what?"

I thought about what Aubrin had said, about people still being loyal to the House of Soranna. The Palatinate needed Aubrin for her prophecies. But they needed the Dowager to prevent . . .

"A rebellion," I said. "Everyone here already hates the Palatinate. If we could reach out to those others that Talian is talking about . . ."

No one argued. But they didn't jump to agree either. I turned to the Dowager, who had moved into the corner, refusing to meet my eyes.

Finally, Da said, "Well . . . we started with a plan to break into Umbramore. How much more planning could a full-scale rebellion be?"

Edilman untied the mage's hands. "Can you help us?"

"How?"

"Information. Tell us what the Lordcourt is planning. Where are they vulnerable?"

Talian stood and nodded. Da returned the mage's spellsphere. "I'll do what I can," Talian said. "Something's happening soon that might be an opportunity. I'll be in touch."

He opened a quickjump ring and disappeared. We waited. There was a chance we were wrong and Talian was rounding up an army of Sentinels and monsters to level Slagbog. When ten minutes passed and we weren't dying, Da clapped his hands.

"All right, everyone, from this moment on, we're the resistance. That's got a nice ring to it, doesn't it? And our first official job is the hardest we'll probably ever have to do."

"What's that, Da?" I asked.

Da pulled open the curtain and pointed out the window to where the mayoress was crossing the town square.

"Telling Oberax."

27

The Dowager's Dilemma

"A secret shared enslaves the teller."

—*The Lymmaris Creed*

When Da first proposed the idea of creating a haven for thieves in Slagbog, Oberax had agreed only because she wanted the village to survive. And while she had no love for the Palatinate, she didn't necessarily want to make them angry either. When Da, the Dowager, and Edilman went to tell her their ideas about turning Slagbog into the headquarters for the revolution, her screams could be heard from either end of the village.

After several hours of discussion, Oberax agreed on the

condition that everyone in Slagbog had to sign on. If even *one* person disagreed, our rebellion would have to find another home. So we had to win over the entire village.

Da came home that night, exhausted but optimistic. "Oberax is going to call a town meeting tomorrow. We'll present our idea and see what happens."

"Do you think everyone will listen?" Aubrin asked.

"Can't say for sure," Da said. "Maybe. I wish we had something that would convince them we can succeed."

I suddenly remembered my discovery at the Abbey and reached into my pocket. "How about this?" I produced the Vanguard and quickly explained to him what it was. "This is how the Scions were beaten. Everyone *has* to rally if they know we've got the ultimate weapon."

Da's eyes nearly burst from his skull. "You haven't told anyone you've got that, have you?"

"Just Aubrin."

Da touched his temple. "Keep it that way. I admitted to the village that we were Grimjinxes. Thankfully, we have a very big family tree with many branches. I didn't say we're the ones on the wanted posters. Or that we have the Dowager with us."

"But you said they thought we were heroes," I said.

He nodded. "Yes, but as Ranjax Grimjinx always said, 'The best truth hides the worst facts.' No need to risk our status as heroes by revealing that the two most wanted people in all the Provinces are here. Add the Vanguard to that and we might as well paint targets on our backs. No, we'll find another way to convince the others."

Aubrin and I touched our temples in agreement.

Surprisingly, everyone came to the town meeting. In the past, these meetings had been poorly attended. But Talian's visit had sent a scare throughout the village. They came to the meeting expecting to be told they were safe.

Boy, did they get a shock.

Gandrick's tavern could safely hold about half the residents. Today, though, it was packed with three-quarters of the village, with the rest crowding around the door and windows. Da stood behind a table against the tavern's north wall, facing everyone. The Dowager stood near the door with Maloch and Callie. I sat atop the bar with Aubrin, while Edilman leaned on a chair nearby.

"I know that when I brought you all here," Da said, "I promised our sole purpose was to break our families out of

Umbramore. But I believe we have a chance to change things permanently so that we don't have to spend the rest of our lives hiding."

"What became of the Sentinel?" Sarquin Scalander asked.

"He's been dealt with," Da said gravely. We wanted people to think we'd buried Talian in the swamp. We'd have a *different* rebellion on our hands if people knew we'd let him go.

"There are just over fifty people here," Gandrick said. "The Palatinate has two hundred mages with an arsenal of spells and thousands of magical beasts at their command. We don't stand a chance."

"Not if we stand alone, no," I blurted out. "But we aren't alone."

Suddenly, all eyes were on me. I swallowed hard and lifted my chin. "The assassin-monks, the most formidable warriors this side of Rexin, are our allies. They've seen people who think like us all over the Provinces. We only have to reach out to them."

Da and I went back and forth, offering arguments for why we should revolt. One by one, people started nodding in agreement. It wasn't long before we'd won over most of the room.

Oberax alone remained unconvinced. Her dark eyes bored into Da, unmoving. It occurred to me that her deal with Da was designed to fail. Only *one* person had to be against the idea of starting a rebellion. Even if we convinced everyone else, Oberax would always be against it.

Soon, the discussion was between Da and Oberax, as they argued the reasons for and against rebelling. It was clear she wasn't going to budge. And the more she argued, the more people seemed to sway to her side. Soon, others were arguing against Da too. We were losing allies.

"This isn't getting us anywhere," I muttered to Edilman. "We can't just have everybody shouting. We need to be organized."

"No," Edilman said quietly. "We need a *leader*."

He nodded across the room. The Dowager watched the debate with a look of distaste. *People are loyal to the House of Soranna.* I couldn't stop thinking about it. They probably hoped the High Laird would come back and drive out the Palatinate. But that wasn't going to happen. The High Laird was gone.

Yet the House of Soranna remained. Problem was: no one knew.

As the yelling reached fever pitch, the Dowager pushed her way through the crowded doorway and into the street.

"Excuse me," I said to Edilman, then followed the Dowager out.

I caught up with her as she approached her house.

"No, Jaxter."

She didn't even turn to look at me.

"You don't know what I'm going to say," I told her.

"You want me to rally everyone."

"Okay, so you do know," I admitted. "You saw how naff-nut it is in there. They need someone to sort it all out. Your father trained *you* to be High Laird. Like it or not, the Provinces are yours to rule."

"Well, I *don't* like it!" Her words were cold. Slowly, she faced me. Her eyes were hard and focused, more so than I'd ever seen. "Jaxter, I told you that I refused to become High Laird because I wanted to devote my life to research. That was only partly true. I also didn't want to be the head of a government I hated. My family has ruled the Provinces for five hundred years. I don't think one family should have that much power over the people."

I never knew this. I knew that, like me, she'd gone against her family's expectations. It was something we shared. I never imagined that she cared about the people of the Provinces so much that she couldn't *bear* to be their ruler.

"Then don't let it be about power," I said, taking her hand. "Let this be about the people."

The Dowager's face fell as she considered. "I'm so old, Jaxter. I'm weak."

"You? Weak?" I said, scoffing. "You, who fought off a horde of vessapedes with a bottle of ashwine and a stick?"

She laughed, remembering our time in the vessapede warrens all those months ago. Drawing her shawl tight, she straightened her back and allowed a calm austerity to wash over her face. I hadn't seen that—her head-of-state face—in a long, long time.

"How's this?" she asked.

"Scowl a little," I said. "You want them to take you seriously."

We walked back to the tavern, where they were no closer to agreement than when we'd left. When they caught a glimpse of the Dowager's stony face, people stepped aside.

She moved to the table with Oberax and Da. Everyone fell quiet.

"There will be no more discussion," the Dowager said flatly. "You're wasting time when there's work to be done."

"What work?" Sarquin asked.

"The annihilation of the Palatinate," the Dowager answered.

Oberax folded her arms. "You seem to think that's easy."

"Easy?" the Dowager said. "Not at all. Make no mistake. What we're proposing is a threat to every man, woman, and child in this village. But it's insignificant compared to the threat that faces every single person living in the Five Provinces. I have no intention of doing anything 'easy.' I intend to strike back and retake what is ours."

The Dowager reached up and pulled the wig from her head. There were gasps as people immediately recognized her. "Protecting the Provinces has always fallen to the House of Soranna," she said, tossing the wig aside. "As heir to that noble lineage, I tell you now that we can and will prevail."

She pointed to the door. "Just outside, there's a road that leads from Slagbog. Anyone who wants the days that follow to be easy, leave now. I have no patience or time for you.

But anyone who wants their life back, anyone who wants the freedom that is rightly theirs restored, stand with me now."

No one moved. No one made a sound.

"You see Slagbog as small and unimportant. That's what the Palatinate sees. People they can starve. People they can divide. People they can *break*. Let me tell you what I see. In Slagbog, I see the first link in a chain. A chain that will grow as we reach out. A chain that gets stronger when we refuse to be alone. We find friends, we find allies. . . ."

She reached over and took Edilman's hand. The abbot bowed respectfully and placed his free hand on his heart, pledging fidelity.

The Dowager continued, louder than before. "We find anyone who feels the same oppression we feel. Everyone we've ever known becomes another link that brings us closer to victory. And the chain we form will grow stronger until we're a flail we can use to drive the Palatinate out!"

I nearly leaped out of my trousers as cheers shook the tavern. Someone at the back stood. Then someone else. The room filled with the sound of chairs being shoved aside as people rose to stand with the Dowager.

Everyone watched Oberax. The par-Goblin scowled,

then hoisted herself up. At first, it looked like she might storm out. Instead, she bowed to the Dowager and clenched her fists, a par-Goblin sign of respect.

No one was left seated.

The Dowager slowly looked around the room, making eye contact with every person. "Time is short. Soon, Xerrus will return for another tribute. I say we make this tribute a message the Palatinate will never forget."

Another cheer sounded from all assembled, louder and more raucous than before. Edilman leaned over to me.

"Congratulations," he whispered. "It'll look mighty impressive in the Grimjinx family album when it says 'Jaxter Grimjinx, architect of the rebellion.'"

The people of Slagbog slowly filed from the tavern and returned to their homes. On her way out, Sarquin Scalander caught my eye and bowed her head. Soon, it was just Da, Edilman, the Dowager, and me.

"Well," Da said, "we've got our work cut out."

"How long before the next tribute is due?" Edilman asked.

"Two weeks," Da said. "Can't wait to see the look on old Xerrus's face." He took a deep breath, then held out his hand to the abbot. "Your monks . . . can they train people to fight?"

Edilman shook Da's hand vigorously. "Hand to hand, swords, spears . . . We can teach the people of Slagbog to turn anything into a weapon."

Da and Edilman started outlining plans for the days to come. But the Dowager got that distant look in her eye, the one she got when she was calculating.

"What do you think?" I asked.

"I fear it won't be enough," the Dowager said softly. "The Palatinate is very powerful. Even with the monks' help, it will take a lot more than this village to mount a meaningful insurrection. What I know about waging war will only get us so far. We need an army."

She was right, of course. But I'd been thinking about what the Dowager had just told everyone. That we'd need every resource to succeed. Every contact, every acquaintance, every friend. Well, we had friends. Lots of friends. And it was time we paid them a call.

"You provide the leadership," I said to her, "and I'll provide the army."

28

Kolo's Last Secret

"Danger is opportunity
spelled with mostly wrong letters."

—*Ancient par-Goblin proverb*

Of everything that amazed me the following day, the most insane was that a ragtag group of rebels listened closely as *I* outlined a plan to recruit an army. Maybe it was my powers of persuasion. Maybe what I said just made sense. Or maybe we were so desperate that we were willing to try anything.

It was probably the desperation.

Supplies were gathered. Maps were collected. The entire village pitched in. We got a good night's sleep and then, just before dawn, everyone rallied in the square. The morning mist down the street parted as a parade of backpack-wearing assassin-monks strode into town, Edilman and Bennock at the head.

Everyone divided into the groups I'd assigned. I walked around to make sure they were ready. Maloch stood near the scaffold, doing a last-minute check through his backpack. A pair of monks did likewise at his side.

"I should be going with you," he said when I approached.

"I know you want to," I said. "Splitting up is the fastest way to get things done."

I moved to Callie and her monk bodyguards. She gripped the straps on her backpack so tightly that her knuckles had gone white. She smiled but I could see the terror in her eyes.

"You okay?" I asked.

She gave a single nod. "I'll be fine. I just—"

"I know," I said. "Don't worry. You'll be great."

"But what if she's forgotten—"

"She hasn't."

Callie clicked her tongue as Edilman moved to each team, issuing instructions. "I can't believe you let him into our lives again, after last time."

"He's had several chances to get revenge," I told her. "I think he and the monks really want to help. And we need them now, in case we run into trouble."

She wasn't convinced. "I'm glad he's not coming with me. Edilman Jaxter is the last person I want by my side in a crisis."

Across the way, I heard Uncle Garax yelp in fear. One of the hardest things had been convincing everyone in the village to release Garax. But he was an important part of the plan.

I went over to find Luda intimidating Uncle Garax near the entrance to the Ghostfire house. As I approached, Luda pulled me aside.

"I should be going with *you*," she said.

Everybody wanted to go with me. I liked being popular.

I shook my head. "Luda, I need you to go with Uncle Garax. You're the only one I trust to make sure he does what he's supposed to do and doesn't just take off. Can you do that?"

She arched an eyebrow. "You doubt my abilities?"

No. The only thing I believed in more than Luda's abilities was my uncle's low tolerance for pain. Something Luda could exploit if he got out of line.

"Who knows when I'll see you again?" I asked. "How about a hug?"

"How about broken bones?"

Life as a rebel had made Luda *sassy*.

Finally, I got to Da. He pulled me in tight and, for a minute, I didn't think he was going to let go.

"At the first sign of danger—" Da started.

"I will honor the Grimjinx name and run like a demented gekbeak in the other direction," I promised. "Are you okay working with Edilman?"

Da glanced across the square where the abbot stood with most of the population of Slagbog. Everyone was armed with *some* kind of weapon, from pole arms and halberds to garden hoes and egg whisks.

"I still don't know that I trust him," he said, "but I have to admit that it feels a bit like the old days. If he can do what he promises . . ."

I gave Da an extra hug. "Come back safe."

"We're wasting time!" Edilman shouted. Bennock and a female monk named Keela moved to my side. I exhaled loudly as Bennock gave my shoulder a squeeze. Everyone nodded to one another. And one by one, our teams departed, each in a different direction.

"Harash porr glagg!" Oberax called out. An ancient par-Goblin blessing: May your good fortune flow swifter than your enemy's. No doubt about it: we needed every bit of luck we could get.

The second morning of our trip started as the first morning had: with pain. Luckily, it wasn't *my* pain.

I hunched over our campfire, cooking a breakfast of gekbeak eggs, while Sister Keela trained Bennock in hand-to-hand combat. He had the punching down. But any time he tried to leap in the air and kick, he ended up in a gnarled heap of limbs on the ground.

When Keela took our flagons to be filled in a stream, I handed Bennock his eggs.

"Eat up," I said. "You're a growing assassin."

Bennock grumbled. "I don't think I'll ever learn."

I shrugged. "You're just a little clumsy. Like me."

"You?" Bennock laughed. "I've hardly even seen you stumble."

"Well . . . I've gotten better. I'm not as clumsy as I used to be. Trust me, you'll get better too."

Bennock sighed. "I think you're confusing my 'I can do this' look with my 'I just want this to be over' look."

Leaning in, I lowered my voice. "You mean . . . you don't want to be an assassin-monk?"

The question caught him off guard. The eggs slipped from Bennock's hands and into the fire. He groaned. I split my own portion of eggs in two and gave him the second half. He smiled with embarrassment.

"Most acolytes come to the Abbey because they want to join the order. I was an orphan and—"

"You were never given a choice," I finished for him.

"They've done so much for me," he said, pushing the eggs around his plate. "It wouldn't be right not to join the order."

"Let's pretend," I said slowly, "that you could do anything. What would you choose?"

"I'd work with Sister Andris," he said without hesitation. "I love the idea of language. I almost wish I was back in the Abbey, helping her translate that message from Aubrin's journal. If I could do anything, I'd study language."

It seemed like every time Bennock and I talked, I realized

how much we had in common. I wanted to tell him about how everyone assumed I'd be a master thief like my father but instead I became the Dowager's scholarly apprentice. I wanted to tell him there was hope. But Keela returned and Bennock suddenly grew quiet.

We finished our breakfast in silence before breaking camp and heading out. An absolutely insane idea popped into my head. What if—when all this was over—I could go back to studying at Redvalor Castle with the Dowager? And what if she would take Bennock on as an apprentice as well? The three of us doing research? We'd be unstoppable.

But a lot had to happen before then. And, at present, not a lot of it seemed very likely.

"I count eight mages," Keela reported, peering through a spyglass.

We crouched behind bushes on a hillside overlooking the Palatinate Palace. Something didn't seem quite right to me. The last time I'd been here, the golden walls had shone and pulsed with magical light. But now they seemed darker, burnished. The whole area was unsettlingly quiet.

Outside the main gate, a small caravan had assembled. Two mages stood at the head, spellspheres throbbing with light in their hands. Just behind them, three vortakaars—lumbering beasts with thorny exoskeletons—dragged their considerable knuckles on the ground, growling softly to themselves. Behind the vortakaars stood four mages. Next in line, a strange assortment of creatures marched in place, just ahead of two massive mangs pulling a large covered wagon. The caravan ended with a pair of mages.

The main gate to the palace swung open. A mage with dark, spiky hair stepped out and didn't bother to close the doors behind him. He wore the robes of a member of the Lordcourt.

"Spellspheres at the ready!" he shouted. "Let's move out!"

The mage climbed into the back of the wagon. A moment later, the caravan trudged forward. They pulled away from the palace, and we watched until they'd disappeared into the forest.

Bennock regarded the palace with shock. "That's it?" he asked. "They're just leaving it wide-open?"

"It's got to be some kind of trap," I muttered.

Our plan had been to sneak in through the same

underground tunnels Maloch and I had used to infiltrate the palace many months ago. As the Palatinate's headquarters, the palace would be crawling with mages. All we had to do was avoid them and get to the gallery filled with glass statues.

Sister Keela shook her head. "We heard rumors that the Palatinate was going to move to Vesta and inhabit the High Laird's old palace."

"But why leave in a caravan?" I asked. "Why not just use a quickjump spell to get to Vesta?"

Nothing about this felt right. But we didn't have time to overthink it.

We approached cautiously, stepped through the door, and entered the cavernous main gallery. As Keela lit a torch, the firelight flickered off a collection of glass statues atop mordenstone plinths. The Shadowhands. But the number of statues had grown since my last visit. It appeared that the Palatinate had continued freezing their enemies with shimmerhex curses even after they seized control of the Provinces.

All the better for us.

"Keep an eye on the door, Keela," I told the monk, "just in case they come back."

I took the vallix skin gloves Aubrin had given me for my birthday from a hook on my belt and slipped them on. They'd protect me from accidentally catching the shimmer-hex curse while I worked.

"So where do we start?" Bennock asked.

I spotted a familiar face in the crowd. A man, about Da's age, held his fist tightly to his chest.

"We start here."

Bennock helped me take the man down off the plinth. I reached into my pocket and pulled out the Vanguard.

"What's that?" Bennock asked.

"Erm, something Callie said might help," I lied. Da and I had decided to keep the Vanguard a secret a mite longer. It was our best weapon in the upcoming battle. We couldn't risk tipping our hand with anyone. Even our allies.

I touched the crystal pyramid to the statue. Deep within the glass, flesh-like color spread. The glass shimmered and fell like melting water to the floor. The man gasped, drawing in a huge breath, and fell forward. Bennock lowered him to the ground. Looking up, the man spotted me.

"Jaxter Grimjinx?" Maloch's da asked.

"Oya, Mr. Oxter," I said.

Bennock and I moved from plinth to plinth. While I liberated people from the shimmerhex, Bennock explained our plan to raise an army. As I'd guessed, recruiting was easy. Everyone here had reason to hate the Palatinate. We had a small battalion in no time.

"Are we done?" Bennock asked.

"Not quite," I said, nodding to the last statue. The one I'd been avoiding. Kolo. A couple of Shadowhands laid the statue on the ground.

I paused, Vanguard in hand. Kolo himself had said that his frail body wouldn't survive being awoken from the shimmerhex.

"Bennock," I said quietly, "can you take everyone outside? I need a moment."

Bennock ushered everyone away, leaving me with Kolo. I stared down at him for a long time.

"You *chose* this," I said, "but I don't think you *want* this."

Kneeling, I touched the Vanguard to Kolo's forehead. The glass washed away. Kolo clutched his chest and howled in pain as he drew a breath.

"Easy," I said, slipping my backpack under his head.

The elderly Sarosan squinted, as though he couldn't quite see. "J-Jaxter?"

"I'm here, Kolo." I gripped his hand. He could barely squeeze back.

"So, you found the Vanguard," he said, a ghost of a smile crossing his wrinkled face.

"You didn't exactly make it easy."

Kolo coughed. "I couldn't risk the Palatinate finding it."

"You were right. About everything. The Palatinate succeeded where the Scions failed."

"The Scions . . . ," he said. "You were in the whisperoak forest?"

"Yes. But how did *you* get in there?"

"As a boy, I was arrested and sent to serve at the Creche. I learned all about the Great Uprisings the same way you did. The knowledge changed my life. That's why Tree Bag has a picture of a whisperoak."

Kolo turned his head and spat. A small trickle of blood oozed from his lips.

"We have to get you to a healer," I said, panic setting in.

The old man shook his head. "You have the Vanguard. You can still stop them."

"But how?" I asked.

"Think about it, Jaxter," Kolo wheezed. "I sent you to retrieve the Sourcefire. Why?"

"When you betrayed the Shadowhands, the Covenant's magic gave you Mardem's Blight," I said. "The Sourcefire was the only thing powerful enough to destroy the Covenant. It was the only way to cure you."

"But I had the Vanguard. It absorbs all magical energy. I could have used that to destroy the Covenant. So why did I *really* want the Sourcefire?"

I mumbled in frustration. This wasn't the time for riddles. I looked around at the gallery walls. Their magical luster had gone dark.

"Because," I said slowly, "the Sourcefire was protecting the palace."

As I said the words, the truth became obvious. Using magic drained energy from any mage. So how did the Palatinate power the palace's magical defenses? They drew power from the Sourcefire, an infinite source of magical energy.

Kolo had planned to blow up the palace. But he couldn't as long as the Sourcefire was protecting it.

"The Sourcefire is the key," Kolo rasped, pulling me closer with his thin fingers. "Only the Vanguard can eliminate the Sourcefire. Remember . . . they can't find the Vanguard . . . with magic. . . ."

I was still confused. Even without the Sourcefire, mages could cast spells. What good would destroying it do?

Kolo shuddered. I felt every muscle in his body tense under my hands.

"Don't . . . let them . . . do it . . . ," Kolo said. Then a great breath left his body. He went limp and died.

I sat next to him for a long time, not moving. Wiping tears from my eyes, I took the empty Tree Bag from my backpack and laid it atop Kolo's body. I felt a hand on my shoulder. Bennock leaned in.

"You okay?" he asked.

My mouth had gone dry. "I don't know, Bennock. I don't know if any of us is okay."

29

A Patchwork Army

"A rogue's deed is truer than his tongue."

—*Ancient par-Goblin proverb*

The worst part of our army recruitment plan was how long it took. By the time Bennock and I returned to Slagbog with a platoon of Palatinate adversaries and recently freed Shadowhands, the next tribute was nearly a week away. We had to be ready to face Xerrus by then.

One thing we hadn't anticipated was what happens when you suddenly add a hundred former statues into a village with a shortage of houses. We had nowhere to put everyone. Thankfully, the assassin-monks graciously opened the doors of the Abbey to take in our new recruits. It was a cozy fit but not crowded.

Crowded happened when Da and Edilman returned.

To hear Da tell the tale, Slagbog's assault on Umbramore was the greatest battle since Mannis Soranna led a Satyran army to destroy the Onyx Fortress of Rexin. Whatever the real story, the mission was a success and the population got even bigger as the Umbramore escapees arrived, led by . . .

"Ma!"

Aubrin squealed as she and I ran to greet our mother. Ma knelt, arms outstretched, and the three of us hit the ground in a hug so powerful it made the Sourcefire look like a candle. Ma had grown a bit thinner but was no less strong when she pulled us into her arms.

"Well, that was an interesting little vacation," Ma said brightly. "I hear you're planning a revolution. Thanks for inviting me."

"We'd never start without you," I said.

A day later, Oberax called a meeting in the square and revealed Slagbog's newest problem: a food shortage. The village had already been on the brink of starvation. Now, with our growing population, food was scarcer than ever. I *never* thought I'd be sad to see a shortage of grubslush.

As we discussed options, the Ghostfire house rolled into town with Luda in the driver's seat. Da and I went to greet them. The house came to a stop, the door flew open, and a howl of pain erupted from inside. A moment later, Uncle Garax staggered out, followed immediately by a small, silver-haired woman with her hand clamped firmly around my uncle's ear.

"Oya, Nanni," I called out. "Glad you could join us."

My grandmother dragged my squirming uncle over to me and Da, hugging us with her free hand. Then she pulled hard on Uncle Garax's ear.

"Don't you have something to say to your brother?" she asked Garax.

My uncle winced. "She hasn't let go of my ear for a week."

"Garax . . . ," Nanni warned.

"No, really, she even holds it while we sleep."

"Tell him!" Nanni yanked so hard that I thought Garax's ear might come off.

"I'm sorry!" Garax screamed, tears falling down his cheeks. "I should never have turned you in to the Palatinate. Grimjinxes don't turn on Grimjinxes, no matter the price." He held out a large scroll of parchment to Da. Written on it, over and over, were those very words: *Grimjinxes don't turn on Grimjinxes*. It had to be on there at least a thousand times. "Please accept my apology. *Please,* Ona, I'm begging you."

Da shrugged. "I guess this'll do . . . for a start."

Nanni released Uncle Garax, who caressed his sore ear like it was a newborn babe.

"Bangers, Luda," I said as the Satyran climbed down. I'd asked her to make sure my grandmother learned about Garax's betrayal. I figured Nanni would have a thing or two to say about it. I also figured those things involved lots of swearing at my uncle.

Luda nodded. "Your grandmother is a formidable warrior. I would not like to meet her on the field of battle."

Who would?

Another day passed. Just as we'd started to figure out how to live with all of us crowded into the tiny village and the Abbey, our newest recruits arrived. Dressed in tattered clothes, a flock of Sarosans emerged from the swamp at dawn. Once inside the village, they immediately knelt, took flasks from their packs, and began the ritual of drinking at First Rise. I wended my way through the crowd, looking for Maloch. Icy fingers gripped my leg and when I looked down, I found familiar dark eyes staring up.

"Reena!"

The dark-skinned girl winked at me as she completed the ritual. When she finished, I knelt to hug her and felt a poke.

"The mages need a lesson learned. Look out, world, we have returned!"

Reena's younger brother, Holm, grinned at her side. They were exactly as I remembered them. Even Holm's poetry was just as horrible.

Maybe even worse.

"I had a feeling the Sarosans wouldn't pass up a chance to pay the Palatinate back for everything they did," I told them.

Reena rolled her eyes. "We're lucky to be here. With Kolo gone, our father—Kendiloxinevlertal—took over as our leader."

"And for those of us who don't understand Sarosan names, your father is called . . . ?"

She giggled. "Kendil. Anyway, you can imagine how happy he was to find out his own daughter was using magic." She opened her fist to show the pendant Maloch had given her so the two of them could stay in touch during the Sarosans' exile. She'd kept it a secret all this time.

But when Maloch sent Reena the message saying we needed the Sarosans to return and fight the Palatinate, she had to tell her father. I'm sure Kendil wasn't *at all* pleased.

"Hey," I said, "where's Maloch?"

Holm nodded across the crowd of Sarosans toward their father. A short, thick rope linked Kendil's wrist to Maloch's. Whenever the Sarosan leader raised his hand to drink, Maloch's hand rose involuntarily. Maloch didn't look amused.

"Father blames him for the magic," Holm explained. "Tied to Mal, it's all quite tragic."

The idea of Maloch being tied to Reena's angry father for the past week made me smile.

Reena and Holm led me over to their father. Reena eyed the rope binding her father to Maloch. "Father," she said, "you promised that when we arrived . . ."

Kendil growled. "He gave you magic."

"Yes, sir," I said, "he did. But if you let him go, I promise that his father will punish him severely."

Maloch's eyes lit up. "My . . . father?"

I nodded. Just then, Mr. Oxter appeared at the edge of the crowd of villagers. Frowning, Kendil untied the rope. Maloch ran to his father, stopped, and offered his hand. Mr. Oxter reached out and hugged his son.

"Some punishment," Kendil muttered.

I gave him a pat on the back. "You spent a week tied to Maloch, sir. Don't you think just *being him* is punishment enough?"

He didn't argue.

Over the next few days, Blackvesper Abbey became a hive of activity. Within the hallowed walls, the assassin-monks trained villagers, Sarosans, and Shadowhands alike. Elsewhere, the Dowager devised attack plans. Despite her hesitance to assume the role of leader, the Dowager proved very effective at strategy, composing a list of targets that could cripple the Palatinate. Still, every day she hoped to hear from Talian. We needed inside help if our insurrection was to make an impact.

Even with our little army coming together, I had a lot on my mind. Everyone was losing sight of one very important fact. And it felt like I was the only one who'd noticed.

I went to the Dowager's house, which had now been changed into a home for all the seers. Aubrin had begun working with the others, collecting prophecies in the hope that they might help us against the Palatinate. The seers were busy scribbling on parchment when I arrived.

Aubrin saw immediately that I was upset. She took my hand and led me outside. "What's wrong?" she asked.

"Have you learned anything?" I asked, nodding toward the seers. "About the Palatinate or . . . anything?"

Aubrin frowned. "Nothing important. The Palatinate is planning something big, we know that. We're just not sure what." She rubbed my back. "But that's not what you mean. Is it?"

I sighed and shook my head. In the rush to get our army trained, no one else had noticed that not everyone had come back from their missions. I felt a knot in my stomach. *I'd* come up with the plan. *I'd* placed everyone in danger. And if anything had happened, I was to blame.

I scanned the village as I did every day at this time. Hoping—praying—for a sign.

"Where's Callie?"

30

The Greater Loss

"Danger past, Castellan forgotten."

—*The Lymmaris Creed*

It was two days before Xerrus would return to claim the Palatinate's tribute. Two days before we struck back and announced our plans to retake the Provinces. Two days until we knew for certain what our army was capable of.

Naturally, that's when everything fell apart.

To take my mind off Callie, I threw myself into a task from Oberax. Just as we'd gotten the housing and food situation figured out, a new dilemma cropped up: Slagbog's *other* other new residents.

As Talian had told us, there were those in the Provinces eager to fight the Palatinate. As word spread underground, more and more of these people arrived, looking to help. We started with fifty thieves trying to save a simple village. Now we were four hundred strong and the headquarters of the rebellion.

The trick was figuring out which of our new residents could be trusted and which might be spies for the Palatinate. Oberax suggested we create a roster of new arrivals. So, with the noon sun high overhead, I took to the streets to catalog everyone. I had just started when Bennock, looking haggard, joined me.

"Aren't you supposed to be training in the Abbey?" I asked.

"Friar Polik told me I should take a break," he said.

"Who did you injure?"

"Your friend Maloch. I hope he heals fast."

We went from door to door. Bennock, in his calm, soothing voice, talked to people, asking for their names and how they'd heard about Slagbog. I watched their body language to determine if anyone was lying. An hour in and everyone's stories had checked out. So far.

We were passing by the cheese shop when the door flew open and Sarquin, followed by her sister, ran out. Bennock and I collided with Sarquin, sending all three of us to the ground. The sack Sarquin carried flew, scattering an assortment of parchments.

"I'm so sorry," Bennock said. He scrambled about on his knees, gathering the papers.

Sarquin didn't hear him. A glint on the dirty street had caught her eye. I followed her gaze to find that the Vanguard had fallen from my pouch. I quickly snatched it.

"We'll get this picked up for you," I said quickly. No one knew we had the Vanguard . . . or even what the Vanguard was. But Sarquin looked a little too interested.

I crawled around, helping Bennock collect the papers, and smiled up at Minss. The silent sister stood near Sarquin's shadow, unmoving. And that's when I noticed.

Minss wasn't casting a shadow.

Bennock squinted at one of the papers in his hand. "Are you working with the Dowager?" he asked Sarquin. "These look like our attack plans. . . ."

I slowly rose. Sarquin smiled. She knew what I'd discovered. Minss was a hardglamour. She didn't really exist.

"Well, now you've gone and ruined my surprise," Sarquin said, reaching into her pocket. "But I guess it was only a matter of time."

She pulled out a spellsphere and barked in the magical tongue. Minss melted into a pool of light that seeped into the ground. At the same time, a glowing patina around Sarquin twinkled and the image of the taller Scalander sister bled away. In its place stood Nalia.

"I've been waiting patiently," she said, "watching you assemble your little army. It's been very entertaining. And now my patience has paid off. Everything I need is here. The Dowager. The augur. And the Vanguard."

Thunder shook the streets of Slagbog as three quickjump rings appeared overhead. Masked Sentinels, accompanied by a regiment of monsters, fell from the portals and started laying siege to the village.

One by one, mud huts ignited as the Sentinels launched their magical assault. Some villagers resisted, grabbing whatever they could find—rakes, pitchforks—and using them to fend off the attack. But many were mauled as the monsters rampaging through the village proved stronger.

"Give it to me," Nalia ordered, "and I'll let you live."

I reached out, Vanguard in hand. But as she went to take it, I swung my arm and touched the pyramid to her spellsphere. A flash threw Nalia back. Her spellsphere fell to the ground, broken in two. Bennock took my hand and we ran.

"To the Abbey!" Bennock called out to the scrambling crowds. Word spread and everyone raced east toward the distant tower. We darted through the chaos. I prayed that my family was already in the Abbey and safe.

A stampede of skaiths—with deadly tusks and spiky tails—lay waste to building after building, reducing them to rubble. The Sentinels walked calmly amid the pandemonium, capturing those who cowered and killing anyone who resisted.

We tried sneaking through alleys to avoid the masses. But just when it looked like we'd found a way out, a bolt of magic struck Bennock from the side, sending the acolyte flying into a mound of hay. Before I could turn to help him, I was tackled and pinned to the ground. I pushed back against the Sentinel on top of me.

"Take this," the Sentinel whispered. I recognized his voice. It was Talian.

He thrust a large piece of parchment into my hand. "Use

it well," he said. Looking past Talian, I saw Nalia weaving her way among the monsters, her monocle flickering in the explosions all around. A Sentinel handed her a new spell-sphere, which she quickly used to kill people who ran from her.

"They're not even fighting her!" I said.

Talian nodded at her. "They were about to. The monocle lets her see five seconds into the future. She can respond before an attack. I'll distract her but I can't be seen acting against them. Go!"

Talian let me up, then ran to join the fray. I helped a dazed Bennock to his feet and we made for the Abbey.

As we passed through the square, we spotted the Ghostfire house. I thought for sure Garax would have taken off at the first hint of trouble. Instead, he was sprawled out near the house's front door, holding his leg and wincing.

"I twisted my ankle!" he moaned. "I can't move."

Behind us, a mud hut collapsed as a magravore stomped it into bits of broken clay. The horde was nearly here. We had to go. Carrying Garax would slow us down. We only had one choice.

"Bennock, help Uncle Garax into the house," I said. As

Bennock did so, I jumped into the driver's seat and gripped the steering levers. Grinding my teeth, I pushed at the pedals below me. Gears churned and the mammoth house rolled forward.

I'd never driven a house before. I didn't do so badly. Sure, I destroyed the village well, leveled the bakery, and mangled a few chimneys. But that's to be expected for a first time, I think.

I pedaled as hard as I could, but the house wasn't built for speed. The fleeing villagers and rebels were outpacing us, charging around the house in a desperate attempt to make it to the Abbey. I spotted a vortakaar that had backed a villager up against a wall. I yanked on the steering levers. The house banked right and bucked in the air as we crushed the vortakaar under our wheel, giving the villager the chance to bolt.

We cleared the edge of the village and aimed for the Abbey. The house's wheels kicked up a massive wave as we plunged through the weed-ridden bog. No matter how hard we rocked left and right, I concentrated on the large doors at the Abbey's entrance. I figured they were just big enough to fit the entire house inside. Just.

Behind me, a window looking into the house opened and Bennock stuck his head out.

"Not to worry you," he said, "but Slagbog is pretty much destroyed and now all the monsters and Sentinels are chasing us. Oh, and they're catching up."

With a grunt, I tried to pedal faster. But the house wasn't having it. "We're too heavy," I said. "Unless we can drop some weight, we'll— What's that?"

I pointed straight ahead. In the distance, mages riding flying beasts swarmed the Abbey, firing bolts of magic from their spellspheres. But I was more concerned about the glowing blue mist swirling at the base of the octagonal tower. It slowly spiraled its way up the Abbey's side.

"Automatic defense," Bennock said. "When the Abbey's under attack, it moves to protect everyone inside. We don't have much time. Once the doors close, it'll be gone."

We needed to pick up speed *now*.

"Switch places with me," I said.

Bennock crawled out the window and squeezed into the driver's seat as I gripped the side of the house and scaled it to the thatch roof. "Keep pedaling!" I shouted down to him. "Aim for the Abbey."

The house lurched side to side. I crawled along the roof on all fours. Taking the dagger from my boot, I sliced the ropes that held the burlap camouflage around the edge of the house. It fell away and we picked up a little speed.

It wasn't enough. As I made it to the back of the house, I saw what Bennock was talking about. Slagbog was a smoldering black stain. A wall of monsters ran straight for us, their snarls drowning out the house's grinding wheels. They'd overtake us before we could reach the Abbey.

I crawled to the wooden crane at the very back. Wrapping my arms and legs around it, I shimmied out to the boulder Garax used to simulate a rampaging braxilar. Just below, a pair of zellix—gelatinous spheres with teeth on every surface—rolled closer and closer to the base of the house. One lashed out, eating a chunk of the back wall in a mighty gulp.

I sawed at the rope suspending the boulder. Below, the second zellix bounced upward, chomping at the air just inches below my dangling legs. As it fell back down, the rope snapped and the boulder plummeted, flattening the zellix with a loud squish.

The Ghostfire house shot forward with a burst of

newfound speed. I cried out as the dagger fell from my hands. Teetering, I quickly hooked my knees around the crane and hung upside down.

"Don't go faster!" I yelled.

Bennock called out, "Go faster? Okay!"

"No!"

The house accelerated. I flailed like a doll in the wind. Soon, our pursuers were far behind. The house became enshrouded in the glowing blue mist. A moment later, we skidded to a stop as the house drove between the Abbey's massive main doors and into the entryway.

I released my grip on the crane and fell to the stone floor with a thud. Before I could stand, Aubrin plowed into me, hugging me close.

"You're safe!" I said, squeezing her back. "Ma? Da?"

"Everyone's here," she said, "except the Dowager. We can't find her."

We heard a cry outside. Peering into the swamp, I spotted the Dowager crawling on all fours just beyond the blue mist.

I darted outside, Aubrin close behind, and threw myself at my mentor's feet.

"I can't stand," the Dowager said, pointing to a bloody gash on her right leg.

Just then, a low moan filled the air. The Abbey doors started to swing shut slowly. Inside, Bennock was shouting for us to come back.

I cradled the Dowager in my arms and Aubrin helped me to my feet. My legs shook as I struggled to carry the injured royal back to the Abbey. Aubrin and I ran as fast as we could. The Abbey was just steps away. . . .

Behind us, we heard a pop and a bloodreaver's screech. Aubrin's small hands pressed against my shoulders and shoved. The Dowager and I flew forward, just barely making it through the crack of the closing doors. Whirling around, I watched in horror as the bloodreaver wrapped its arms around Aubrin. They disappeared together in a cloud of black smoke.

"No!"

The tower entrance slammed shut. The Abbey shuddered. Everything blurred. My wailing protests disappeared with all other sound as the Abbey moved.

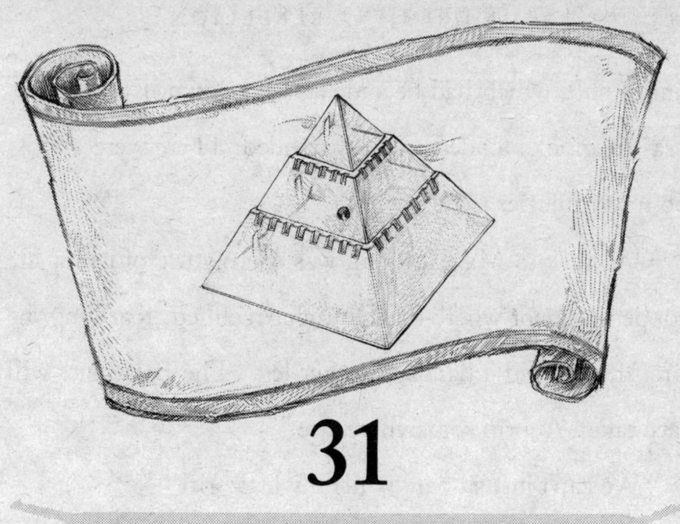

31

Battle Plans

"The thief who steals poorly, ends poorly."

—*Irinas Grimjinx, thief-bard of Jarron Province*

"Edilman Archalon Jaxter, turn this Abbey around right now!"

Warriors used swords. Mages used magic. Mothers used middle names. And it was no contest which weapon was the greatest.

Of both my parents, Ma was the least likely to crumble under pressure. When she unleashed someone's middle name, however, it typically meant she was in a blind panic.

She, Da, and I followed Edilman through the Abbey's

dining hall, which had become a triage room. Everywhere, assassin-monks tended to the wounded. There were almost too many injuries to deal with.

Contrary to Ma, Edilman was the picture of calm. He stopped at a cot where the Dowager reclined. Kneeling, he carefully applied a bandage to her leg. "The Palatinate will have taken Aubrin somewhere else."

"We can't just sit here while my little girl—"

"Allia," the Dowager said, "the Palatinate needs Aubrin's abilities. They won't hurt her. We need time to come up with a plan."

Ma seethed but said nothing else. Da took Ma's hand and led her from the dining hall. I sat on the edge of the Dowager's cot.

"It's not your fault," she said.

"I didn't say anything," I told her glumly.

"I know you, Jaxter," the Dowager said softly. "You blame yourself for losing Aubrin."

Of course I did. I blamed myself for Aubrin. I blamed myself for not noticing that Minss was a hardglamour sooner. I blamed myself for letting Nalia live among us, gathering our secrets even as she pretended to support us. I blamed myself for Callie still being missing. I'd failed as a thief, as an apprentice . . . and now as my sister's protector.

As if she could read my thoughts, the Dowager shook her finger at me. "This isn't over, Jaxter Ona Grimjinx."

Oh, by the Seven. Now *she* was using middle names.

"We'll find your sister. And we'll use our army to turn the tide."

"How?"

She sighed, her eyes glazing over with a wistful look. "I don't know yet."

I plunged my hands into my pockets. There, I found the parchment that Talian had handed to me during the raid on Slagbog. I pulled it out and looked it over.

"Dowager," I said, "I think *I* might know how. . . ."

The Abbey came to rest on the outskirts of a desert. The mesas provided the perfect camouflage, and the combination of searing heat and sandstorms meant the chance of being discovered was slim.

That same weather also made the Abbey unbearably hot. Tempers flared as people gathered in the abbot's chambers to discuss the information from Talian.

"This means nothing!" Kendil said, pointing to Talian's parchment on the table near the Dowager.

"That's not true," the Dowager said calmly. "It's a map. We just don't know what it means yet."

Ma joined the Dowager at the table. "This details a route that goes from the Palatinate Palace north to Vesta."

The Dowager's finger traced numbers spread out along the route. "These are dates. Milestones, maybe?"

I peered at the map and the date next to the Palatinate Palace. "That's the day Bennock and I freed the shimmer-hex prisoners. The same day we saw that caravan leave the palace."

Suddenly, the room got very quiet. Kendil and Mr. Oxter, who seemed the most agitated, became quickly interested.

"So," the Dowager said, "I think we can assume this map is the route the caravan is taking. The question is: what are they transporting?"

Everyone threw out theories. Weapons, prisoners . . . no one could agree on what it all meant. The discussion got heated and people started shouting. I closed my eyes and blocked it all out. I thought about what I knew. I kept coming back to one question: Why a caravan? Why not just use magic to get to Vesta?

What if they *couldn't* use magic?

"It's the Sourcefire."

It came out a little louder than I'd planned. But it was loud enough to cut through the bickering. Everyone froze and looked at me. I explained how the Sourcefire was used to protect the palace from attack.

"It would be the *last* thing they'd remove," I concluded. "And now they need to move it to Vesta to use its power to protect their new headquarters."

"Why use a caravan?" Edilman asked.

I thought back to the day Maloch and I tried to steal it. "Because they can't use magic to transport it."

"That's right," Reena said, jumping to her feet. "One of the mages tried to take the Sourcefire from Jaxter using magic and that Nalia woman told him magic couldn't be used on it."

"Technically," the Dowager said, "the sigils carved on the box that contains the Sourcefire protect it from magical transportation. To keep rogue mages from stealing it."

We all had the same idea. While the Sourcefire was

being transported, the Palatinate was vulnerable.

"Then we strike in Vesta now!" Luda boomed. "Without the Sourcefire, the High Laird's palace is defenseless. We take down the Lordcourt."

"We'd be just as outnumbered there as we were in Slagbog," Da pointed out. "Even without the Sourcefire, the mages can defend themselves."

"Then we go for a smaller target." The Dowager's soft voice filled the room. "Talian's told us *how to take the Sourcefire*. According to this, they'll be traveling through Obsidian Canyon tomorrow night. A perfect place for an ambush."

Ma's eyes grew big. "If we had the Sourcefire, we could bargain with them. We could get Aubrin back."

"I suspect we could bargain for more," the Dowager said. "Like an end to all hostilities. Jaxter's right: they *need* the Sourcefire. If we capture it . . . their reign is over."

Everyone looked around. We'd just survived a humiliating defeat . . . but suddenly, the possibility of success seemed very, very real.

"What are the caravan's defenses?" Kendil asked me.

"No more than nine mages and a handful of monsters,"

I said. "This is supposed to be a secret. They don't want to draw a lot of attention to how weak they are until the Sourcefire reaches Vesta. They've got just enough to defend it from marauders . . ."

". . . but not enough from our army!" the Dowager finished. "Abbot, start rounding up anyone who can still fight. We don't have much time."

"No!"

I don't think I'd ever shouted at my parents before. But then, I don't think I'd ever been this angry at them before.

As the residents in the Abbey prepared to sleep, Ma and Da pulled me aside into the monks' library.

"There's no arguing, son," Da said.

"Thirteen is old enough to enlist in the Provincial Guard," I argued. "I want to fight."

I didn't want to fight. I was scared to death of fighting. But everyone I loved was going to be in the middle of the battle. I couldn't just sit here while my sister was the Palatinate's prisoner.

"We've already discussed this with Kendil and Mr.

Oxter. You'll be staying behind with everyone who's under-age," Ma said.

"Bennock is fighting with the monks," I pointed out.

"Edilman is the closest Bennock has to a father and he's allowing it," Da said. "That's his choice. If it were up to me, Bennock would be joining you."

Ma pushed my glasses up from the tip of my nose where they'd fallen. "You have an important job to do but it won't be in the middle of a combat zone."

"You want me healing the wounded?" I asked. It was insulting. Raising the army had been *my* idea. How could they exclude me now?

"The monks will be busy fighting," Da said. "After them, you're our best healer."

I continued to protest but their minds were made up. I wouldn't be anywhere near the fighting. "Get some sleep," Ma said, kissing my forehead before she and Da retired.

But I couldn't sleep. I was angry. I was frustrated. Fists clenched, I stomped off down the Abbey's corridors. I wandered for hours, shouting out the occasional curse word.

I was all but exhausted when I rounded a corner and found Edilman leaning against the wall. I got the idea he'd been waiting for me. He pulled the mask from his face and sighed.

"Feel better?" he asked.

"Talk to them, Edilman," I said. "Tell them I should be part of the fight."

Edilman shook his head. "I agree with them. You're more valuable to us tending the wounded."

Scowling, I pushed past him.

"Jaxter."

I stopped but wouldn't look at him. "What?"

"Sister Andris finished translating the message."

I drew a deep, long breath. The message meant for the mysterious Eaj. The message Aubrin had been sure would save the day. The message she'd told me to translate and then leave the Provinces.

I started to walk away but Edilman persisted. "Jaxter, do you *really* not know what it says?"

I spun around. "No, and don't you dare tell me. Aubrin said that once I knew what the message says, I'd have to leave the Provinces to save my life. But I'm not leaving. Not while she's still a prisoner. So, as long as I don't know what it says—"

"I don't think it works that way." Edilman looked down at his feet. He was trying to be gentle.

"I don't care!" I snapped. "I don't care about the message. I don't care what you think."

Edilman flinched. My words drew a line between us. But I meant it. I didn't care.

"I just want my sister back," I said. "Unless the message tells me how to do that . . ."

He shook his head. "It doesn't."

"Then we're done here." I stormed away, angrier than ever. Returning to the dining hall, I threw myself down on my cot. Arms crossed, I glared at the ceiling. It was going to be a long night.

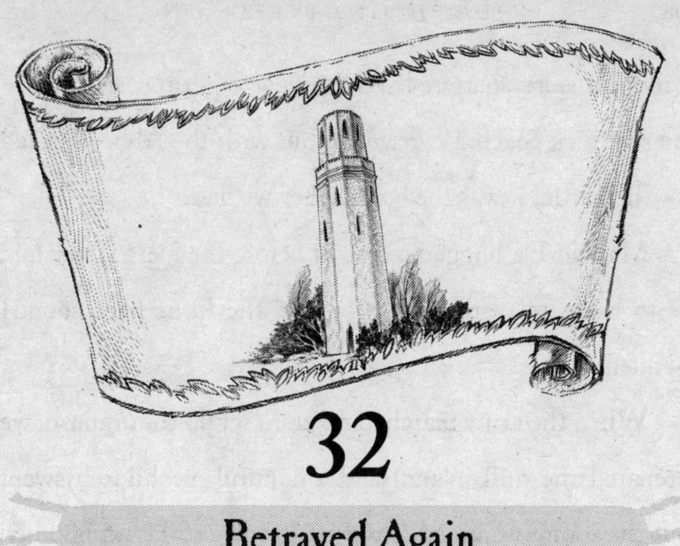

32

Betrayed Again

"Where trust sows, vengeance reaps."

—Ancient par-Goblin proverb

The next day, the Abbey materialized in a valley just south of Obsidian Canyon. We found an abandoned flour mill near a stream about an hour from the canyon's entrance. This became our home base. Nanni and everyone underage would remain safe in the mill, mixing healing salves and preparing to tend to our wounded when the battle was done.

The mill wasn't much. The huge waterwheel on the side creaked and shook as it turned in the lazy stream. All the windows were shattered. And a coat of grime a thumb's-length thick covered *everything*. But with the Abbey needed for the battle, it was the best shelter we had.

Ma and Da hugged me tight before they left. They told us to listen to Nanni and promised they'd be back soon. I nodded.

When the army marched north to set up the ambush, we prepared the mill. Nanni and a handful of children swept out the rooms and made up cots. Reena and Holm huddled over a small bowl filled with viscous poison. They were teaching the seers how to soak the tips of wooden needles in the poison before carefully inserting the needles into their blowguns. The seers were enjoying it a mite too much.

Maloch and I sat quietly at the kitchen table, using the herbs from my pouches to make burn ointment. Every so often, Nanni poked her head in and leered at us.

"Just this morning," she said in a low rumble, "the two of you were fighting tooth and nail to join the battle. Why are you suddenly so helpful?"

"Just doing our part," I said cheerfully.

As night fell, Nanni took the seers and the other children

upstairs to tuck them in. Reena and I turned our ears toward the staircase.

"Can you tell us a story?" we heard Pressia, the youngest of the seers, ask Nanni. My grandmother gave an exaggerated sigh, then launched into a par-Goblin fairy tale about the naughty children who woke the Grundilus from his slumber and paid for it with their lives.

"She did it!" Reena whispered. Earlier, when we'd asked Pressia to help, the young girl was happy to be part of a secret plan. She'd promised to keep Nanni busy just long enough.

"All right," I said, nodding to the others. Maloch blew out the candles. Reena and Holm brandished their blowguns. Together, the four of us left the mill and headed north.

Our parents said we couldn't fight. They didn't say we couldn't watch.

Moonlight shone on the entrance to Obsidian Canyon. The four of us knelt behind a cluster of rocky spires. If all had gone according to plan, our army was already deep in the canyon, waiting to ambush the caravan when it arrived.

We waited. Moments later, eerie white light flickered to our left. Two mages, walking single file, came into view. A tether of wispy white light rose from their spellspheres to a massive globe of throbbing energy that illuminated their path. They were soon followed by the Palatinate caravan, which disappeared into the canyon. Once we could no longer see them, we crept out and followed at a safe distance.

The walls of the canyon narrowed. The caravan gathered in tightly as the party ventured into the bottleneck. Maloch ushered us all to a nook, a safe place to watch. I held my breath as everything got quiet.

"Come on, Garax," I whispered under my breath.

As if my uncle had heard me, a loud thud echoed off the canyon walls. The earth shook. Another thud, then another, each louder and closer. Suddenly, the air was rent with the tortured cry of a braxilar. Not one but three distinct howls filled the bottleneck.

Just as we'd hoped, the caravan came to a halt. The mages spoke among themselves, trying to pinpoint where the sounds were coming from. The door at the back of the covered wagon flew open, and the mage in charge jumped out.

"Why have we stopped?" he demanded. A new volley of braxilar screams issued a response. Farther down the bottleneck, a flash of blue fire gave the appearance that the creatures were on their way.

"Lord Aztan," one of the mages said to the man in charge, "that village we stopped in last night . . . they said there were stories of wild braxilar near the canyon."

I smiled. *We'd* planted that rumor. All part of the plan.

Aztan spat on the ground. "You idiot. We *created* the braxilar. There's no such thing as a wild one. There's only braxilar that need to be brought back under our control. Go take care of it."

Three mages nodded and slunk down the bottleneck toward the continued howling. The creatures protecting the wagon shifted restlessly, as if responding to the feral cries. Aztan shouted a word in the magical tongue. The control medallion around his neck glistened with golden light. The matching amulets worn by the creatures responded with a similar glow and the monsters immediately fell silent.

Aztan moved to the head of the caravan and shouted down the bottleneck. "What do you see?"

The answer came as three pained human screams. More

bursts of blue fire lit the air. With a wave of his hand, Aztan ordered two more mages to assist the first three. Reluctantly, the pair ran down the bottleneck toward their screaming comrades.

Zzzzisssh!

A flaming arrow seared the air just over our heads and buried itself in the ground at Aztan's feet. Before the mage had a chance to move, our army of rebels charged, leaping from their hiding places.

Aztan and the three remaining mages took out their spellspheres and responded with a spectacular display of power, firing bolts of pure energy into the throngs of attackers. Within seconds, the caravan was masked in a cloud of smoke.

The creatures with wings took to the air, swooping down to attack the rebels. A platoon of Sarosans, hidden on a ledge halfway up the canyon wall, drove the monsters back with their crossbows.

The battle grew quieter; it seemed like it was almost over. The blasts of magical energy became far and few between. The smoke slowly started to lift. The caravan had been vastly outnumbered. From the darkness of the bottleneck, Uncle

Garax and a group of assassin-monks came forth, training their weapons on the unarmed mages who'd gone to investigate the braxilar.

Within minutes, the mages were relieved of their spellspheres and bound. The Dowager limped over to Aztan, Ma and Da at her side.

"Surrender," she demanded, "and your lives will be spared."

Aztan's face spread into a maniacal grin. "But the fight's hardly begun."

That's when I saw it: a pinprick of light in the shadows. Then another. And another. One by one, a constellation of lights appeared up and down on both sides of the bottleneck walls. As one, the rebels craned their necks. Spellspheres. The meaning quickly sunk in.

They were surrounded.

The canyon exploded. Each dot of light shot a torrent of raw energy at the caravan. The rebels scattered as fire and earth flew through the air. The detonations sent people falling to the ground. The captured mages quickly broke free and ran to the shadows, where scores of masked Sentinels stepped from the darkness.

With expert precision, the Sentinels advanced, spell-spheres afire. The assassin-monks pulled out the smoke pellets I'd given them and created another camouflage cloud. But it took only a few words of magic before the smoke had vanished, leaving the mages with a clear shot at the rebel troops.

I lost sight of Ma, Da, and the Dowager. The battle, which had seemed like a victory for the rebellion, quickly changed. Swords melted as magical energy sliced through the ranks. Crossbows ignited, disintegrating into glowing embers.

Next to me, Maloch pulled a dagger from his belt.

"You can't go in there," I told him. But Reena and Holm also had their blowguns at the ready.

"They need all the help they can get," Maloch said.

I took the dagger from my belt, preparing to go with them. But a sound from above—an earsplitting squeal that pierced through the sounds of battle—changed everything. I looked up to see a black cloud descend into the canyon. As it got closer, I realized it wasn't a cloud.

It was a flock of spiderbats.

The flying creatures swept over the combatants, dousing

the Sentinels in their anti-magic webbing. Before long, the spiderbats were everywhere: crawling on the canyon walls, landing on the monsters, defending the rebels.

"Woooo!"

A new sound from overhead. Six spiderbats, webbing dangling from their backsides, had woven a basket. Callie, with two assassin-monks, stood triumphantly in the basket, fist high in the air. The six spiderbats gently lowered the basket to the ground near us. The assassin-monks at Callie's side joined the fight.

"Sorry we're late," Callie said, running to our sides. "The trip from the aircaves took forever and it was hard to find you after Slagbog was destroyed."

I threw my arms around her. "I thought you were . . ."

She grinned. "Takes more than that to get rid of me."

The tide of the battle shifted a third time as the spiderbats returned the advantage to the rebels. Sentinels fought to free themselves from the webbing that prevented them from casting spells.

As the fighting continued, Aztan stumbled away from the center of the battle, took out his spellsphere, and spoke an incantation. *Crack!* A quickjump ring opened in the air above, sending the flying spiderbats scurrying away. As the glowing ring widened, a steady current of monsters fell into the combat zone.

I scanned the scene, looking for something—anything—to help. That's when I noticed: the fighting had moved closer to the bottleneck. The wagon was defenseless. And we had a direct line to it.

I could end this all by capturing the Sourcefire.

"Who's ready to do something that's really stupid and maybe a little brave?" I asked. Everyone nodded.

"Reena and Holm, distract Aztan so the quickjump closes." I pointed at the mage. "Maloch and Callie, cover me. I'm going for the wagon."

We moved as one. Reena and Holm charged at Aztan, firing poison darts with every step. The distraction forced him to close the quickjump while he fought his new attackers. Meanwhile, I ran for the wagon. Maloch scooped up a fallen sword and fought off anyone who got too close. Callie cast spell after spell to fend off the approaching monsters. Soon, all my friends were engaged in their own battles, leaving me alone.

Wild bolts of magic homed in and exploded harmlessly,

the Vanguard in my pocket protecting me. I got to the wagon and climbed into the back. The only light inside came from the far end where a crystal box held a churning ball of multicolored flame. The Sourcefire.

I made for the box but froze halfway when I heard the door slam shut behind me. Actually, it was the menacing growl *after* the slam that made me stop.

Turning slowly, I met the eyes of a sanguibeast no taller than me. I cursed quietly. I should have known they wouldn't have left the interior completely unguarded.

I pressed up against the table that held the Sourcefire and reached for my dagger. The sanguibeast's teeth gnashed, sending rivers of spittle in every direction. Just as my fingertips grazed the dagger's hilt, the creature stopped. It backed up and said in a gravelly voice, "Is brother of Bright Eyes?"

"Gobek?"

The sanguibeast shrank. Soon, it was gone, replaced with the Creche's caretaker.

"What are you doing here?" I asked.

"Is protecting Sourcefire," the shape-shifter said softly, grief filling his eyes. "Gobek is failing duties."

"But why are you helping the Palatinate? Aubrin said they caused your pain."

Gobek muttered. "Is always pain for Gobek. Is made from magic? Is to be in pain. Gobek is having nowhere else to go."

I held out my hand. "If you help us, I promise to find a way to end your pain."

Gobek looked uncertainly at my hand and then licked it. I took that as a yes.

Outside, it sounded like the fighting was getting closer to the wagon. I stood and faced the Sourcefire. The crystal box looked just as I remembered it except for one thing. A large golden disc, etched with magical sigils, sat affixed to the top. It resembled the medallions mages used to control their army of beasts.

"What's this for?" I asked, pulling at the disc. It wouldn't budge.

"Is not sure," Gobek said. "Is not for Gobek to know—"

Gobek's voice cut off. I spun around to find the former Creche keeper in the arms of an assassin-monk. The monk had hoisted Gobek in the air, clamping one hand around his mouth. Just past him, in the doorway, stood Edilman and

Bennock. All three monks were frowning.

"Edilman," I said. "We can end this now if we—"

But Edilman ignored me. He marched down the length of the wagon and pushed me out of the way. He caressed the Sourcefire's box. Then, without looking back, he raised a single hand. Suddenly, Bennock grabbed me and held my arms behind my back. Skinny as he was, Bennock was strong.

"What the zoc?" I asked.

Edilman nodded at Bennock. The acolyte reached into my pocket, retrieved the Vanguard, and tossed it to Edilman.

"Bennock . . ." I yanked my arms. But Bennock held tightly. The only satisfaction I got was the look on his face. Bennock felt guilty.

Edilman's free hand ran across the top of the box. He took a deep breath and touched the Vanguard to the disc on the Sourcefire box. Sparks shot up as the disc went dark. The abbot flicked his hand, sent the disc flying, and tucked the crystal box under his arm.

A lump filled my throat. This had been Edilman's plan all along. He'd planned to steal the Sourcefire in the chaos.

"Don't do this, Edilman," I pleaded. "Please. It's not worth it. You said we all need to fight together. You said—"

Outside, the air filled with a dozen dissonant roars. Something was different. The battle didn't sound the same anymore. The monsters were much more vocal. Not as subdued as before.

"Time to go," Edilman said. He dropped the Vanguard as Gobek and I were shoved to the floor. Edilman exited with the other monk. Bennock looked back into the wagon once more, then closed the door.

I got to my feet but before I could take a single step, the wagon tipped, falling on its side. Gobek and I were tossed against the wall. The disc landed next to Gobek's head.

Outside, we heard screams: human, Aviard, par-Goblin. The screams were quickly drowned out as the monsters' roars took over. I grabbed the once-glowing disc.

"*This* is how they controlled all the monsters," I said to myself.

Callie and I had wondered how they maintained constant control when magic exhausted mages. This was how. The Sourcefire powered the control medallions through this master medallion. And now that the master was dead . . .

"Is not controlling monsters now," Gobek whispered.

The wagon shook again. I cried out as we rolled over and

over like a wheel. When we finally stopped, I snatched the Vanguard and scrambled out the door with Gobek.

Madness. Rebel and mage alike bolted helter-skelter as the monsters ran amok, destroying anything in sight. The spiderbats, realizing they were beaten, took off. Everyone else ran from the canyon as fast as they could. I looked around for Ma, Da, or anyone. That pause was enough time for a pair of skaiths to cut off my exit from the canyon.

The skaiths snarled and leaned back on their hind legs, ready to pounce. Suddenly, Gobek jumped in the air. In one swift move, he transformed into an Aviard. He grabbed me under my arms and flew us up out of the skaiths' grasp.

Gobek's wings flapped hard, taking us higher and higher. I looked down. From here, the shiny obsidian in the canyon looked like it was on fire. People poured from the bottleneck, scattering to avoid the rampaging monsters and running into the wastelands beyond.

"There!" I shouted to Gobek, pointing to where I saw Ma and Da running. Gobek dove and landed us in front of my family.

"By the Seven!" Ma cried, throwing her arms around me. "What are you—?"

"The mages can't control the monsters anymore," I said quickly.

"We'd figured that out," Da said.

"Where's the Dowager?" I asked. I scanned the crowd but she was nowhere in sight. And there was no sign of Maloch or Callie. Or Reena and Holm.

A plume of blue flame from a braxilar shot over our heads.

"We have to go!" Da shouted.

With Gobek at our side, we all joined hands and fled into the night.

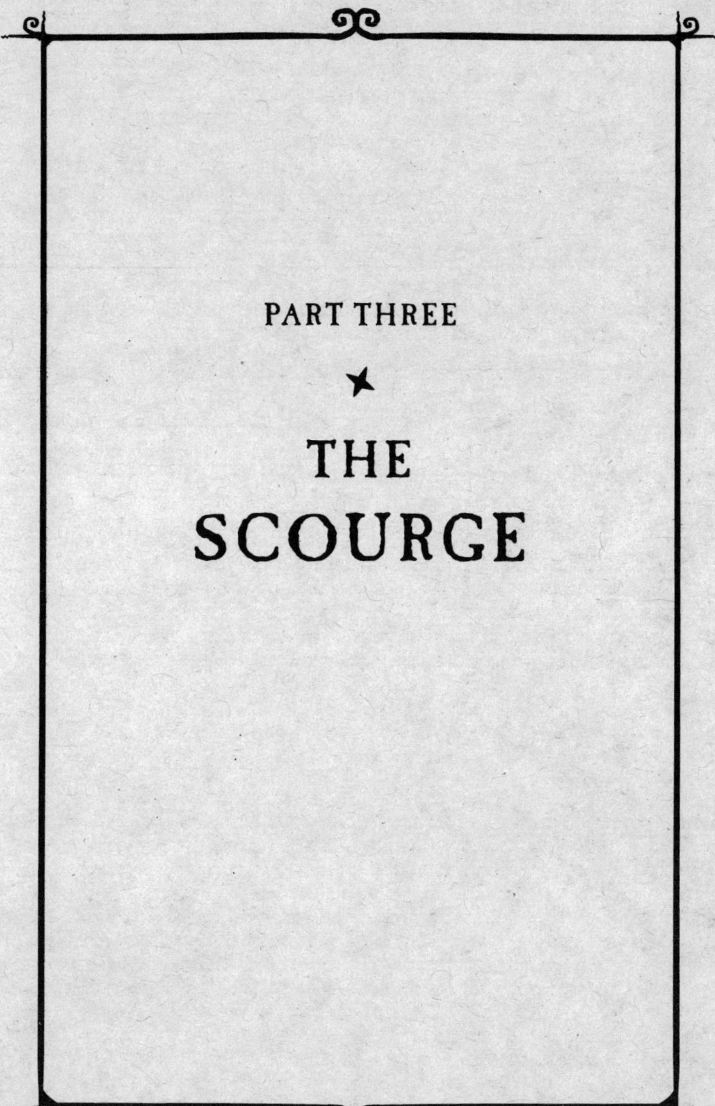

PART THREE

THE SCOURGE

33

A Plague of Monsters

"A lie too-oft told casts the shadow of truth."

—Lyraken Grimjinx, architect of the Kaladark mine plunder

It was called the Scourge, that much we knew.

In the three weeks following the Palatinate's fall at the Battle of Obsidian Canyon—when they lost control of their monster army—the stories that filtered through the Provinces were wild and rampant, two parts fiction to one part fact. Sifting through the tales proved difficult. But no matter how gruesome the story, some facts remained the same.

The trouble started as a wisp on the horizon, a long black

cloud mingling among the white. If you stared long enough, the wisp grew wider and darker. In an hour, it blotted out the skyline completely. The wisp became a wall that stretched from land to sky. And as it drew closer, you could hear it.

Distant chatter. Insects chirping in the forest at sunset. Then the chatter became a rattle, like hail beating on a steel roof. When the black wall eclipsed the sky, the noise became a unified wail. Pain, agony, torture. The sound nightmares make when they're afraid.

By the time you heard the wailing, the stories all agreed, it was over. By then, the Scourge was upon you. Thousands and thousands of monsters descended, wiping out an entire town-state in a matter of minutes, leaving a mound of fiery embers. And nothing more.

Everything we ever knew was gone. Governments vanished. Communities disintegrated. Da said there was a name for what was happening: anarchy.

But only one name meant anything to anyone.

The Scourge.

★

"That one?"

"Elios."

"That one?"

"Sorivol."

"How about . . . that one?"

"Xaa. Everyone knows that."

Years ago, when Nanni first moved into our house back in Vengekeep, she and I would spend whole evenings up on the roof. There, we'd lie for hours and she'd teach me all the constellations in the sky. She said it was important for a thief to know them. They could guide you home if you ever got lost. Now, as we sat side by side on a different roof, she quizzed me on which stars I remembered. It was like the good old days.

They seemed so long ago.

"I was afraid you'd forget all this, moving off to Redvalor Castle with the Dowager. I bet *she* doesn't quiz you on your constellations," Nanni said with a sniff.

Not exactly. The Dowager and I used her telescope to look at the constellations, studying their movement in the sky and trying to learn more about them. I didn't tell Nanni that though. I liked letting her think that the stars were something only she and I shared.

"You know," I said, "some people think that stars are big balls of fire in the sky."

Nanni frowned. "Well, that's just naff-nut. The sky's a dumb place to keep fire."

We leaned back on the old flour mill's thatched roof, staring past the overlapping moons toward the starry sky. I balanced near the edge of a gaping hole that opened up into the dusty attic below. Not the safest place, to be sure. But the roof was filled with holes. Safe was relative.

Far below, in the mill's basement, what remained of the rebellion had gathered to discuss strategy. The Obsidian Canyon survivors had returned here three weeks ago to regroup. As stories about the Scourge's carnage filtered in from all corners of the land, the Dowager made one thing very clear: we needed to build a new kind of army. We weren't trying to liberate the Provinces from the Palatinate anymore. We were trying to save our land from destruction.

Most nights—like tonight—the "strategy talks" involved lots of arguing. *Everyone* had an opinion on what we should do next. These opinions tended to be very loud. After a while, Nanni and I would get tired of it all and head up to the roof. Here, we could at least pretend the world wasn't coming to an end.

Nearby, a giant wooden waterwheel creaked as it turned, scooping up tubs of water each time it dipped into the rushing stream three stories down. I'd grown to love that creaking sound. I had no choice. The wheel's axle was right outside my bedroom window. I heard it all night long.

I peered out to the eastern horizon. In the distance, a parade of tiny lights marched in a single-file line.

"There go some more," I said. Every day, we saw numerous bands of refugees heading south. Many followed the stream just outside the mill. Sometimes, they came in small groups. Other times, entire villages wandered by.

"*Harash porr glagg.*" Nanni whispered the par-Goblin blessing as she did whenever we saw refugees escaping from the devastated north.

"Wish they were closer," I said. "We could use some more news."

This was how we learned what was going on in the world. With no governments, money was meaningless. Most people traded in two currencies these days: weapons and food. But we knew there was something of far more value out there.

Information.

When people wandered by, Ma and Da would grill them about where they'd been and what they'd seen. Then the Dowager would try to recruit them to join us. No one did. They just kept moving south. It was safer, so they said.

"We've heard the news," Nanni said glumly. "None of it's good."

She was talking about what we'd learned just last week. A family from Merriton told us how the Scourge had descended on their town-state and reduced it to rubble. Just as the attack started, Blackvesper Abbey appeared outside the city gates. The monks, ready to fight, had barely started to emerge before the entire swarm of monsters reduced the tower to rubble. There was nothing left of the Abbey. Or the monks.

And if there were no survivors, then that meant Bennock . . .

"It hasn't all been bad," I said to distract myself. "Quite a few places have been spared." In the early days of the Scourge's onslaught, all we'd heard about was the devastation. We'd only recently started hearing about places the Scourge had left alone.

Nanni grunted. "That makes things worse. They attack randomly."

Every refugee who'd shared information with us had said the same thing: the Scourge's attacks made no sense. Some massive cities were laid to waste; others were spared. Tiny villages without any means of defending themselves were wiped off the map. How could we fight an enemy when we had no idea where they'd strike next?

"They're monsters," I said. "It's not like they have to use logic. Maybe we need to think like monsters."

"What we need," Nanni continued, pointing straight down, "is for everyone to quit bickering so we can figure out what to do next."

She had a point. The resistance hadn't accomplished much in the past three weeks. Unless you count disagreeing, in which case we'd achieved master status. The one thing we could agree on was that the Scourge needed to be stopped before it destroyed everything. But we had no idea how.

"It's strange the Scourge left Port Scaldhaven alone," I mused. We'd learned about this from a group of refugees only yesterday. "It's the second largest city in the Provinces. You'd think they'd destroy cities with large populations. It would cut back on resistance."

"I've been to Port Scaldhaven," Nanni said. "Highly overrated. The Scourge probably left it alone because the monsters couldn't get a decent cup of singetea there."

I laughed. "That's it! They're only attacking places that make great singetea. They want the rest of us to suffer without it."

Nanni chuckled. The idea was absurd, of course. I pictured the Scourge on a search for the best singetea and only attacking those towns that possessed it. If that's what they were really doing, then suddenly their attacks would make sense.

Yes . . .

The attacks would make sense if all the places under siege had shared something.

My mind raced. What if all the places that the Scourge had destroyed were *linked*? What if—no matter how big the town-state or how small the village—they all shared something in common? Something important to the Scourge.

I leaped up, stepped onto the top of the waterwheel, and rode it down. Just before it disappeared into the stream, I jumped off and ran toward the mill's front door.

"Jaxter Grimjinx," Nanni called down, "what are you doing?"

"Just the usual: saving the Provinces," I yelled back up. "I get it now. The attacks aren't random. *The Scourge is looking for something!*"

34

Is Death

"Choose allies slowly. Lose allies slower still."

—*The Lymmaris Creed*

I cursed myself for not seeing it sooner. Huddling in the dark and fearing for your life can really be murder on your deductive skills.

I ran down the stairs to the basement. There were fewer people now than when I'd been here earlier. Most, I guessed, had grown tired of the yelling and gone upstairs to the second floor where we all slept.

Our leaders stood around a large table in the room's center. As usual, Kendil and Mr. Oxter were at each other's throats, seeing who could outshout the other. Luda stood nearby, watching them carefully. These days, most of her time was spent keeping those two from coming to blows. By contrast, Ma and Da sat calmly at the far end of the table, playing a round of giggly dice to pass the time.

"It's very simple," Kendil was shouting. "If we take refuge in a town the Scourge has already spared, we'll be safe."

"We don't know why the Scourge spared them," Mr. Oxter countered. "It may only be a temporary reprieve!"

As the argument got louder, Maloch gathered the seven seers, who were quietly playing card games in the corner, and led them upstairs. He often did this when things got heated. The seers had been through enough, he reasoned, and didn't need to hear any more.

It had been some time since any of them had had a vision of the future. At first, I thought it was stress. Callie had said stress interfered with a seer's abilities. And maybe that was true. But I began to suspect a far more sinister reason for the recent lack of prophecies.

They can't see anything, I thought, *because there's no future to see.*

The Dowager paced back and forth, ignoring the heated debate. She'd been walking with a pronounced limp since the

Battle of Obsidian Canyon. It was her only wound. She was considered lucky. Some of the survivors still hadn't recovered from the burns and deep gashes they'd received. Many others—Oberax and most of the Sarosans—had never returned from the Canyon.

Every so often, the Dowager cast her eyes at the tabletop. It was covered with scraps of paper, each black with scribbles that represented the sum of our knowledge about the Scourge. In the center of the table was a large map of the Provinces. Every Scourge attack had been marked with a large red X. Like me, she suspected that the attacks weren't random at all. She thought that if she glared at the map long enough, the answer would come to her.

This time, it had worked. Because I was here with the answer.

I grabbed the map, took a quill, and started circling all the places we knew the Scourge had been but had ignored.

"We haven't been focusing on the fact that the Scourge is sparing some towns," I told the Dowager, loud enough to get everyone's attention. "They're selective in the places they're attacking. Which means . . ."

". . . they're looking for something," the Dowager finished softly.

Nearby, Reena helped Holm to his feet. A large cloth bandage wove around his head diagonally, covering his left eye. Odds were he wouldn't see out of it again. The siblings took their places at their father's side along the broad edge of the table.

Reena scowled. "What could a plague of monsters possibly be looking for?"

A few people glanced over at Callie. As an apprentice mage, people kept expecting her to have more information on the Scourge than she had. Her face flushed.

"You'd have to ask the Palatinate," she said coolly. "They didn't share all their secrets with us apprentices."

The chances of asking the Palatinate were slim to none. Some stories suggested they were hiding. But most people believed the Lordcourt had led all the mages far away from the Provinces to a distant land where they could start over. Part of me hoped that was true. And that they'd taken Aubrin with them. At least she'd be safe.

Ma studied the Xs and Os on the map. "If we knew what

these places had in common, we could predict where they'll strike next."

"And bring the fight to them," Da said.

I hunched over the map and focused on the three latest attacks. Laying my battered copy of *The Kolohendriseenax Formulary* on top of the map, I pressed my quill against the book's spine and drew a straight line that ran through the recent attacks, linking them all. Previously, the attacks had been all over the place. Now, there was a pattern.

"Whatever the Scourge is looking for," I said, "they've figured out where it is and they're heading straight for it."

The Dowager's eyebrows went up. "Bangers, Jaxter!"

Murmurs erupted around the room. People who'd been quiet for days suddenly stirred. This was our first real breakthrough.

Luda tapped a point along the line, just below the most recent attack. "This mill is in the direct path of the Scourge."

Leave it to Luda to kill an inspiring moment.

The Dowager did some fast calculations. "Given the time that's lapsed between attacks," she said, "I estimate they'll be here in a week."

Kendil stood. "We have to evacuate."

The Dowager disagreed. "We're not going anywhere. Any time we buy ourselves by leaving won't be enough. No, we stay here and we make a stand."

The room fell quiet. We'd vowed to stop the Scourge and now we were getting our chance. But from everyone's sullen faces, I could tell no one believed we were ready.

"Our defenses are poor at best," Luda said, her arm sweeping the room. The few weapons that had survived our last battle were strewn about. Most had broken blades. Several bows needed to be restrung. In addition, we'd failed to recruit any of the refugees who'd fled south. We were only a hundred people and barely armed.

"Well, then," Da said, a lilt in his voice to lighten the mood, "I suggest we get a good night's sleep. We've got quite a bit of work to do in the morning if we're going to prevent our own executions."

There was no avoiding it. We would *have* to be ready to face the Scourge in a week. Resigned, the group broke up, most heading upstairs to the rooms we'd converted into bedrooms. I leaned over the Dowager's map again. If we had any hope of surviving, we needed something with power. . . .

An idea flashed in my head. "Ma," I said softly, pulling

her aside, "you fancy a quick trip to the Palatinate Palace tomorrow?"

Ma scratched her head. "But it's empty."

"I have an idea."

"Is it a completely and totally insane idea?"

"Do I have any other kind?"

"Of course not. You're my son." She mussed my hair. "Let's get some sleep and we'll head out in the morning."

We went upstairs to the room we shared with three other families. As candles went out one by one, Ma and I joined Da and Nanni along the wall where we made beds on old blankets. Slowly, the rebellion fell asleep.

The room became still but I was restless as ever. I hated this feeling. It was like there was something hiding in the corners of my eyes. Something that should have been obvious but I couldn't see it. I tossed and turned and wriggled.

"If you don't stop that," Nanni whispered in the dark, "you'll be sleeping outside in the stream."

I struck a flint and lit a small candle. "Sorry, Nanni. I can't stop thinking about the Scourge. We agree they're looking for something. What could it be?"

"Is death."

The soft words came from Gobek. The strange creature hadn't said much since the battle. He kept to himself, often curled up in a corner, as he was now. I couldn't tell if he was adding to the conversation or just talking in his sleep. Then, his eyelids flicked open and he stared at me from across the room. He spoke again, his voice quiet and dreamlike.

"Is death."

35

Callie's Hope

"A marked thief is a failed thief."

—*The Lymmaris Creed*

Traveling by quickjump spell, while certainly speedy, is not a fun experience. As you pass through the ring, a wave of dizziness grips you. There's a moment where you're in two places at once: your top half is where you're leaving and your bottom half is where you're arriving. And for just an instant, it really feels like your two halves won't be reunited.

There's also the fact that arrival always involves falling out of the sky. I don't know what thrill-seeking mage invented the spell, but it's clear they were completely naff-nut.

The danger is compounded when the place you're traveling to is totally dark. As I leaped through the ring, darkness swallowed me. Unable to see the ground, I hit the stone floor beneath me hard and grunted. I scrambled to my feet, lit a torch, and found myself in the gallery of the Palatinate Palace where I'd rescued the shimmerhex prisoners not that long ago. The room was empty and cold.

I looked up at the quickjump ring, still glowing above me. "Come on down!"

Luda and Ma emerged next, followed by Uncle Garax, who howled the whole way. Finally, Callie arrived, the ring vanishing the second she landed.

"I really like that spell," Callie said, clearly pleased. "Could come in handy if I'm ever in a tight spot."

And, I thought, *it works better without the Vanguard interfering.* I'd left it with Da for safekeeping.

Ma agreed. "I just hope the binding spell works as well. *That's* more important."

"Explain to me again," Uncle Garax said, crossing his arms grumpily, "why you've dragged me into this?"

"Because everyone else back at the mill is busy," I said, "making weapons, fortifying the walls . . ."

". . . and we wouldn't want you to slink away during the confusion like the vermislug you are," Ma finished, giving my uncle a sweet smile.

Garax humphed. He was a reluctant member of the rebellion, to be sure. But even he knew he had nowhere to go. He was mostly here because we needed the help.

Callie and I led the way from the gallery, followed by Garax. Ma and Luda brought up the rear. Callie and I hadn't spoken much since she arrived with the spiderbats in the canyon. She'd spent most of her time practicing magic. We all knew magic was the best way to fight the Scourge. If attacked, Callie could be our best hope.

"Hey, Cal," I said, "remember when I was teaching you to be a thief? And you'd go 'ta-da!' every time you succeeded? Do you do that with spells too?"

She grabbed a handful of cobwebs from the wall and threw them at me with a smirk. We laughed. It had been a long time since we'd laughed together.

"Thanks," I said.

"For what?"

"For not saying I told you so when Edilman betrayed us."

Callie grinned sheepishly. "You don't need me gloating.

I'm sure you're beating yourself up over it just fine."

I groaned. Every night since the Battle of Obsidian Canyon, I'd dreamed of that final encounter with Edilman. How he'd destroyed the control medallion and left with the Sourcefire. It replayed over and over in my mind and I awoke every morning, angrier than ever.

And it wasn't just Edilman. Every dream also featured an appearance by Bennock. In some ways, his betrayal hurt more. But I only had myself to blame for trusting Edilman. "What was he thinking?" I asked.

Callie tilted her head. "I suppose we'll never find out now."

And then, just as quickly as my anger had risen at the thought of Bennock's betrayal, a rock settled in my stomach to think that he was now dead. Further proof that no good came from being around Edilman.

"If it makes you feel better," she said slowly, "I was starting to trust him again too. I think *we all* needed to believe him. Nothing's sure anymore. Before all this, you were going to be the Dowager's intellectual heir and I was going to be a mage. Believing that Edilman could help us change things meant we were going to get all that back."

I nodded. "I guess that's impossible now."

"It doesn't have to be. When this is all over, I'm going back to my studies. I'm going to find a new teacher and become a full mage."

"Are you serious?" I asked. "After everything the Palatinate's done . . ."

"But that's exactly why. People are going to hate magic more than ever. I believe good can be done with magic. I don't want people to forget that. I hope to show that not all mages are evil."

As terrified as I was at the idea that I might not be able to return to Redvalor Castle someday and study again with the Dowager, I felt better knowing Callie had her life all figured out. If anyone could remind people that magic wasn't just evil, it was Callie.

She led us confidently through the abandoned Palace to the laundry room. Once, this room crackled with magical energy as enchanted tubs washed the robes of the mages who resided in the Palace. Now, it was lifeless and filled with the stench of fetid water.

Garax and Luda pulled a square stone from the middle of the floor, revealing a shaft and a ladder. One by one, we descended into a network of caves. I grimaced. In all the months we'd spent hiding from the Palatinate, I was grateful we hadn't hidden in any caves. I'd had my fill of them.

I took the lead and guided us through the earth-walled tunnels until our path ended in an expansive cavern. Callie spoke a word to her spellsphere. A ball of light appeared near the cavern ceiling and lit the area with a pale gray glow.

From wall to wall, the floor was covered with hundreds of tinderjack plants. Some of the volatile plants shook, getting ready to expel their fireblossom and expose the explosive pods within. Thankfully, Kolo never got the chance to blow up the Palace with this crop. Now we'd put it to a better use.

"It'll be tricky getting these back to the mill," I said, "but *this* should give the Scourge something to think about."

"I always said you were brilliant, Jaxter."

We all whirled around at the voice behind us. Talian stood in the tunnel from which we'd just emerged, his spellsphere shimmering in his hand. His right hand was scorched, the fingers fused together. Just behind him, a small group of cloaked mages stood, hands at their sides.

Callie ran and threw her arms around her cousin. Talian returned the gesture, then pointed to the cloaked figures behind him. "These are the other mages who helped fight the Palatinate from within. We've been living here since the Scourge was released. We didn't know where to find you. What have you been doing?"

Ma quickly explained how we'd turned the old mill into our base and were preparing for the Scourge's imminent arrival. Talian listened carefully and nodded.

"We can help you bind the tinderjack pods so you can get them through the quickjump safely. It won't hurt to have some explosives on hand. But . . ." Talian paused. "You may change your minds on what to do once we tell you what we know."

36

Message Received

"Rich coats oft mask poor hearts."

—*Ancient par-Goblin proverb*

When we returned to the mill hours later, we were met with cheers as hundreds of tinderjack pods—bound safely with magic so they wouldn't detonate—fell through the quickjump ring, increasing the power of our arsenal tenfold.

The cheering stopped, however, when we brought Talian and the other mages through. The restless rebels started shouting. Swords were brandished. Ma raised her voice, trying to keep everyone cool, but it did no good. The mages huddled together as curse words flew in their direction. My blood ran cold as a voice from the back yelled, "Kill the mages!" and the rebels surged forward.

The mages pulled out their spellspheres, ready for a fight. But Ma threw herself in front of Talian.

"Stop!" she shouted. Remarkably, everyone did. She straightened her tunic and pointed to the mages. "They're allies. This is Talian. He's the one who told us about the caravan in the first place. They've been working against the Palatinate to help us."

Kendil stepped forward. The few Sarosans who'd survived the battle stood behind him. Reena and Holm stood at their father's side.

"We will not work with mages," Kendil declared. The Sarosans shouted in agreement.

"Oh, yes, you will."

The Dowager's voice cut through the din. She stepped through the crowd and walked right up to Kendil. She looked up at the much taller man and didn't bat an eye.

"The Scourge is comprised of creatures of great magical power. I understand the Sarosans' hatred of magic. But it will take an equally powerful magic to defeat the monsters.

If you disagree, you and your people are free to leave. Right now."

The room erupted in more arguments, some saying we should work with the mages, others demanding their removal. As the shouting grew louder, I threw back my head and shouted.

"The Palatinate is in Vengekeep!"

Silence. With that one statement, we were united again. If only for that moment. I nudged Talian.

"Once the control medallion was destroyed," the young mage said, "the Palatinate lost control of the monsters. They knew they had no hope of regaining control without the Sourcefire. So every last mage gathered and went south."

"Why Vengekeep?" Mr. Oxter asked.

"When the Lordcourt realized that the Scourge had started the destruction in the north, they went to the farthest southern town-state. They've used magic to enhance the Vengekeep's existing defenses. The hope is that the Scourge will weaken by the time it gets that far south and it will be easier for the Palatinate to destroy."

"But it's not getting weaker," the Dowager said. "From everything we've heard, the Scourge is stronger than ever."

Talian nodded. "I know. We"—he pointed to the other mages—"have been looking for a way to weaken it. But the monsters have destroyed every magical stronghold they find."

"Aubrin," Da said. He moved across the room and took Ma's hands. "Is Aubrin in Vengekeep?"

"Most likely," Ma said.

"She's the only one who can warn the Palatinate before the Scourge attacks," Talian said. "They'll be keeping her safe."

I knew my sister. She wouldn't do anything to help the Palatinate. Even if warning them meant they could protect her.

Magical strongholds. Talian had said that's what the Scourge was destroying. That's why they spared some towns and destroyed others. But what did that accomplish? Why attack only where magic was present . . . ?

As the discussion continued, I plunged through the crowd and examined the Dowager's map again. I ran my finger down the line I'd drawn through the last three attacks. I continued moving northwest to southeast across the Provinces until . . .

"The Scourge is going to Vengekeep," I said.

The Dowager examined where my finger had come to rest. It was at the very end of the line I'd drawn.

"Well, now we know what the Scourge is looking for," Mr. Oxter said. "They're seeking revenge on the Palatinate for enslaving them."

No, I thought. These creatures were driven by instinct. Revenge didn't feel right.

"If they're going to Vengekeep to destroy the Palatinate," Kendil said, "then I say we let them." A grumble of support echoed throughout the crowd.

"The zoc you will!" Ma said. "If the Scourge is headed there, I'll warn the Palatinate myself if it means they'll protect my daughter."

The arguing resumed, louder than ever. And there it was again: the feeling I was overlooking *something.* I squeezed my eyes shut, trying to block out the furor. No, there was another reason the Scourge was headed to Vengekeep. I just couldn't grasp it. I needed to think.

As everyone shouted, I crept from the room and walked out the front door of the mill. A cool fall breeze chilled my bare arms. I strolled past the field where Uncle Garax had parked the Ghostfire house and down to the stream, following it south. With silence at last, I focused my thoughts on what we knew.

The Scourge had destroyed magical strongholds. *That's* what they all had in common. And the Scourge was *made* of magical energy. They must have been able to sense magic.

So maybe they *were* on their way to Vengekeep because they sensed that's where all the mages had gone. That or they sensed something else . . .

I probably would have figured it out right there and then if I hadn't been distracted by a hand that clamped around my mouth from behind. I'd walked so far that the mill was no longer in sight. Before I could react, an arm gripped me tightly around the chest and dragged me into the forest.

I struggled and screamed but my captor held tight. We went deeper into the darkness of the woods until I saw a distant campfire.

When we arrived at a small clearing, I found a hooded figure kneeling next to the fire. Suddenly, my captor let go. I whirled around to find Bennock standing over me. I looked into the acolyte's eyes. They were fierce but sad. Like he knew this was wrong but he had no choice. His firm stance told me I'd never succeed if I tried to get away.

"Have a seat, Jaxter," the hooded figure said.

"I'd heard you were dead, Edilman," I said. "At least, that's what I hoped."

"Give me a chance to explain," Edilman said. His voice sounded pinched and weak. "You owe me that much."

"I owe *you*?" I stepped toward him. "You're the reason the Provinces are burning!"

Edilman reached out, holding Aubrin's journal. "Read it."

"What?"

"I told you before the battle that Sister Andris had finished translating the message. The message you were so sure would turn the tide of the war. Read what it says."

We glared at each other, the only sound coming from the crackling fire. Finally, I opened the journal and scanned the text. Sister Andris had made small notations in the margins. A translation appeared under the message, written in a shaky hand. With each word, I grew more and more disbelieving. And by the time I got to the end—the signature—I knew something was wrong.

"How gullible do you think I am?" I said, glaring up at Edilman. "You wrote this translation yourself."

Edilman shook his head. "Sister Andris would be very

angry to hear you say that. She slaved over it. I'd ask her to verify that but . . . she's dead."

"It's not possible," I said. "That message—"

"—is in a language that predates all known languages," Edilman said. "Very few people living today could craft a message using it. But there it is. And it answers your question very neatly."

Edilman bound up, closed the distance between us in a single, giant step, and stabbed the message with his finger. "Yes. You owe me. I stole the Sourcefire, Jaxter," he said, his mouth so close I could feel his breath, "because *you* told me to."

37

The Abbot's Story

"Welcome a bitter enemy when a false friend comes knocking."

—*Corenus Grimjinx, clan father*

I couldn't take my eyes off the rows of unfamiliar symbols. Below each squiggle sat the corresponding translation in Sister Andris's handwriting. As hard as I tried to deny it, I knew that Edilman was telling the truth. The message read:

Edilman,

I don't have time to explain. When the rebels attack the Palatinate caravan, you must get to the Sourcefire first and steal it. Take the Vanguard from me, destroy the master medallion, and then leave. Once you're safely away, hide the Sourcefire in the Keep at Vengekeep. Under no circumstances are you to mention this message to me until after you've hidden the Sourcefire. You're looking for redemption, Edilman. This is how you earn it.

It was signed with my name.

"I *couldn't* have written this," I argued. "I don't know this language."

Edilman leaned against a tree and sighed. "You're very bright, Jaxter. Don't start being stupid now."

No. I wasn't stupid. I knew exactly how this was possible.

"She saw it," I said, opening to the message and reading it again. "Aubrin said she saw a hand write this. It was *my* hand. She copied down the message she saw in the vision."

Edilman tapped the journal. "At some point—maybe tomorrow, or next month, or in ten years—you're going to write that message. At the same time, your sister will sneak a peek from the past and see it."

He leaned forward and pointed to a single word under my name. "What's this bit?"

Sister Andris's translation read, "Guddlesark." I smiled.

"When I was little, I had an imaginary friend named Guddlesark. I never told anyone about him. I think I put that there to . . ."

Edilman leaned back. "To convince yourself you wrote it?"

"But what was all that 'Eaj' nonsense?" I asked.

Edilman poked himself in the chest. "Edilman Archalon Jaxter. E-A-J."

My stomach burbled. Why would I tell him to do this? The Sourcefire theft made everything fall apart. We could have ended this after the attack on the caravan if we'd stuck with the plan and used the Sourcefire to bargain with the Palatinate.

I felt suffocated. If this was all true, everything was *my* fault. I couldn't hold it in anymore and, as Edilman jumped back, I threw up all over the ground.

Bennock put his arm around my shoulders and handed me a flagon of water. I drank the whole thing in three mighty gulps as I sank to my knees.

"If it means anything," Edilman said softly, "I have a theory that you will write that message once life is back to normal. You tell me to steal the Sourcefire because you know for sure that it's the *only* way to make things right. You know that if you don't write that message, things will turn out much, much worse."

Worse? The Scourge was tearing the Provinces apart. There was no clear way to stop them. How could things get worse?

"I'll have you know," Edilman went on, "this wasn't easy. I had to sneak into Vengekeep in the middle of the night, carrying a box filled with glowing magical fire. Not the best way to stay inconspicuous. And your note didn't mention how to get into the Keep."

I pictured the Keep. The entrance was marked by a stone dome in the very center of the town-state. A stone warrior guarded the dome's door, his arm outstretched as if ready to strike. To open the door, you had to place a magic dagger in the warrior's hand. A dagger that was kept by the Castellan.

"So I got a chance to work on my burglary skills," Edilman said. "I was a mite out of practice. But I broke into the Castellan's house, stole the dagger, placed the Sourcefire in the Keep, returned the dagger so no one would be any the wiser, and left town before the Palatinate showed up and took over."

I'd barely heard anything he'd said. I still couldn't quite fathom that I was responsible for all this. I peered at the translation again. "What does this mean? About redemption?"

Edilman pulled his knees into his chest. "After the balanx attack a year ago, I fled Vengekeep. Got lost in the woods for days. I nearly starved to death. Then the Abbey appeared out of nowhere. It knew where it was needed.

"The monks took me in and nursed me back to health. They saw I bore the brand of the High Laird. They *knew* I was marked for death. But they didn't care. You see, their abbot had just died. And when that happens, the Abbey leads them to a new abbot."

He laughed. "They thought it was me. They thought *I* was meant to be their new abbot. And I was willing to play the part. It was going to be my greatest con yet. Imagine the heists I could pull with a legion of assassin-monks at my command. So I donned the abbot's mask and threw myself into my best disguise yet."

His voice cracked and he fell quiet.

"And then?" I prompted.

"And then," he said, "I got caught up in my own lie. I learned everything I could about the order, hoping to strengthen their allegiance to me. But the more I learned . . . the more I saw how reverent they were, how strongly they believed in their cause. . . . It stopped being an act. The Abbey brought the monks to me because I was in need. I just didn't understand what it was I needed."

As his story ended, I understood what Edilman had needed. A lifetime of treachery had caught up with him. He needed redemption.

"So, you took the Sourcefire to Vengekeep and hid it in the Keep like I told you to," I said. "Then what? We heard the Abbey was destroyed."

"In the end, the Abbey's desire to help those in need was our undoing. After Vengekeep, the Abbey went to where it sensed it was needed. We ended up in Merriton just as the Scourge descended on the city. The beasts tore the Abbey to pieces as soon as we appeared." Edilman placed a hand on his acolyte's arm. "Bennock pulled me from the rubble. The other monks weren't as lucky. Bennock and I barely escaped with our lives."

I looked at Bennock. The acolyte added a log to the fire. I couldn't be angry with him anymore. He'd been following his abbot's orders . . . who'd been following my orders.

"Come back with me to the mill," I said. "We have to tell everyone about the Sourcefire."

Edilman laughed gravely. "I set one foot into that mill and my head will be removed from my body. Besides, the Sourcefire won't do you any good. You can't use it to bargain with the Palatinate anymore. Your new enemy is the Scourge."

The Sourcefire won't do you any good . . . No, the Sourcefire wouldn't do *us* any good. But the Scourge . . .

"I have to go," I said, rising.

Edilman grunted. "Go with him, Bennock. You've been a good acolyte to an order that doesn't exist anymore. No one in the mill will hurt you."

"Yes," I said. "Come with me."

I hated the idea of both of them alone in the wilderness. I'd feel a bit better if I knew Bennock was safe.

But Bennock crossed the campsite and knelt near Edilman. "I'm staying with you, Abbot."

Bennock's honesty might have prevented him from ever becoming an honorary Grimjinx. But his unshakable loyalty would have made it hard to deny him the privilege.

I made to leave when Edilman's voice stopped me. "So do I have it?"

I looked back. "What?"

"Redemption," he said.

I swallowed. "I think you're the only one who knows the answer to that."

Edilman sighed. He clapped Bennock on the back and nodded.

"You always were too smart, Jaxter. Guess I just have to keep looking."

I hurried through the forest. If my theory was right, we could end all this madness fairly easily. But only one person could tell me if that was true.

I had to find Gobek.

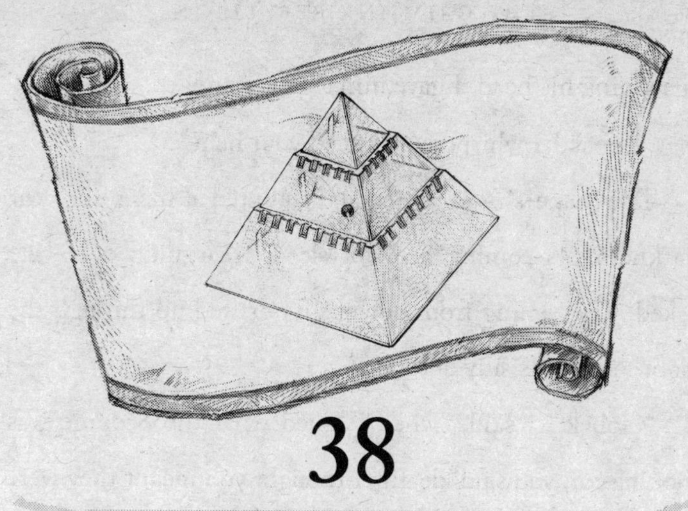

38

War from Within

"Steal with one hand, wish for wealth with the other. See which hand fills up first."

—Baloras Grimjinx, architect of the First Aviard Nestvault Pillage

When I burst through the door of the mill, I could still hear everyone arguing in the basement. They were trying to decide if they should join forces with the Palatinate against the Scourge or attempt to stop the monsters on their own. No one was giving any quarter.

I heard a familiar moan from above. I shot up the rickety staircase to the second floor. The area was filled with great vats where giant blades once ground singegrain into flour. I searched until I found Gobek in the corner, his arms cocooning his head. I gave him a gentle nudge.

"Gobek," I whispered. "I need your help."

The shape-shifter stirred and squinted at me in the near darkness. "Is coming here for sleep. Is arguing over?" he asked. The yelling from downstairs drifted up through the floorboards. "Is silly question."

"Gobek," I said, "when I asked what the Scourge was looking for, you said 'death.' I thought you meant they were looking to *cause* death. But that's not right, is it? You meant the Scourge is looking to die."

Gobek sat up, wincing as he did. I thought of him back in the Creche, always suffering. *Is being Gobek, is being in pain,* he'd said.

"Is not really death," he rasped. "Gobek is making poor choice of words. Is problem with Gobek."

I sat next to him on his blanket. "The Scourge is nothing more than magical energy given physical forms, right?"

Gobek nodded. "Is not meant to be. Is painful for something of one world to be forced into another world."

"So, ever since it was created," I said, "the Scourge has wanted nothing more than to be magical energy again. The monsters are looking for a way to destroy their bodies and return to their natural state."

"Is very smart," Gobek said, patting my knee. "Gobek is not belonging in this world, Scourge is not belonging in this world. Is forced by mages."

The creature grimaced. This was why he was in constant pain. And since he was made of magic, death wouldn't come easily to Gobek.

"The Scourge is looking for the Sourcefire," I said. "It's the only thing powerful enough to destroy it. That's why it was only attacking places where it sensed magic. And now that it's far enough south, it can sense the Sourcefire in Vengekeep."

Gobek nodded. There was only one way to stop the Scourge: give it exactly what it wanted.

"Thanks, Gobek," I said, shaking his hand. The shapeshifter smiled a pained smile and lay back down in his makeshift bed.

I raced downstairs and into the basement where the climate had changed dramatically. The room had divided neatly down the middle. The Dowager and the mages on one side, the Shadowhands and the Sarosans on the other. The few rebels without a clear allegiance to one side or the other seemed to shift back and forth as each side's arguments became more or less persuasive.

I found my parents and Nanni sitting atop a pile of crates in the corner, watching the whole thing with looks that ranged from mildly amused to utterly disgusted.

"This is why the Sarosans have always fought against the evils of magic!" Kendil pointed at Talian as his voice broke above the din. "We always knew it would come to this. Mages brought this upon us. We cannot use magic to solve the problem!"

"Right now," the Dowager argued, "magic is the only way to stop—"

"The Sarosans have fought magic with natural means for years," Reena said as she stood firmly at her father's side. "If everyone had just listened to us and had magic outlawed—"

"I don't agree with the Palatinate's methods," Talian interrupted, "but there would be more order with a magical government in charge."

This caused an all new outburst of anger that shook the timbers.

"Oh, that was a bad move," Da whispered.

"Let's see him get out of this," Ma said in return.

It only got more heated from there.

"Is that where this is headed?" Mr. Oxter said, turning to the Dowager. "Are we to defeat the Scourge, only to put mages back in charge?"

The Dowager rubbed her temples. "We're losing sight of the problem at hand. The Scourge will be here in days. We must decide if we're to take a stand against it here or try to forge an alliance with the Palatinate."

The arguments swelled to the point where words were indistinguishable. It was all just noise.

"You're all wrong!"

How I managed to bellow loudly enough to be heard above all that, I'll never know. But there I was, standing on a crate, hands cupped around my mouth, and suddenly—finally—the room was silent.

I pointed to Kendil. "The Sarosans have spent years trying to get everyone to believe like they do, saying that magic is evil." When I saw Talian nod out of the corner of my eye, I whirled on him. "And mages staged a revolt because they wanted to impose their beliefs on everyone. Both sides have been fighting to get people on their side but neither stopped to ask everyone what *they* wanted.

"You can't force people to believe what you believe. You can't take something and force it to be something it's not. That's what the Palatinate tried to do. They created monsters from magical energy, something it was never meant to be. And now we're all paying for it. Haven't either of you learned anything? There's not just one way—your way. We need to use everything we've got—everyone's skills—or we're going to die."

No one moved or spoke. Also, no one looked particularly happy that I'd spoken in the first place. Except the Dowager. She looked proud.

"Now, listen," I said more quietly, "I've figured out what we need to do."

"Are we really going to sit here," Kendil said, turning his back to me so he could face the rest of the room, "and listen to a boy who's nothing more than a second-rate *cutpurse*?"

As one, my family stood. We weren't about to take that kind of slur. I expected the Shadowhands, fellow thieves to whom such an insult should have been unforgivable, to speak up in our defense. They didn't. I looked at Reena, Holm, and Maloch. They stood by their respective fathers in silence.

"Enough!" the Dowager said. "Every minute we spend fighting among ourselves, we . . . Jaxter?"

Ma and Da led the way, followed by Nanni, and I brought up the rear as we went upstairs. Once we were gone, the arguing below started up again.

The four of us went down by the stream. Nanni skipped rocks against the current as Da paced back and forth.

"Everything we've done," he spat, "and they just see us as cut—as cut—as *that word*."

"Jaxter," Ma said, "what were you about to tell everyone?"

I told them everything. Meeting Edilman in the woods, Aubrin's journal, how the Sourcefire was hidden in Vengekeep, and how the Scourge monsters wanted the Sourcefire to rid themselves of their bodies. All three of them listened to me closely.

"You're right, son," Da said. "We could end this if we give the Scourge what it wants."

"Can't wait to see the look on old Nalia's face when she learns the Sourcefire has been under her nose this whole time," Ma said.

"But the Palatinate isn't going to help," Nanni pointed out. "If we tell them where the Sourcefire is, they'll only use it to enslave the Scourge again. Then we're right back where we started."

"It's simple," I said. "We go to Vengekeep, rescue Aubrin, and get the Sourcefire."

Da pointed to the mill with his thumb. "They can't agree on anything. They won't help."

"Not them, just us," I said. "You heard Talian. The Palatinate has made Vengekeep impenetrable. They've got enough defenses to fight off a siege for days, weeks maybe. But they're expecting an attack from the Scourge. . . ."

I pulled the Vanguard from Da's pocket and held it up in the moonlight.

"They're not expecting the Grimjinxes."

39

The Prisoner

"The insult not well endured
should be well avenged."

—*The Lymmaris Creed*

We'd tried.

Ask any of the 127 Satyran deities and they'd all swear by the Omnipantheon that we Grimjinxes had *tried our hardest*. We'd played within the system. Some of us had taken jobs as Protectorates. Some of us had worked in phydollotry shops. Some of us had tried to raise armies. What did that get us? A status as refugees, caught between power-hungry mages and the bloodthirsty monsters they'd created.

There was only one way to finish this. And it wasn't by

playing within the rules. It wasn't by listening to our allies fight among themselves. It was by striking out on our own and smashing every rule, law, and edict into a million pieces.

In other words: being our true selves.

I lay on my stomach near Vengekeep's southern perimeter wall where the trees were thickest. As the moons peeked out from behind the thick cloud cover, I raised my spyglass and watched the pair of Sentinels who paraded along the top of the wall. Each held a glowing spellsphere, ready for action.

Nearby, Nanni ducked to hide in the shadows. She walked slowly toward me, drawing a line in the sand with a long stick. Occasionally, sparks flew when the stick touched the invisible magical barrier Nanni was outlining. As she finished, Nanni joined me on the ground.

"Anything interesting?" she asked.

I nodded. "Couple gaolglobes near the tree," I reported. "Few other traps. Nothing we can't handle."

A faint rustling in the tree above told us Ma was on her way down. She dropped next to us as the Sentinels on the wall pivoted and turned their gaze in our direction. Seeing nothing, they continued their patrol.

Ma held up my fob watch. "I like punctual guards," she

said, "and those two are *very* punctual. Move like clockwork." She kept an eye on the watch's second hand as the Sentinels marched past. "And . . . turn."

On Ma's cue, the Sentinels spun around on their heels and began walking back in the other direction. "We've got a six-second window," Ma said, "where neither of them will be looking in this direction."

"Six seconds?"

Da had just joined us, crawling over fallen logs and bushes from where he'd been spying.

"Six whole seconds?" he repeated. "That's very generous of them! It's like they're *begging* us to break in." He held up Ma's rubyeye, which he'd been using to spot magical traps between us and the wall.

"Everyone know what to do?" Ma asked, pulling a black cowl over her head.

Nanni picked up the tinderjack pod filled with explosive powder. "Is this thing safe?"

"Not at all," I said.

Nanni tucked it under her arm. "Oh, bangers. Well, good luck!" She touched her finger to her temple, then scurried off into the dark of the woods.

We kept an eye on the Sentinels marching back and forth. Ma nodded her head in time with the watch's second hand. "Ready?" she asked. "Go!"

Atop the wall, the Sentinels looked away. I jumped to my feet and brought my toes right up to the line Nanni had drawn. Reaching out, I touched the tip of the Vanguard to the invisible barrier. The air rippled, a cascade of sparks fell to the ground, and the magical shield dissolved. We belly crawled forward until we reached the base of a giant mokka tree just a few feet from the wall.

Hidden behind the mokka, Da dug his fingers into the tree's trunk. As he pulled, a curved section of bark hinged open like a door, revealing a ladder inside the hollow tree. Ma produced a small lantern and led us down the secret passage.

We came to a horizontal tunnel that took us under the perimeter wall. Ma looked admiringly at the walls.

"This takes me back, Ona," she said to Da with a wistful sigh. "Remember those late nights digging this out?"

Da grinned. "How could I forget?"

The long tunnel ended in a ladder leading up. Da climbed first. He pressed on a square stone overhead. The trapdoor swung up on a hinge and Da disappeared into the ceiling. Ma and I followed him, emerging into a very familiar room. Iron bars, rickety furniture, smelly hay bales. The Grimjinx summer home.

Also known as the Vengekeep gaol.

I pushed the trapdoor shut with a thud.

"Who's there?" a voice hissed in the darkness behind us. Ma held her lantern at arm's length. There, huddled in the corner, was a man wearing rags. He held a hand up to his face to shield his eyes from the light.

"Castellan Jorn?"

Jorn had looked better. He'd lost a lot of weight and was almost unrecognizable. His skin was pale and his eyes had sunken deeper into his head. One look at us and he collapsed to his knees.

"Wasn't my life bad enough?" he moaned. "Why did *you* people have to come back?"

"Castellan, what are you doing here?" Ma asked.

"The Palatinate arrested anyone who remained loyal to the House of Soranna!" he spat. "That woman—that *Nalia*—moved into my house."

"With the rest of the Lordcourt?" Da asked.

Jorn shook his head. "She's the only member of the Lordcourt still alive. She leads the Palatinate from *my house*. Can you believe it?"

"And are you?" I asked.

The Castellan stammered. "A-am I what?"

"Loyal to the House of Soranna?"

I'd never liked Jorn much. None of us had. We thought he was slimy and only out for self-glory. But he gained our respect that day when he held his flabby chin up and said, "Now and always."

"Splendid!" Da said. "Then you won't mind us giving the Palatinate what for, I take it?"

The Castellan, purely out of habit, started to object. But he changed his mind when he realized that, for once, we were all on the same side. "How can I help?"

I held up a sketch of the relics. "The Palatinate stole these four magic relics. They use them to control the Sourcefire."

The Castellan nodded. "Yes, but I heard they lost the Sourcefire. The relics are useless now."

"But do they still have the relics?" Ma asked.

"Of course. Nalia keeps them in a safe in my house. . . .

Wait a minute. . . ." The Castellan studied the floor. "How did you get in here?"

"The tunnel, of course," Ma said. "It comes out just past the perimeter wall."

You'd think the Castellan would have been more grateful, seeing as we'd just rescued him. But he couldn't let it go. "There's a tunnel that leads from the gaol to just outside Vengekeep's walls? How long has that been there?"

Da beamed. "We dug it out right around Jaxter's first birthday."

The Castellan's cheeks puffed up in rage. "You mean that every time I had you locked in here, you could have gotten out?"

"Yes, but we didn't," Ma said sweetly, as if that made everything okay. "We only built it as a precaution. Thankfully, you were never very good at making charges stick."

The Castellan burbled a bit. When he calmed down, he said, "Then let's take your tunnel and leave—"

"Can't do that," Ma said. "We didn't break into gaol for fun . . . although it was sort of fun. No, we've got something to do."

Ma pulled a perfect replica of the gaol cell key from her tunic pocket. Reaching through the bars, she unlocked the door from within.

"A key?" The Castellan's breathy whisper was nearly as loud as his shouting voice. "You've got a key too?"

"Of course we do," Ma said. "One of my finest forgeries."

His fists clenched, the Castellan shook with silent fury.

As the cell door swung open, we crept out and toward the stairs that led up into the Protectorate's office.

"You can't go there!" Jorn said. "The Sentinels use this as headquarters."

"That *is* a concern," Da said.

"We'll just have to go out the other way," Ma said. She walked over to the far wall and pressed a discolored brick at waist height. Click. Ma shoved the wall forward, revealing a dark passage. Jorn stood there, dumbfounded.

"You had *another* way out of gaol?" he asked.

"Comes out near the bakery," I said.

"I hate you people," Jorn muttered, shaking his head. "I *really* hate you people."

"Now, Castellan," Ma said, hooking her arm around

Jorn's and leading him into the passage, "I know you've been down here a long time but I'm sure you hear things. So tell us . . . where is Aubrin?"

We descended the stairs into the catacombs below the town-state hall. A familiar, dank smell met my nose. My last trip down here hadn't been much fun. I didn't imagine this one would be any better.

"Why would they keep her down here?" I asked, looking around. The walls were still lined with racks holding glass tubes that contained hundreds of prophetic tapestries. The room we were in was the first of many identical rooms. There was no telling where Aubrin was.

"It's like Jorn said," Da reminded me. "The Palatinate figures this is the safest place in the event the Scourge attacks. They need to keep Aubrin safe."

"Speaking of Jorn, do you think he'll be okay? Should we have left him with—?"

"He's a grown man, Jaxter. He'll be fine."

Ma nodded to a pile of crates and barrels, labeled as food

and water. The pile went all the way up to the ceiling. "My guess is the Palatinate plans to hide down here when the Scourge comes."

"Hiding won't do any good."

The small voice pierced my heart. Aubrin stood in the doorway to the next chamber. Shackles bound her wrists to the wall and she looked like she hadn't slept in a week.

Ma ran to her. "Are you okay?"

Aubrin pointed to the tubes containing prophecies. "Of course. Since I've been down here, I've made a *fortune.*"

Prophecies. Fortunes. If Aubrin was making bad jokes, she was fine.

As Ma picked the lock on Aubrin's shackles, my sister sighed. "It's been fun lying to the Palatinate about the prophecies I've had. I told them the only way to defeat the Scourge was for everyone in Vengekeep to dance the Aviard two-step. I don't think they believed me."

Da patted her on the shoulder. "That's my girl. You don't tell those bad mages anything."

Aubrin took my hand. "Jaxter, listen, I have to tell you about the vision I had yesterday. It's very important—"

"Yes, please do. I'm all ears."

I stiffened, instantly recognizing the voice behind us. Nalia stepped into the room from the staircase, her spell-sphere aglow.

"How did you know we were here?" Ma asked.

Nalia chuckled, a magical shimmer roiling across her monocle. "The infamous Grimjinx clan. Your heists are legendary. I suppose it was only a matter of time before you came up with a plan that wasn't totally foolproof . . . or rather a plan where someone realized it was more valuable to turn you in."

Footsteps sounded behind Nalia. The shadowy figure that stepped into the room hung his head low. He shuffled as he moved to Nalia's side.

It was Uncle Garax.

40

The Key and the Keep

"There is no gaol more fortified
than a thief's disgrace."

—Ancient par-Goblin proverb

"Garax!" Da said through clenched teeth. "You followed us here from the mill!"

"Of course I did," Garax said, shrugging. "You lot, sneaking out in the middle of the night. I figured you were turning your backs on everyone and going out on a really lucrative heist. Didn't expect you to come here."

"Money's useless these days," I said. "They can't pay you."

"What the Palatinate's got is better than money, isn't it?" Garax asked. "There's a horde of monsters tearing the land apart. I figure my best bet for safety is with these magic folks. So, yeah, I warned them you were here." He nodded at Nalia and lowered his voice. "But, you know, when the Scourge is gone and everything's back on track, you're gonna pay me, right?"

"What happens next," Nalia said, her eyes fixed on Aubrin, "depends on the augur. I want you to tell me everything you know about the Scourge. I want to hear every vision you've had. You've been refusing to tell me for weeks. And I had no way to persuade you. But now . . ."

Nalia spoke a word. A bolt of green lightning shot from the spellsphere, striking Da on the chest. He howled and fell to the floor, writhing in pain. Ma dropped to her knees to help him.

"I'm all right," Da said weakly.

"Now, augur," Nalia continued, "I have some incentive for you. You're going to tell me about the Scourge, or I'll kill your family. One by one."

Aubrin looked up at me, tears filling her eyes. I put my hand on her arm and nodded. "Tell her what you know, Jinxface."

"Listen to your brother," Nalia said. "You're beaten. I'm

the only one who can help you now. Their rescue plan has failed and—"

Suddenly, the entire room shook as an explosion sounded over our heads. Nalia looked around. She saw my entire family smiling back.

"Or," I said, winking at Nalia, "this was all part of a clever plot to lure you away from the Castellan's house so my grandmother could destroy the relics."

Nalia's eyes grew twice as large as she pieced it all together. She glared at Uncle Garax, who smirked and waved.

"So sorry to lie to you, your evil awfulness," Garax said, tugging at his shirt collar. "Don't get me wrong. I'm really terrified of you. But I betrayed my brother once, you see, and I learned that there's something out there I fear more than you and the Palatinate and the Scourge put together: *my mother.*"

Garax crouched, ready to lunge at Nalia. But the mage used her monocle to see five seconds into the future. Before Garax could move, she barked a word of magic. A shaft of white light pulsed from the spellsphere and turned Uncle Garax to glass.

Exactly as we planned.

With Garax distracting her, I made my move. The Vanguard, safe in my pocket, shielded me from her magic monocle. I tackled Nalia at the waist, sending her spell-sphere flying. An instant later, Ma and Da were tying the mage to the tapestry racks.

"You won't need this anymore," Ma said, slipping Nalia's monocle into her pocket as the mage thrashed helplessly.

I pulled the Vanguard from my pocket and touched it to Uncle Garax. The glass fell from him like running water. He gasped for air.

"I can't believe I agreed to let her do that to me," Garax said, shaking his arms to get the feeling back. "How did you know she wouldn't just kill me?"

"We didn't," Ma said.

"So it worked, then?" Da asked Garax, securing a gag around Nalia's mouth.

"They never doubted my performance for a second," Garax said proudly. "Oh, they were a mite cautious when I drove the house up to Vengekeep's gates. But once I told them who I was, they let me right in. They figured if I ratted you out once, I'd do it again. See, I told you that first time would pay off."

Da called Garax a name I don't feel comfortable repeating. Let's just say he called him a liar.

"So they didn't search the house?" I asked.

We'd ridden in the Ghostfire house from the mill and hidden it in the woods while we checked out the town-state's defenses. When Ma, Da, and I went through the tunnel to the gaol, Nanni hid in the house. Once the mages let Garax drive the house inside Vengekeep, Nanni sneaked out and rigged the Castellan's house to explode with the tinderjack.

"Why would they?" Garax said, flashing me a smile. "They trusted me. Like our great-great-grandfather Alphorax Grimjinx used to say, 'Trust is—'"

"Whoo!"

Nanni waddled down the stairs, a plume of smoke wafting off her head. Her face was blackened with soot and her eyes were wide with shock. "That tinderjack is powerful stuff! Where can I get some more?"

Da pulled tightly on the ropes that bound Nalia's wrists. "Did you find the relics?"

"Blew 'em all up," Nanni said. "And most of the Castellan's house. We don't have to pay for that, do we?"

"Where is the Castellan?" I asked.

"He's setting diversionary fires a few streets over," Nanni said. "The Sentinels won't know where to look first. Which reminds me, we need to get moving. They'll be here soon."

We all ran up the stairs, out of the town-state hall, and into the street. Citizens of Vengekeep had already appeared to watch the Castellan's beautiful mansion burn to the ground.

Da clapped his hands together. "All right, everyone. You know what to do now. We have to keep the mages as far from the Keep as possible." He nudged me with his elbow. "You ready, son?"

I nodded, hoping the churning of my stomach wouldn't tell another story.

Uncle Garax reached behind his back and produced a small bag. "You'll be needing this. When I first arrived, they took me right to the Castellan's house. I nicked this when Nalia wasn't looking." From inside, he pulled the magic dagger that opened the Keep. Garax squinted at it in the dark. "That's funny, I coulda sworn it was glowing before. . . ."

Ma reached for Aubrin's hand. "I'm going with Jaxter," Aubrin said. "I can help him." Ma looked skeptical but nodded once in agreement.

"All right, everyone . . . scatter!" Ma said. Da, Nanni, and Garax ran in different directions. The people of Vengekeep applauded. Just then, scores of mages in long flowing robes emptied into the road, spellspheres at the ready. They fired bolts of magic after my departing family, who dodged this way and that before disappearing from view. The mages, not even noticing me and Aubrin, gave chase.

"Let's go, Jinxface!"

We sprinted through the shadowy streets toward the ancient Keep.

"Jaxter, listen to me," Aubrin said, puffing as she ran. "I had another vision yesterday. A vision about you. This one was much clearer. I know what's going to happen."

"I know, I know," I said. "I promise to avoid big pillars of light. We don't have time to talk about it now."

"But I was wrong!" she said, squeezing my hand. "It wasn't a pillar of light. It was—"

An explosion to our left, followed by a scream, sent us falling to the ground. I peered down an alley into the next street over. Nanni, holding her skirts up, ran nimbly away from a pair of pursuing mages. She gave us a friendly wave as she passed.

"Come on," I said, yanking Aubrin up and continuing forward. We wove through the streets we knew so well until at last, far from the fighting, we came to the Keep.

The face on the stone warrior that guarded the Keep door had long since eroded away. I took a deep breath, walked up to the statue, and placed the dagger's hilt in its hand. The statue should have slid aside to reveal the door. But nothing happened.

"Did I do it wrong?" I asked Aubrin.

She went up and spun the dagger upside down, placing the stone blade into the warrior's hand. Nothing. I grabbed the dagger and examined it. Had Uncle Garax grabbed the wrong dagger? Why wasn't it . . . ?

"Oh, no."

Aubrin crinkled her face. "What is it?"

My temples throbbed. "Uncle Garax had this on him when he was hit with the shimmerhex."

"So?"

"So I used the Vanguard to free him. The Vanguard negates *all magic.* It got rid of the shimmerhex *and* the dagger's magic. It's useless. We have no way to get into the Keep!"

And that's when we heard it.

The sounds of fighting in the streets fell away. In the distance, a dissonant wail, rising in pitch, grew closer and louder. Aubrin and I climbed the warrior statue, stood atop the Keep's dome, and gazed northwest.

Sentinels patrolling the perimeter wall stopped and gaped. On the horizon, the stars started disappearing, one by one. Xelos, the small moon, had just begun to rise. Slowly, a black shadow crept across its surface, eating the moon bit by bit.

I felt Aubrin slip her trembling hand into mine and squeeze. We were too late.

The Scourge was here.

41

Attack of the Scourge

"Leave sacrifices to the brave and bold."

—Ancient par-Goblin proverb

As the approaching shriek of the Scourge grew louder, more and more citizens of Vengekeep poured into the streets. People pointed to the flying mass—a darkness separate from the night sky—as it covered the city like a cloak.

One by one, my family—having evaded the mages—gathered at the entrance to the Keep. Nanni was limping now. Uncle Garax was doubled over, wheezing. Ma and Da huddled together, eyes glued on the horizon.

"This is a little too familiar," Da said grimly.

Like Da, I was also thinking about when the balanx skeletons attacked Vengekeep. But back then, there were only a handful of balanx. And we knew exactly how to defeat them. The one weapon we needed now we didn't have.

Aubrin and I climbed down and I explained what had happened with the dagger. "The Scourge will be here any minute. We have to find another way in."

By now, panic had rippled through the crowd. Parents clutched their children and looked frantically around for a place to hide. Ma immediately took charge.

"Ona," she said to Da, "you and Garax go to the armory. Find something to smash in the Keep door. The rest of you, help me get everyone into the catacombs. It's the safest place."

Ma and Da kissed before Da and Uncle Garax charged off toward the armory. As Ma and Nanni began herding people toward the town-state hall and the entrance to the catacombs, Aubrin held tight to my wrist and pulled me back.

"What is it, Jinxface?"

"We have somewhere else to be."

With that, she pulled me in the opposite direction. We moved against the crush of people following Ma. Aubrin led me to a spot near the western perimeter wall.

I looked around. "Aubrin, we need to find something to help us get into the Keep."

"Trust me," she said, looking around expectantly.

I rolled my eyes. "If you had a vision that will help us, just tell me you had a vision."

"I had a vision."

"See? Was that so hard? Look, we can't just sit here waiting for the vision to come true. What we need is a battering ram."

With a mighty *crack*, the wall next to us disintegrated, sending bits of mordenstone flying through the air. Aubrin and I fell to our stomachs. As dust floated in the air around the newly formed hole, the rounded head of a battering ram poked through.

Coughing, Aubrin and I got to our feet as people—humans, Aviards, and par-Goblins—ran in through the gap in the wall. Leading the way, sword in hand, was a flighty-eyed woman who stopped only briefly to admire her handiwork.

"That worked better than expected," the Dowager said.

Soon, more familiar faces arrived. Maloch, Callie,

Reena, Holm . . . each holding a weapon and ready to fight. The rest of the rebel army entered the city and immediately began setting up small catapults and other weapons.

A quickjump ring opened with a snap above us. Talian fell through the ring and landed near the Dowager.

"The Palatinate is trying to escape out the north gates," he reported, "but my mages are keeping them inside the city. They'll be forced to fight with the rest of us."

"Good work," the Dowager said. She took my chin and raised my face to look at her. "Later, we're going to have a very long talk about leaving me behind and why it's never a good idea. But first, maybe you should tell us what's happening here."

I quickly explained the situation and how we needed to get into the Keep. "When we left, everyone was arguing. How'd you get them all to follow you?"

"You're joking, right?" Maloch said, tossing his head at the Dowager. "You should have heard the speech she gave. Shamed us all. Made Reena's da cry. She rallied everyone and here we are."

"But how did you find us?"

"How do you think?" Talian said, nodding toward the

hole in the wall. Through the settling dust, a tall silhouette stormed into the city, a halberd in one hand and a battle-ax in the other. As the Satyran soldier assumed a stance next to the Dowager, she glared down at me.

"You will *never* be able to hide from me," Luda said.

Clearly.

A ball of green flame soared over our heads and incinerated the Laughing Par-Dwarf tavern. Two hulking skaiths dropped from the sky and onto the perimeter wall. With dangerous tusks and spiky tails, they began tearing the wall to shreds. The Scourge had arrived.

The Dowager put a horn to her lips and sounded the war cry. "This ends now!" she declared. The rebels responded with a guttural cheer and ran forward to combat the monsters.

The Dowager pointed to Talian. "You, Callie, and Luda, get Jaxter to the Keep. Do whatever it takes to get him inside." Then she went to join her troops. My heart stuck in my throat. I had a terrible feeling it was the last time I was going to see her.

With Luda and Talian leading the way, Aubrin, Callie, and I dashed through the chaos. Monsters appeared at every turn, digging into the cobblestone streets and crushing anything in their paths.

None of them had reckoned on Luda, though.

Slashing in every direction, the Satyran tore a path for us, dispatching creatures with each swing of her weapons. Talian and Callie helped, firing blasts from their spellspheres, until the constant use of magic weakened them. Aubrin helped Callie while I threw Talian's arm around my shoulder and moved forward.

As we rounded a corner, three massive graglars—feline prowlers with three mouths—blocked the quickest path to the Keep. The creatures snarled, baring their teeth. Luda didn't even hesitate. She ran straight at them, weapons singing through the air as she went. The graglars attacked her from every angle. Luda spun wildly, inflicting damage with every blow. But the graglars weren't giving up.

"Go!" Luda called to us.

We sidestepped the melee and continued on to the Keep just ahead. Dodging creatures at every turn, we ran directly for the stone dome. We'd almost made it when a bloodreaver appeared with a pop and threw us all to the ground. The creature leaped onto Talian's back, then lurched forward and sunk its fangs into the mage's side.

Talian screamed. Blood gushed from the wound. The bloodreaver shook its head back and forth, trying to rip Talian's arm from his body.

"I dropped my spellsphere!" Callie cried. Aubrin and I dug through the dirt, searching for the iron marble as Talian wailed in agony.

Just as we found it, a loud squish made the bloodreaver freeze. Its jaws slackened, it released its grip on Talian, and it fell over, twitching. Just behind, Bennock stood, his sword protruding from the creature's head. He put his foot on the bloodreaver and yanked to retrieve his weapon.

"You were right," he said to me. "I *am* getting better."

Just behind him, Edilman strode toward us. He bent over and examined Talian. "He's unconscious. Aubrin, look after him."

I smiled at Bennock. "Where did you come from?"

"When you left the mill, we stowed away in the attic of your uncle's moving house," he said.

"You were with us the entire trip here?"

"Every night," Edilman said. "Just so you know, Jaxter: you snore."

Bennock nodded. "You do."

I ignored them and pulled the once-magic dagger from my belt. "This is the key to open the Keep door," I said, handing it to Callie. "But it got touched by the Vanguard so it's useless now. Can you . . . magic it?"

"I could do that," Callie said, studying the dagger. "Or I could do this."

She spoke a word, her spellsphere pulsed, and the stone warrior disintegrated, revealing stairs that led deep into the ground.

"That works too," I said. "You've gotten good, Cal. You'll be the head of the Lordcourt in no time." I turned to Aubrin. "We'll be right back."

"Come on," Edilman said, leading us down into the Keep.

The Keep itself was very small: a perfectly square room with a row of waist-high columns on the far side. The Sourcefire sat atop a column in the center, magical fire swirling in the crystal box.

"It's not very big," Bennock said. "How is that going to destroy the entire Scourge?"

"It only looks small," Callie told him. "A thousand years

ago, it took a hundred mages an entire day to secure the Sourcefire in that box. It's more than enough to take care of the Scourge."

The sounds of Vengekeep's destruction had grown so loud we could hear it through all the earth and stone above us. Chunks of dirt fell from the ceiling. "Let's open it," I said, reaching out.

But Callie snatched my arm. "The second we open that, the Keep will be flooded with fire. We'll be incinerated."

Bennock nodded. "We need to take the box into the forest and find a way to—"

Another crash from above. A section of the ceiling collapsed, burying Bennock and Edilman under a river of rock and sand. Callie and I fell to our knees to dig them out. I pulled Bennock from the debris quickly but as Callie went to help Edilman, he screamed. The three of us tossed rocks aside until we freed his leg, now crushed and unusable.

Edilman gripped the wall and pulled himself up onto his good leg. "We don't have time to take this anywhere," he said quietly. He muttered in par-Goblin and put his hands on either side of the box's lid.

"It's magically sealed," he murmured. "We're sunk."

I reached for my pouches. Empty. I couldn't counter the magical lock. And if I used the Vanguard, I risked accidentally destroying the Sourcefire inside. Just like how I'd neutralized the dagger when I freed Uncle Garax from the shimmerhex.

A mighty crack sounded behind us as the stairs we'd descended split. Soon, they'd crumble away and we'd be trapped down here.

Over my shoulder, Callie exhaled sharply. She stared at the crystal box hatefully. Swallowing, she walked past me and stood at Edilman's side. "I can undo the lock. But the second I do, the box will automatically open."

Her meaning was clear.

No. No, there had to be another way.

"Magic can't be used on the Sourcefire," I argued.

Callie shook her head. "Magic can't be used to *transport* the Sourcefire. Magic is the only way to open the lock."

How could she sound so calm? My heart was hammering. This wasn't fair. Callie *had* to survive. She had to show the world that mages could be good.

"Jaxter," she said, "you and Bennock get Edilman out of here."

But Edilman waved us away. "I'll slow them down. And it'll take the two of them to get Talian to safety." He held out his hand. Callie took it. "Together?"

"Who would have thought?" Callie said with a quiet laugh. "You and me."

"Abbot," Bennock said, voice shaking. "What are you—?"

"I'm going to count to fifty," Edilman said softly. "You've got that long to get as far away from here as possible."

"No, Edilman," I said, "this isn't the way."

The Keep lurched. A stream of sand poured down in front of the stairs, threatening to cut off our exit. Edilman turned his back to us. Callie held her spellsphere out. Their free hands gripped each other tight.

"One . . . two . . . three . . ."

None of this felt real. I looked to Bennock. The acolyte gaped, pale faced, and tugged at Edilman's arm. Edilman didn't budge. "You can't do this, Abbot."

". . . four . . . five . . . six . . ."

I reached for Callie, but she hissed a magical word and sent me and Bennock flying across the room. "Jaxter, go!" she said firmly.

Numb, I touched Bennock's shoulder. The acolyte

wouldn't move. He stood there, eyes fixed on his abbot.

". . . eight . . . nine . . . Jaxter, get Bennock out of here . . . ten . . . eleven . . ."

Edilman kept counting. Callie joined in the count. They wouldn't even look at me. Edilman paused only to whisper in par-Goblin, the same word he'd uttered earlier. I knew then there was no stopping him.

"What did he say?" Bennock asked.

"'Redemption,'" I said.

Bennock strained against my grip. "Abbot . . ."

It took all my strength to get Bennock to move. He fought me every step of the way, screaming that he wanted to stay with Edilman. I took one last look at Callie. If she was afraid, it didn't show. She just squeezed Edilman's hand harder.

Eyes burning with tears, I dragged Bennock from the Keep.

42

The Death of Jaxter Grimjinx

"A bad thief never gets a good lockpick."

—*The Lymmaris Creed*

The dome at the Keep's entrance collapsed just as we bolted out from underground. You couldn't see the cobblestone streets for all the ruin. The next block over, a wall of fire consumed everything in its path. The Scourge made short work of the few buildings left standing.

The imminent danger snapped Bennock out of his daze. Together, we picked up Talian and, with Aubrin at our side, we dashed for whatever cover we could find.

We ran until our legs burned. Suddenly, the entire ground

heaved, shattering the street around us. Thrown forward and up, we landed near the ruins of the widow Bellatin's house. Behind us, the Keep exploded. The earth blew apart when a massive discharge of green-blue energy shot up with a roar like continuous thunder.

The Sourcefire was unleashed.

I gaped where the entrance to the Keep had once stood. *Callie . . . Edilman . . .*

The Sourcefire twisted and churned like a tornado of light, red and orange bolts of energy shooting out from the swirling green-blue flames. It pierced the night sky, dancing in place from an unseen chasm. Strangely cool but powerful winds blew around the Sourcefire, whipping debris everywhere.

Aubrin crawled to me. We lay flat and covered our heads. I looked to Bennock, whose face was racked in pain. When the explosion threw him, he'd fallen on a broken wagon wheel. One of the spokes had pierced his thigh. He pressed his hand against the wound as his face grew paler by the minute. Talian remained unconscious nearby.

Above the tumult, a wall of noise, built from a thousand separate cries, overpowered the terrible sound of the

Sourcefire. The Scourge as one had stopped its rampage against the town-state. The creatures had seen the Sourcefire and were doing exactly as we'd predicted. They ignored everything in their path and charged toward the column of magical fire.

Problem was, we were right in their way.

"Stampede!" I cried. I grabbed Talian's legs while Aubrin hooked her arms under Bennock's. We dragged our friends from the path of the oncoming herd and took refuge behind what remained of a bakery.

The Sourcefire's unyielding winds did nothing to stop the Scourge. The monsters smashed any piece of flying debris that dared interrupt their progress. The first to arrive on the scene were a handful of bloodreavers, clawing their way across the broken ground. As one, they leaped straight at the Sourcefire with a final cry . . . and vanished. No flash. No sound. They just disappeared, like they'd never really been there.

Flying creatures followed suit, gliding serenely into the Sourcefire from a multitude of angles. The ground trembled as wookilars and skaiths and baxrons alike ran at top speed into the fire to be painlessly consumed. Seconds ago, they'd all been part of a murderous frenzy. Now, as they vanished, the Scourge looked peaceful at last. The feral braying faded as one by one the beasts cast off their physical forms and returned to pure energy.

And then we were alone. The threat of the Scourge was over. We'd won.

But the echoing thunder of the Sourcefire continued. The red bolts of lightning that snaked out from the center of the vortex grew more powerful, igniting the rubble. A doom-filled crack sounded as more of the earth at the base of the tornado fell away, engulfed by the fire.

"Is it me . . . ," I asked, my throat going dry, ". . . or is it getting bigger?"

The Sourcefire started churning faster. Its base grew wider still, inching its way across the square. Talian stirred and produced his spellsphere. "I have to call the other mages. We have to contain it."

I eyed the expanding girth of the Sourcefire. Callie had said it took a hundred mages a day to contain the Sourcefire once before. We didn't have a day. The Sourcefire would consume all of Vengekeep in an hour. Or sooner.

Talian glared at his spellsphere. It flickered with light,

then went dark. "I'm—I'm too weak."

I reached out to Aubrin. Her eyes were red and wide with terror. Tears glistened down her cheeks. I pulled her close to reassure her.

But Aubrin wasn't looking at me. She looked past me. At the Sourcefire.

And I realized: she hadn't seen a pillar of light in the vision where I died.

She'd seen a pillar of fire.

That was what she'd been trying to tell me. She'd had a clearer vision and knew it was fire I was destined to walk into. This fire.

But why would I ever walk into the Sourcefire? Especially when we only had a few minutes before it expanded enough to destroy us all.

"Aubrin, what—?"

As I reached for her, I felt something press against my leg. My hand slid down my side to a ripped pouch. And the Vanguard.

Only the Vanguard can eliminate the Sourcefire, Kolo had said.

Struggling to my feet, I held my arm back and pitched

the Vanguard right at the approaching tornado. But the gale force winds made it impossible. The crystal pyramid landed just steps away. There was only one way to deliver the Vanguard into the heart of the Sourcefire.

"No, Jaxter!" Aubrin cried. She tried to snag me but I dodged her grasp and retrieved the Vanguard. We both knew what had to happen next. We'd finally arrived at the purple marble.

"I love you, Jinxface!" I called over the turmoil. Then I turned and ran at the Sourcefire.

I ducked as wooden poles and hunks of thatch hurled past. The broken cobblestones made me trip and stagger. But I forged on, my hand to my eyes to fight off the wind.

It won't hurt, I told myself. *It can't hurt.*

Suddenly, I was struck from the left. I hit the rocky ground, pain shooting through my body, as the Vanguard tumbled from my grasp. Powerful arms held me in place.

It was Gobek.

The creature pinned me down, the expression on his face both pained and sad.

"Gobek," I shouted over the wind. "You have to let me go. I have to destroy the Sourcefire!"

"Is wanting Gobek to suffer more?" he asked. "Gobek is not belonging here. Gobek is wanting to be free."

"If I don't take the Vanguard into the Sourcefire, it'll expand and destroy all the Provinces."

Gobek ripped the vallix skin gloves from my belt and used them to pick up the Vanguard. Being made of magic, touching the Vanguard would have ended him. Even with the magic-resistant gloves protecting him, the flesh on his arm sizzled and blistered. He suddenly looked very tired and very ill. "Is not your time," he said, almost too quietly to hear.

"But it *is* my time," I said. "Aubrin's seen it. Please, Gobek, you've got to let me—"

Gobek raised his arms and the skin across his body began to shift. The color changed. He grew taller, leaner. A tangle of messy brown hair with unruly cowlicks spread out over his head. A pink, four-pointed star formed on his shoulder.

A moment later, I was staring at an exact replica of me.

"Is taking care of Bright Eyes." The voice from this other me was Gobek's. He looked like me but I could still see the enormous sadness and the pain. More than that, I saw hope.

Then, without another word, he took the Vanguard and

walked calmly up to the expanding Sourcefire.

He didn't stop to brace himself. He didn't look back. He was at total peace, just as the Scourge monsters behaved when they were erased from existence. Gobek held the Vanguard in a clenched fist high above his head and stepped into the Sourcefire.

It was like the night winked. The light from the Sourcefire collapsed in on itself and my ears popped as a giant whoosh pulled all the air into the empty crater. Where the explosion that released the Sourcefire had thrown us away, the destruction of the Sourcefire drew everything nearby toward it.

I flew toward the crater, as if tied to an invisible rope. Massive piles of house shot through the air around me. My arms flailed, grasping to hold on to anything. I managed to dig my fingers in at the edge of the chasm while debris rained down past me.

Then everything was still. Completely and utterly still.

I wriggled and fought to pull myself up and out of the crater. "Help!"

A moment later, Aubrin's dirty but smiling face peeked over the edge of the crater. "You're alive." She grabbed my forearm and pulled while I scrambled up the side of the crevasse. But she wasn't strong enough. The earth where my hand dug in slowly started to give way. . . .

Aubrin's hands slipped. I fell back, only to be snatched by two gigantic hands and hauled up to safety. Before I could thank my rescuer, I was crushed in a life-threatening embrace. It wasn't until I wheezed for air that Luda let me go. I crumpled to the ground and coughed until I could breathe again.

"You . . . hugged . . . me . . . ," I said to the Satyran.

Luda cleared her throat. "I did no such thing," she proclaimed tersely. "I was just making sure you weren't damaged. You seem to be working fine. Carry on."

Talian and Bennock, leaning on each other, limped over. Aubrin took the empty pouches from my belt and used the fabric to dress their wounds.

"Help . . ."

We almost missed hearing the voice, weak and shaky as it was.

"There's someone trapped under there," Bennock said, pointing to a collapsed house near the edge of the crater.

Luda led the way and we started tearing bits of timber

and thatch from the wreckage, searching for the survivor. A small hand shot up from down below, a spellsphere pinched between its thin, bleeding fingers.

I peered into the debris. "Callie?" It wasn't possible.

With a roar, Luda tossed a beam twice her size into the crater, revealing my battered friend, her legs pinned under the wrecked house. Callie smiled faintly. "Ta-da."

Aubrin squealed but I couldn't make a sound. I'd have fallen over if Bennock hadn't been there to hold me up.

"But you were in the Keep," Aubrin said.

"It was Edilman," she said. "When I released the magical lock, he threw his body on top of the box to keep the lid from opening. It bought me enough time to open a quick-jump ring."

"Did the abbot—?" Bennock pawed hopefully at the remains of the house.

But Callie shook her head. "I wasn't going to leave him, but he knew if he moved off the box, we'd both die before we could make it through. So he shoved me into the ring and it closed behind me."

Luda and Talian gently eased Callie out from under

the rubble. She cried out as her legs emerged, mangled and bloody.

"So you quickjumped into a demolished house?" I asked, trying to take her mind off it. "Some mage you are."

Callie snarled. "It wasn't demolished at the time, you garfluk. I can only quickjump to places I've been. For some reason, the first place I thought of was your house. I'd forgotten how close it was to the Keep."

I took a step back. I hadn't realized it but she was right. The house I'd grown up in was gone. Aubrin's arm slid around my waist and we hugged.

"You did it," she whispered. "You changed the future."

I ran my fingers through her short hair and glanced down into the gaping hole where the Keep had been.

"Yeah. The future will never be the same."

43

Birth of the Procoran

"The mills of justice grind slowly,
but they grind finely."

—*Corenus Grimjinx, clan father*

We spent the night among the ashes of Vengekeep. As dusk came, everyone helped gather food and carve out shelter from the heaps of debris. Grievances were set aside. We weren't thieves and mages and Sarosans and soldiers. There, huddled in the ruins, we were all just survivors.

The next morning, we attended to our dead. I carved Edilman's name into an arrow-shaped slab of mordenstone. There was nothing to bury but I couldn't let his death go unnoticed. Side by side, Bennock and I placed the stone in the cemetery just outside Vengekeep. The inscription under his name bestowed the greatest honor I could think of. It said: "A Grimjinx to the end."

Then we joined the Sarosans, deep in the woods, as they mourned their losses. Reena wept uncontrollably in her father's arms while Maloch stood stoically at her side. I bowed my head in respect as the flames of a funeral pyre took what remained of Holm. I'd heard he'd died saving his sister from a braxilar. Like a true warrior-bard.

When the funerals finished, the unclaimed dead—Nalia and many mages—were lined up down one of the few undamaged streets. They'd be tended to later. The Dowager vowed to show them more respect than they'd shown the Provinces.

Talian and the healers had worked on Callie until late into the night. They relieved as much pain as they could, but in the end they had to tell her she'd never walk again. The news didn't faze her for a second.

"Maybe I'll surprise you," she said with her usual knowing smile.

Of that, I had no doubt.

At breakfast, what remained of the rebellion's leadership

gathered to talk about the only thing left to discuss: the future.

"We must spread the word," the Dowager said, "and start rebuilding the Provinces as soon as possible. We can't do that until everyone knows the Palatinate and the Scourge are gone."

Kendil nodded. "Before our exile, the Sarosans happily wandered the Provinces. We'll resume that sacred tradition and share the news."

"And what do we tell everyone?" Ma asked. "Yes, it's important they understand the danger has passed. But life just can't go back to normal."

"I don't think it *should* go back to normal," Da said. Quizzical looks spread through the group. "Look, Mannis Soranna created the Five Provinces from the ashes of the Great Uprisings. Well, we've got plenty of ashes to go around again. Why not start something new?"

Talian disagreed. "We wouldn't be here today without the Dowager. Isn't that a sign she should lead us—?"

"It most certainly *is not*!" The Dowager looked up from her plate. "Ona is quite right. It's time to start over. The Five Provinces were created because there was a *need* for them. Things have changed. I don't know if that need exists anymore."

Mr. Oxter chuckled cynically. "So, what do you think we *need*?"

Everyone looked expectantly at the Dowager. I thought she was going to be ill. But when our eyes met, I gave her a small nod. Her chin went up and her shoulders went back.

"We need freedom. To believe what we chose to believe, to be what we chose to be. For too long, the people of our land have defined themselves by what they've always known: the leadership of a High Laird. We neglected personal responsibility. We need to leave the cradle and make our own decisions.

"There is no more High Laird. The house of Soranna is gone. So what will *you* choose? I know the people of these Provinces. They're good people. They're smart people. They can govern themselves."

It really was a shame she didn't want the job of leader because, at that moment, I think every person there would have followed her anywhere. As she stood, we all stood.

"When we spread the word of the Palatinate's fall, we'll also speak of the future. A future that belongs to everyone, where there is equal say for all throughout the land. A new government will address the new needs of the new land. Everyone will be represented. No voice will go unheard."

Some muttered their approval. Some applauded.

I hoped the new government would have amnesty for thieves.

"Success means ignoring the petty grievances of the past. That is how we'll forge a new order. A new government. And we'll call that new government . . ."

She paused. Everyone held their breath. The Dowager leaned over and whispered in my ear. "I don't want to make a mistake. What's the par-Goblin word for 'wisdom'?"

My mind raced. I hadn't come expecting a quiz on ancient languages. "Um . . . *procoran*."

She rose and said to all, "And our new government shall be called . . . the Procoran!"

A cheer went up from the crowd. The applause was deafening. Nanni appeared at my elbow and whispered in my other ear. "Jaxter, why did the Dowager name our new government after the par-Goblin word for 'naive'?"

Oh. Right. Procor*an* is "naive." Procor*us* is "wisdom."

Funny how so little separates those two words. I was always getting them mixed up.

I shrugged. "Too late now."

Energized, the crowd went to work. The Sarosans gathered supplies for their trek across the land. Others, led by Castellan Jorn, started sifting through the debris, hoping to resurrect Vengekeep.

"Very wise, that Dowager," the Castellan told the workers closest to him. "We *should* start over again. There's nothing saying we have to call the new city Vengekeep, is there? Now . . . Jornville. That has a *lovely* ring to it."

Crews formed to find anything worth salvaging, Uncle Garax took point on top of what remained of the Ghostfire house. He directed people where to search, chastised those he didn't feel were working fast enough, and needled all with reminders of what the Dowager said about working together.

"And just how are *you* going to pitch in?" I asked Garax.

"What do you think I'm doing now?" he retorted. "Supervising is exhausting work, y'know."

Shaking my head, I walked away to let him have what was hopefully his last delusion of grandeur. With the Ghostfire house destroyed, his prospects for employment in the new world didn't look especially good.

I joined up with the Dowager at the demolished cartographer's shop. It was in better shape than most. The roof had collapsed and the walls were buckled, but a convenient hole where there had once been a window made it easy to access the shop's supply of maps. The Dowager was sorting through rolls of parchment, placing them in piles according to Province.

"I'm all for this Procoran," I said. "But I'd really love to have just *one* leader right now who would tell my uncle to zoc off."

The Dowager's eyes narrowed. "Why? Are you applying for the job?"

I coughed, choking on my own surprise. "Er, no. I'm a better apprentice. I just want to get back to Redvalor Castle and start working again."

The Dowager was quiet for several moments. Her lips pulled back in a sad smile. She lowered herself to the ground and motioned for me to join her. "Jaxter, weren't you listening? Everything's changed. There may not even be a Redvalor to return to. And even if there is, I'm not the

Dowager anymore. I'm just . . . Annestra."

"So . . . what will you do?"

"I'll help the new government get started. I won't run it, you can be sure of that. But this could be my chance to mold something new. The Palatinate was able to quietly exterminate plants and animals that resisted magic because the monarchy didn't care. I could make sure the Procoran *cares.* And you're welcome to join me."

"Me? I'm not a politician."

"Neither am I. The Procoran will need advisers. The research that we've already done will go a long way toward helping the Procoran protect anything in danger of extinction. But I know that's not what you wanted when you became my apprentice. And I'll understand if you want to go back to your family. I'd miss you, Jaxter. But you need to do what's best for you."

She kissed my cheek and resumed sorting maps. *You need to do what's best for you.* So many times, I thought I knew what that was. Thief. Scientist. But maybe none of it was true.

I wandered the shattered streets, not sure where I should go or what I should do next. I found myself at the crater and the ruins of our house. A flood of memories came back. Da presenting me with my first lockpicks. Ma carving my profile into a forged silvernib. All that took place here. I hated that it took the destruction of the house to remind me.

"It's very nice rubble."

Bennock, approaching from behind, nodded at our former home.

"It's a good thing the theme of the day is 'starting over,'" I said, kicking at what used to be the front door. "Don't really have much choice."

"I may have lived secluded in an abbey all my life but even *I've* heard stories of the Grimjinxes. I say it's three months before you and your family are back on your feet. Make it two, if *you're* involved."

I smiled at the praise but I wasn't feeling it. "So, what will you do now?"

I wasn't the only one who'd lost his home. Bennock had lost more: the only family he'd ever known. The former acolyte traced sigils in the dirt with the toe of his boot. "I'm not sure. Kendil said I'd be welcome with the Sarosans. It might be fun to travel with them."

"Oh."

"You sound disappointed."

"Well, you said you wanted to study languages. My da speaks six fluently. He's no assassin-monk but I'm sure he'd be willing to teach you. You could always, you know, move in with my family. Or, they'd be more than happy to teach you to be a thief. You'd make a good one."

Bennock titled his head, uncertain. "That's a compliment, right?"

"We're Grimjinxes. It's the highest compliment we can give."

"Are *you* moving back with your parents?"

I tried to picture what that would be like. I couldn't. I tried to picture what staying with the Dowager would be like. Again, I couldn't.

"I don't know, Bennock. The Dowager . . . I mean, Annestra's going to assist the new government. She wants me to help her but . . ."

"But what?"

"I gave up being a thief to be her apprentice. Now I'm supposed to give up being her apprentice to be . . . I don't know what. Can't I just *be something* and stick with it?"

"Who says you're supposed to be one thing, you naff-nut?

Jaxter, you *are* a thief. You *are* a scientist. You're all those things. Nobody's just one thing."

"But the par-Goblins said, 'The path of thievery never forks.'"

"Right. The *ancient* par-Goblins. They were legendary thieves. Where are they now? They fell apart, probably from listening to their own advice. Maybe if they'd found a way to be something other than thieves, they'd still be around. Don't limit yourself because of something a bunch of dead par-Goblins said a hundred years ago. It's like the abbot always said to me: the future's up to you."

Bennock gave me a playful punch in the arm and strode away. As he mentioned Edilman, I felt a knot form in my stomach. *I* had a future to decide. Edilman didn't.

Because of me.

44

Everything Changes

"Until thieves write history,
time will glorify the High Laird."

—*Jaxter Grimjinx, scientific liaison to the Procoran*

I sat on a pile of mordenstone and twisted metal—all that remained of Vengekeep's gates. Flattening my legs so I could use my lap as a desk, I stretched a piece of parchment across my thighs. In one hand, I took the quill and inkpot I'd found in the remains of the Ghostfire house. Aubrin's journal lay spread out next to me, open to the page with the message for "EAJ." *My* message. Sighing, I dipped the quill into the ink.

My hand hovered over the parchment, unmoving. It

should have been a simple matter. I didn't even need to learn the ancient language. I just had to copy what I saw. But I couldn't stop thinking about what that would mean.

Aubrin would have a vision of me writing the message. The message would get translated by the assassin-monks. And as a result, Edilman would steal the Sourcefire.

And then he would die.

How could I do this? How could I write this message, knowing what was going to happen?

"You're doing that now? *Here?*" Aubrin shuffled up the broken street.

"I might as well get it over with," I said. I pressed the tip of the quill to the parchment. But I still couldn't write.

"It's hard," Aubrin said. "But you know it has to happen."

"If I do this," I said, "Edilman dies. Holm, Gobek, Oberax . . . they all died because of this one message. What if I don't write it? What if I never tell Edilman he can be redeemed by stealing the Sourcefire? Won't that save him?"

Aubrin knelt at my feet. "Remember the marbles back at the Creche? How they all have to fall into line for a prophecy to come true? Well, sometimes the marbles don't fall in line. Some marbles never come to be."

She picked at the rubble and found two round stones. "The visions show what *could* be. When I was in the Creche, the other seers shared *their* visions with me. In some"—she held up one of the stones—"you didn't write that note. And as a result"—she held up the other stone—"Edilman didn't steal the Sourcefire. Which means he didn't break the Palatinate's control over the beasts. Which means the beasts never turned against the Palatinate in the canyon. They kept fighting alongside their masters . . . until everyone in the rebellion was dead."

She tossed the stones aside.

I swallowed. "That . . . could have happened?"

She shrugged. "Maybe. These prophecies aren't exactly precise. I don't think they can ever fully predict what will happen. People are just too . . . random. We make choices. Choices change everything. It's why I didn't know Edilman was going to die. He made a choice no one could foresee."

I thought about what Edilman had told me. He said that I would write this message because I knew for sure how things played out. I knew it was the *only* way to make sure things worked out for the best. And he was right. Not writing this would make things far worse.

With steady hands, I copied the message from Aubrin's journal onto the parchment. It was unnerving, knowing that right this very moment—well, several months ago—Aubrin was having a vision of my hands replicating the language I couldn't read. She didn't know it was *me* writing it, only that it was important. The most important thing I'd ever write.

I finished the message, folded the parchment, and wrote *EAJ* on the outside. "That should do it."

Aubrin paged through her journal. "I can finally throw this away. I don't ever want to have any more visions like this."

"Well," I said, "you can't control that, now can you? You *are* the augur. Most powerful seer in generations, I hear."

She pinched my arm and walked back toward the camp.

Choices change everything.

She was right. I used to think I *had* to be a thief. Then I thought I *had* to continue studying with the Dowager. Both were true. And both were false. I had a choice. I *still* had a choice. Move home with Ma and Da. Go off with the Dowager. I bet I could even have chosen to follow the Sarosans all over the land if I wanted.

Not that I would ever, ever do that. First Rise is far too

early to get up just for a drink of water.

I lay back and closed my eyes, just so I could feel the sun on my face. I banished thoughts of prophecies and colored marbles. None of that mattered. I knew now that I could—and would—make anything happen. It wasn't just about who to live with. I could be the next Castellan of Vengekeep. I could rise to the exalted stature of Master Thief of Jarron Province.

I could be something that had never, ever occurred to anyone.

I simply had to choose.

Right there and then, I chose to take a nap.

Hey, choosing your future is exhausting work, y'know.